THE
BIG GAME

DUNCAN DRYE

This book is entirely a work of fiction.
The names, characters and incidents portrayed
in it are the work of the author's imagination.
Any resemblance to actual persons, living or dead,
events or localities is entirely coincidental.

Copyright Duncan Drye 2006

All rights reserved.
No part of this book may be reproduced
in any form or by any means,
without prior permission of the Author

Cover Design & Artwork

Gerhard Geldenhuys

ISBN 1448679230

At his best, man is the noblest of all animals; separated from law and justice he is the worst.

Aristotle

Prologue

It felt as if the hair on the back of his head were glued to the floor, then he realised it was. David Churu fought his way to consciousness. One by one his senses kicked in; each was a shock. He could not move his head one millimetre; he began an inventory.

He was naked and spread-eagled on smooth concrete. Restraints pinned his wrists and ankles. Hard pegs were forced into his ears. The end of a scaffold board blocked his view of the ceiling. The only smell was disinfectant. The only sound was a terrified pig, whenever the light dimmed, the pig squealed.

Then through the fog he realised three things.

Two long nails faced him in the scaffold board.

They weren't pegs in his ears, as he still could hear.

It was not a pig, the sound was slightly deeper, it was human.

He snapped back into consciousness. The pig-human squeals had stopped. There was the sound of footsteps approaching. Nothing else had changed.

The footsteps stopped, out of his range of vision, "Good morning Colonel Churu," a deep, cultured voice, in heavily accented English, "how are you today?" David tried to speak, but just produced a dry cough which sent pain coursing through his scalp and ear canals.

"Well that's enough small talk. It's my job to find out who's involved in your revolution. That can either take a long time or short time, it's your decision, but the result is always the same."

"There is … no … revolution," David croaked.

"Then the answer is the longer time."

From close behind his head came the sound of a plastic chair being dragged, then accepting the weight of the sitter. The leather sole of an expensive shoe entered his field of vision.

A sigh, then again the accented English. "I thought it would be nice to put you and your wife in adjoining rooms. I had a chat with her earlier and ... eventually ... she was very helpful."

David was swept with a cold nausea, despite the distortion, he recognised Sita's screams. He began to shout...

"Be calm Colonel, I believe she knows very little, for the moment she is sleeping peacefully. So it's you who must provide me with the details. But first let me explain your situation. We call the contraption above you, the seesaw. I designed it myself and whilst not fast, it always gives our ... interviewees plenty of time to consider their options. As we're rarely in a hurry," he searched for an elusive word, "clearness ... no clarity ... this instrument has the great advantage over cruder methods, in that your answers have clarity, at least in the early stage they will not be blurred by pain."

With obvious pride he continued, "You can't see this, but on the top of the board above you is fixed a bowl and above that a water pipe. On the other end of my seesaw is a weight. I turn the tap and depending how fast it drips ... you will hear it through those pipes screwed into your ears ... these two nails," a long manicured index finger pointed to each bright nail in turn, "will descend. Now the subtle part," his voice became slightly animated, "the success of my job is greatly affected by leaving people hope. When I leave this room, you'll have to decide if your feelings ... or love ... for your co-conspirators outweighs ... you see here the parallel with weight? outweighs your fear of blindness.

Now I have added another ... aspect ... by the simple act of making these nails," again the pointing finger, "by making these nails of different lengths." He paused giving David time to consider the significance, "even when the first nail has pierced you, like the man with only one kidney, you can still function normally; you will then have some time, whilst the increasing weight of water drives on the first nail ... to think ... and to consider your options. Now before I leave, do you wish to talk about your friends?"

David's voice had dried, his tongue swollen, he made a rasping sound. The hand re-appeared now holding a plastic bottle, a drinking tube was placed gently between his lips, and then timed to David's swallows, the bottle was squeezed.

"That's better, try again."

"There is no revolution."

The plastic chair creaked as he arose, "Not what your lovely wife told me Colonel. Now this is very important, tied around your finger is a string, when you're ready to talk, just give it a pull and day or night someone will appear."

The footsteps receded, at the end of a corridor a door slammed.

David lay and listened to the total silence. Suddenly it was broken by the sound of a single drip hitting the bottom of the metal bowl.

1

GHANA - WEST AFRICA

Despite air conditioning in the arrivals lounge of Kotoka International Airport, the air was hot and sticky. It was the second Wednesday of the month, so as usual Tom McRae was standing watching the first trolley pushers arrive from London Heathrow. His scarred and shaven head and bulky torso incongruous in the freshly pressed white shirt, blue blazer and grey trousers, he looked as comfortable as a farm labourer in a wedding suit. In one stubby fist he held the board displaying: *XTREME TOURS* and in the other a clip board.

He always felt the stirrings of fear when he scanned the faces. It had not happened in over thirty Wednesdays, but one day he would experience the jolt of recognition when his eyes met an old colleague, and ex Sergeant Thomas Wellington McRae of the Second Battalion Parachute Regiment would be exposed as a holiday rep.

Prominent among the throng of returning Ghanaians were two European men, one very tall with close cropped grey hair, the other younger and dark. Their eyes locked on his board.

"Herr Schmidt and Koeffe?" offered the older man. McRae directed them to the minibus.

Next was a tall good looking couple in their 30's, hands together on the handle as they pushed their cart. In Tom's opinion the man's hair was too long, but the woman was a beauty: long brown hair and despite her safari shirt and trousers, he could see she had a stunning figure. That could be trouble, he thought to himself as he checked off Mr M. Bray and partner.

Behind them was a short, plump, worried looking man in mid 20's, he shuffled past McRae fiddling one handed with his

P.D.A. the other hand fighting to control the baggage cart. At the end of the concourse he stared around in confusion, eventually his eyes settled on the Xtreme sign; he waved and dropped his machine. Tom sighed in resignation; it was going to be a tough two weeks.

Approaching and skirting *techno man* as he scrabbled for his battery on the floor, was a powerful man in his early 50's. Holding his arm was a girl less than half his age dressed in short skirt and high heels, more suitable for a Paris nightclub than an adventure holiday. As Tom ticked off Mr. Serovec and partner, he thought it should have said *not wife* in brackets.

Techno man had retrieved all his errant parts and approached McRae. "I should be on that," he pointed at the clipboard with his clutch of plastic.

"Name?" growled McRae.

"Henning," he replied in a West coast American accent, "Paul Henning junior."

"Gotcha, join the group outside at the bus, only two more to find."

The flood of arrivals had reduced to a trickle, but approaching was a young, stick thin couple dressed in matching browns and green. He glanced at the remaining names and read Mr and Mrs Goff. "Oh no, it's got to be a fucking Rupert," he mumbled.

"Hey there," the man waved as if swatting a fly and hailed him at full volume, "are you for the Goffs?"

McRae grinned to himself; sounds like a medical problem, which I guess they will be; a pain in the arse. He nodded and directed them to the bus.

The woman's voice was identical to her husband's, even in volume, "have you got our guns?"

"All organised," McRae called over his shoulder, striding ahead leaving them to pursue with their recalcitrant baggage cart. Let the fuckers know who's boss right from the start, he thought.

He herded his nine passengers and their luggage aboard the tatty Mercedes minibus. The wide-open windows blasting them with 40deg heat and 80% humidity as they honked their way through the chaos of baggage and taxis. It was a short ride to the other side of the airport where a Gulfstream 2 executive jet awaited them. High on its tail was the war shield emblem of the President of the Democratic Republic of Gamasi .

McRae stood in the shade of a wing and checked the trio of local baggage handlers as they professionally abused the nineteen items of expensive luggage into the aircraft's hold. Slipping a five-dollar note to each, he watched as they piled back into their buggy and roared off. He stood in the pool of shade staring at the distant terminal complex; timing a rivulet of sweat as it made its way slowly down his back, finally to be absorbed in his waistband. McRae was an expert at waiting. The ability to wait was one of the most important attributes of a good soldier and Tom had been a good soldier, one of the best until an anti personnel mine robbed him of his left leg just below the knee.

"Eat and sleep whenever you can and learn how to wait," he always told the rookies, "that's what makes a good soldier."

The male Goff emerged from the aircraft and stood at the head of the passenger stairs. "Hi!" he called down to the back of the man waiting below in the shade. McRae counted, at seven the call was repeated.

"Hi there," a pause whilst he thought vainly for a title, "hey, you sure our guns have been loaded?"

McRae paused just enough to unsettle, then half turned, "No."

Goff frowned, "No what? Do you mean they're missing?"

McRae paused again: never answer quickly was the very best way to destabilise a fucking Rupert, "No."

Mrs Goff appeared next to her husband, "Trouble Robert?"

"Not sure, communication probs."

Accustomed to disciplining Labradors and horses from the time she could walk, Fiona Goff could take a monosyllabic Scotsman in her stride. "Are our gun cases aboard, or not?" she bellowed.

McRae studied the distant terminal as he considered her question. "Not," a pause, "but as I told you just now in Arrivals: it's organised." As he spoke, distorted by the heat haze, a small convoy of vehicles appeared from behind the terminal buildings: a small Honda van sandwiched between two Police 4x4's, both with lights flashing.

The older German appeared behind the Goff couple, his English perfect despite his irritation, "Are we going to be long, it's hot as hell in here."

McRae glanced up at the speaker, "Better get used to it, it'll soon be worse." He stepped out of the shade to meet the leading police car.

With her free hand Lorna lifted the weight of hair off her sweating neck and peered through the round window next to her. It must be that English couple shouting about guns to the holiday rep. Can't see him, but I guess he's standing down there under the wing. Wonder if the woman is going to be shooting, it's usually a guy-thing and the part of them I find hard to take, this obsession with guns.

She glanced at the man holding her right hand. Mike has it as well and I don't even know if its his only obsession! I must be mad! I've only known him for three weeks and here I am, thousands of miles from home, on a fourteen day holiday with him. To make it even more mad, it's a hunting holiday. She flapped her hair with her free hand to cool her neck. I guess it's not strictly three weeks, I smiled at him loads of times over the years, whenever we passed in the building. Once we even shared an elevator, pity about the other five people in there as well. But that was when Stephen and I were together, I'd never do more than look. Her thoughts drifted back to that time, dwelling on how things had changed since the Stephen time.

Six great years and sharing the apartment for nearly five. Sure we worked too hard, didn't make enough time for each other, but we both knew where we were going. We knew, or thought we knew, it would all end in a bunch of kids and a home away from the madness of New York. But September eleventh 2001 changed all that. If I'm honest, I guess I knew the second I heard news of the impacts, even as I kept hitting my speed dial for his mobile. Throughout the blurred hours of maybes: maybe his battery's flat? maybe he left his phone on his desk? maybe it was hanging in his coat when he stepped out? Then gradually the cold acceptance that he'll never call, ever again. That morning was the last time I would ever see him, speak to him, share a joke, hold him. She felt the cold lump of Stephen's absence.

It's the toughest thing I've ever done, getting back into life again. Up to three weeks ago, all the dates were crap, none worked, not always their fault, guess I just wasn't ready. Girlfriends began to despair of me. Then three weeks ago as Kathy and I sat in the bar around the corner, just as I was being counselled again about *getting back in the saddle*, Mike walked in. Smiles followed, an offer of a drink, Kathy suddenly discovered a prior engagement, the palpable chemistry, the meal, the first kiss, the invitation back to his for a nightcap, the frantic mind blowing sex only five hours after we exchanged our first words. She smiled to herself. You tart Lorna, and now you've been in the saddle every night since, plus the odd lunchtime and early evening as well.

Airway bills in one hand, McRae checked off the weapons and ammunition, while the police lounged and chatted by their vehicles. One by one he carefully slid the selection of expensive stainless steel, polished wood or leather-bound gun cases out of the van, checked their labels and contents before passing them to the co-pilot standing at the hatch for stowing.

Again in his mind he questioned the documents. Nine guests, but only seven of them shooters after you deducted the Russian tart and American Beauty, yet nine rifles detailed.

The first was housed in battered mahogany and labelled Michael Bray. He snapped open the catches and checked the Swedish PSG-90 lying snugly in its foam bed. A reliable gun and this one had seen a lot of use.

The Goffs had matching dark brown leather cases. Embossed in gold on each was a small stag at bay. Not a new brace of Parker Hales, but very well maintained.

Suddenly the numbers made sense. Four guns were listed as owned by the older guy, Herr W. Schmidt. Four much travelled stainless steel cases containing a Swiss Sig Sauer, two German Unique Alpines and a Walther WA2000.

A brand new, hand built Patriot Genesis with its protective wrapping untouched was listed to the plump young American, care of a Los Angeles address.

In stark contrast was the rifle listed to Serovec, the burly Russian. Housed in a battered military case, it was a WW2 classic, a Mosin Nagent. Although in pristine condition the wear marks of a thousand hours service were written clearly on every surface. McRae stared at the most coveted sniper rifle of the twentieth century. Responsible for more US deaths in Vietnam than any other weapon, it was still the first choice of the old school assassin.

Lorna glanced away from the window, as Schmidt snorted and sprung from his seat to join the English couple at the door. The German, or maybe he's Scandinavian, is pissed with waiting. She had noticed him on the bus, the way he carried an air of frustration, like a coiled spring. This vacation won't help him she thought.

She smiled at Mike and squeezed his hand, he glanced up from his novel. "Good?" she asked.

"Great" he smiled back.

Oh I could eat him, she thought with a slight shiver. In fact I think that's exactly what I'll do the moment we check into our hotel! She returned to her window and watched McRae. He was inspecting a variety of long thin cases, and then checking them against a sheaf of papers. Guess they must be the guns, she pondered, as the Scotsman carefully passed the cases to someone below her.

It's the actual killing I can't take. Ever since Dad taught me to shoot I couldn't kill anything. I get 100% at clay pigeons no problem, and I enjoyed the .22 target shooting – targets no problem, blood, fur and feathers are. But Dad loves it and calls me a hypocrite, which I guess is sorta true. *If you can't kill 'em, don't eat 'em,* is his favourite defence. To which I always respond, *you didn't build your car, but you drive it.* At least once a year he takes off with little brother to a remote corner of the world, to kill some furry life form. Once he invited Stephen, but there was no way he'd go, not even to bond with future pa-in-law. I guess my biggest row with Dad since he left Mom, was about his trip to Australia to shoot wild horses. Now it seems Mike's the same.

She thought about Mike's first mention of this vacation, just a few days after meeting him. That night over dinner when he had broken the news with studied indifference, *did I mention I'm off on vacation to Africa soon?* It had been a shock and a disappointment and she half waited for an invitation to join him. After days of gentle hints had elicited no response, she asked Kathy what she thought, at their next after work affair-debrief session.

"Be direct, tell him you've time owing and you could come."

"I'm scared he's already arranged to go with an old flame."

"All the more reason to ask then," Kathy retorted.

The next Saturday morning as they lay entwined in bed, she plucked up courage. "I've got loads of vacation owing, and I haven't been fussed with holidays for so long," she paused, but he did not fill the gap, "I could always come to Africa ... if you want me to that is."

He hesitated those few seconds too long before replying, "that'd be really fantastic, but it's kind of a guy thing."

She had tried to smile despite the chill in her stomach. He had begun to stroke the long scar that was hidden under his hairline, a habit she had noticed whenever he was stressed.

"That's ok, are all your buddies going?"

Again the pause, "no….I don't know any of the party … it's a sort of … package tour."

She had felt herself regressing to teenager, hating herself, she had become brisk and businesslike. "Well I'll do breakfast then," she firmly extricated herself from his arms and throwing on a robe flounced into the kitchen and banged around the bar. Why are you doing this you stupid possessive cow, she had berated herself, whilst beginning to panic as the minutes stretched. Just get back in there and tell him to go and do his hunter-gatherer stuff and you'll be waiting when he returns. She heard the toilet flush and the sound of bare feet approaching. "Coffee?" she called, a de-fusing offer ... no answer.

He padded silently up behind her, grasped and twisted her sheen of hair, lifted it ... time stood still. She recalled the first hint of breath on the back of her neck, then the abrasion of stubble moving around to the side of her neck, her ears. She gasped for breath, her nipples hardened, he placed his other hand on her waist. Unbidden, a little sigh as he teased her ear. "Will you come to Africa?" he whispered.

She had cleared her throat, "I'll think about it." He pressed her urgently against the bar and she had reached around behind her and smiled, "Ok if I fix coffee later?"

Mike realised that he had been staring at the same page for ten minutes. Despite this being one of the best books he had ever read, he could not concentrate. When could he tell her the truth about this holiday, when would be the best time? You and your gonads Bray, he chided himself, when're you going to learn? He thought back to that Saturday morning in his apartment. There was no way he was going to risk their relationship by bringing her to Gamasi: so why was she sitting next to him, holding his hand on the shuttle aircraft, less than two hours from their hotel? He must tell her as soon as they arrived and if she went ballistic he would just turn it into a romantic holiday – the most expensive holiday in history!

Fuck, fuck, fucking fuck. That fateful morning in his bathroom he had worked out what he was going to say to defuse the situation; he still knew as he walked into the kitchen; he sorta knew as he spotted the delicious outline of her ass through the white silk robe, it was getting a bit blurred as he reached forward for a peace offering nuzzle ... then the old one eyed trouser snake had taken control of his mouth. "Will you come to Africa?" the snake whispered and here we are! fuck, shitting, fuck! ... but it all comes down to the fact that there are some things in life you want to do, but this vacation is something I've gotta do!

McRae handed the signed documents to the senior policeman, who flicked through them to ensure the one hundred dollar bill had been included. Good old US dollars, the Scotsman thought as he climbed aboard the aircraft, certainly make the world go round.

He completed a final head count of his seated guests.

Bray and Karrol were in the centre seats, the American's hair masking his face as he read a paperback, whilst she stared out of the window.

The Upper Class Twats were at the rear of the cabin, in animated conversation with the taller German. Whilst Koeffe, the shorter one, was reading his holiday details.

Both Russians were silent and engrossed in their own thoughts. There was only one empty seat left, next to the door. This involved him sitting next to the fat, sweaty Californian. As the co-pilot sealed the door McRae announced in the closest he ever came to levity, "Next stop, Kamba International shit hole."

Paul Henning shifted damply in his seat as the Xtreme tours man sat down next to him. He hated people touching him. He pressed as far away as possible from the Rep., tucked his elbow in and fiddled with his PDA.

Johan Koeffe turned over another page and came to the Xtreme Tours holiday itinerary.

THE BIG GAME

Wednesday
17.30hrs local time.
Forty-minute flight from Accra to Kamba, capital city of the Republic of Gamasi.
Limousine transfer to the internationally renowned Hotel Ambassador on Amutu Avenue.
Dinner from 19.30hrs in the hotel's internationally famous five star gourmet restaurant."

Thursday
Breakfast from 07.30hrs including a choice of American, English, Continental or African.

Johan was unsure what constituted an African breakfast.

10.00hrs A lecture by General Gboja on how the people of Gamasi had shrugged off the legacies of imperialism due to the inspiration and the guidance of their beloved father, President Amutu.

Johan noted that the shrugging did not extend to breakfasts.

12.30hrs Lunch
14.30hrs Meet in the hotel foyer for a conducted tour of the sights of Kamba, including a visit to the world renowned Amutu Free Hospital.

As only two hours had been allotted to the tour, Johan assumed the sights were very limited.

19.30hrs Dinner in the hotel. Followed by a display by the National Heritage Dancers, illustrating in dance the ethnic diversity of Gamasi.

Friday
Following breakfast an ideological discussion entitled "The enemy at our door."
Conducted by the poetically named Mr Milton Keats.
12.30hrs Lunch
14.30hrs Aggression assessment by General Gboja and assistants, in the Gaiety Ballroom.
19.00hrs A reception and dinner at the Presidential Palace by kind invitation of President Amutu. Meet in hotel foyer at 18.30hrs.

Saturday
Collection from hotel foyer at 10.00hrs for transport to the shooting ranges at the Amutu Military Academy.
13.00hrs Lunch at the Academy Officers Club.
14.30hrs A tour of the "sites of insurgence."
19.30hrs Dinner at the hotel and afterwards the opportunity to sample the world class facilities offered by the Republic of Gamasi's premier hotel.

The itinerary for Sunday and the following nine days simply said:
All active participants will be collected from the hotel foyer at 10.00hrs and returned at around 18.00hrs after a full day in the service of the Peoples of Gamasi.
A packed lunch will be supplied, plus cold non-alcoholic drinks – vegetarian by prior arrangement.
The last item, 20.00hrs on the final evening was:
Farewell Gala Dinner.
Wednesday 09.00hrs meet in hotel foyer for transfer by limousine to Kamba International Airport.
10.00hrs 40 minute return flight to Accra.

Realising that his mind had drifted off half way through, Johan started reading from the beginning again.

In the front seat Paul Henning pondered for the hundredth time why he was on this vacation; he was not a vacation person. He recalled the day he had chanced upon the Xtreme Tours' website and his curiosity had been aroused. The only holiday company he had ever heard of that would not accept booking without *"acceptable personal references."* But why had he followed the maze that resulted in him sitting in this plane today? I guess it's just the hacker in me, the more they played hard to get, the more I wanted to book a vacation.

He thought back to when he was a kid. Three times a year, Mom and Dad would prise him out of his bedroom. He would stay in the car, or the hotel room all the time and play with his Sega, as soon as the car pulled up at home again he would return to the dark electronic world that was his bedroom.

He recalled with horror, when he was fourteen they had dispatched him to Summer Camp. After a few days of ritual bullying the other kids had ignored him, after feigning a leg injury, so had the staff. Ten days left to endure with only his Sega to keep him company.

Now aged twenty-four, he was a multi-millionaire game designer, generally acknowledged as one of the best in the world. All those years alone, hunched over a keyboard had paid off big time. He had no interests apart from work. No interest in clothes, sex, cars, or property. He still lived with Mom. Dad had left at some point, but it had hardly entered his consciousness.

He had outgrown his bedroom and now worked in the dining room with the drapes closed. But why was he here now, on another continent, in the heat, with a load of strangers. He guessed there were two reasons, one real and one spurious. The real one was his desire to build his ultimate game *"Sniper."* The other was his New Year's resolution to get out more!

As the executive jet arrowed into the sky, Johan Koeffe was still staring blindly at the holiday itinerary and also wondering why he was aboard. For him it was simple - the need to keep his job. He glanced at the hawk-like profile of his boss nodding in agreement with the young English couple. He had "switched off" their conversation, bored and slightly repulsed by their stories of killing herds of assorted animals. Despite his fluency in the English language, he found their accents difficult to understand.

He thought about his boss. How slowly his respect for this man was becoming tinged with distaste, a distaste that he must hide for the sake of Krista, their sons and his huge bank loan. Many years ago, he had worked under Schmidt at the world's biggest manufacturer and installer of moving stairs and walkways. Then Schmidt had gone on his own and within ten years, built his company into a serious rival. Two years ago the call had come, Johan had accepted the offer that he could not afford to refuse.

But power had changed his ex boss; always a tough and diligent manager, he had become a ruthless and egocentric owner. They no longer had reasoned discussion, now there was only *Schmidt's way*. Johan had lost count of the times Krista had pleaded with him not to quit and he knew he couldn't. Somehow every month, they always managed to spend his very generous salary package.

Then a few months ago the *invitation* for an all expenses paid vacation. *An opportunity to bond outside the workplace, it will do us both good*, was how Schmidt had put it. Refusal had not been an option, just maybe the tyrant wanted to change? Whatever the reason Johan was not happy. He was good with a gun and excelled at clay pigeon shooting. Sometimes with top clients, he would go game shooting, as long as he didn't have to handle the dead birds. But this was different, so different in fact that he had problems believing the outline Schmidt had given him.

2

As each drip hit the surface of the water above him, David Churu considered the implications of his impending blindness. He would never see Sita or his children again.

Never seeing his sons as teenagers or adults would be the worst, but there were a thousand other things he would miss. What am I thinking? From the moment I entered this prison, I knew I would never see them again! Political prisoners always disappear. They drive the bodies out of town and throw them into the river.

David recalled the old Gamasi joke. *What's Amutu's opposition called?* The answer, *crocodile shit,* seemed even less funny than usual.

He had kept the number of his conspirators to a minimum, but as the time got closer he had to speak to the people of power within the country. He had been very careful, but it would appear not careful enough; one of them must have spoken to Amutu's secret police.

He stared upwards and was sure the scaffold board had moved. He closed one eye and sighted on a mark on the ceiling, but it had been his imagination; it was still in the same position.

What will I do when it descends? Is there any point in closing my eyelids? It'll only gain minutes, maybe only seconds, before the nail pierced the tender skin and enters my eye.

He hated himself for the moments when he had considered revealing his co-conspirators. He knew that it would make no difference to the result, whatever he told the man in the expensive shoes, Colonel David Archibald Churu would very soon be crocodile shit.

He thought about his trusted friends within army and civilian life who believed that Amutu and his bunch of criminals should be removed as soon as possible. Part of him, brought up on English schoolboy stories, where right always overcomes evil, believed they could not fail. I still believe it, but I guess I'll not be around to witness it.

3

LONDON

The Foreign Secretary stared at the traffic silently inching along the rain-slicked street beneath his window. "So what's so important about tantalite ore?" he asked the civil servant behind him.

"It's an essential element used in the production of mobile phones, computers, jet engines and much, much more."

"I see. And presumably it's rare?"

With studied care the man leafed through his folder until finding the correct page. "Very limited supplies world-wide. Some in Brazil, Canada and Australia. A little in Nigeria, but the vast majority to date is in the Congo which our Chinese, German and American friends have already tied up."

The Minister turned from the window and studied the world map on the wall by his desk. He traced a small crescent shape with one soft white finger, "Please remind me about Gamasi, Gerald."

The civil servant focussed on the ceiling high above him, "Used to be one of ours when it was the Reunion Coast. Granted independence in '58, still a member of the Commonwealth, but only just. Population around five million. Totalitarian state run by a President ..." He studied the ornate cornice for inspiration.

"Gerald, I don't expect you to know all this by heart," he flashed his electoral smile, (just to keep in practice.) "Feel free to refer to your file."

The civil servant turned to the front page and read silently for a few moments, "Ah yes ... President Charles Amutu studied law here, at the University of Essex. Came to power via an army-supported coup in 1987, Christian and from the majority tribal group, as are most of the army. Flirted a bit with the Chinese, but still an Anglophile ... values tea with Her Majesty. Exports mostly cassava and timber."

The politician sank into his chair and waved a languid invitation to sit, "And is he secure ... as head of state I mean?"

"At this moment - he runs an extremely tight ship. But this discovery would put him under severe pressure; this is bigger than finding oil."

The Minister considered. "Does anyone else know about these reserves?" he nodded at the folder, "apart from our chaps."

"No one. Obviously we can delay completion of this mineral report but..." he tailed off.

Two plump hands flicked in acknowledgement, "yes, yes, understood, no one can keep the lid on this sort of stuff for long, but some ... manoeuvre time is always good in these circumstances. We need to talk to our people in...?" he raised his eyebrows.

Again the quick scan of the first page, "Kamba Sir, in our time it was Elton, but they re-named it recently, it means *horn,* as in bull and relates to the shape of the country."

The Foreign Secretary rolled the capital's name around in his fleshy mouth a few time like fine claret, "Kamba, Kamba. Please have words with our man in Kamba as soon as and then we'll have another chat."

The civil servant sensing his dismissal rose and headed for the door. With his hand on the worn, ancient brass handle, he was stopped.

"Gerald, does that report go into facts and figures?"

"Yes Sir, in great depth ... all projected of course."

"No problem, pop it on the side table, I'll have a look later."

After lunch the Minister settled behind his desk and began to leaf through the folder. He studied a page of figures, made a few calculations on the reverse side and whistled softly. Eyes still fixed on his bottom line of figures; he groped for his phone.

It was answered on the third ring. "Ah Graham, do you think the P.M. could spare me a few minutes this afternoon? Oh, and perhaps you could arrange someone from Trade and Industry as well … yes, yes actually it is pretty urgent."

4

REPUBLIC OF GAMASI

They felt like visiting royalty when they stepped off the plane. No passport control, or customs. Three black Mercedes with darkened windows were parked near the base of the stairs. The fourth vehicle was a van to bring their luggage straight to their hotel.

"I could get to like this!" Mike whispered as their white shirted chauffeur held open the door of the first car for them. They sat in air-conditioned silence as the rest of the party were ushered to their cars.

The Goffs seemed to be having a dispute with McRae.

Lorna stared at the corrugated iron hanger and sheds, all in varying degrees of disrepair. The hanger doors were open each end, inside she could see the profiles of three helicopters. In a patch of shade just outside the nearest door, five men in unbuttoned coveralls lounged in plastic chairs; slowly they passed around a very long cigarette.

Mike followed her gaze, "Chinese choppers."

Lorna gave him a quizzical glance, "The cigarettes?"

"No, the helicopters. Chinese made, relatively cheap but good, though if I was a pilot I wouldn't want those guys servicing them."

McRae climbed in next to their driver on the other side of the thick glass partition and the cavalcade surged forward. As they paused at the airfield gates, both sentries saluted and stood to attention.

Lorna noticed that one wore scuffed army boots and the other new white trainers with no laces. The gate sign on one side announced, *Amutu International Airport*, whilst the other displayed, *Gamasi Air Force Base*.

Paul Henning sat and stared forward at the blur of half completed, breezeblock houses glimpsed on either side of the car. Their drivers switched on sirens and sped down the centre of the road, leaving the traffic stationary on either side. They flashed past a mix of overloaded trucks, battered cars and small motorbikes, but the vast majority were home made carts drawn by skeletal donkeys and mules, all dwarfed by their towering loads.

The road from the airport into Kamba skirted the coast and in the distance he could see a vast building project where the Atlantic ocean joined an estuary. Enormous yellow earthmovers graded the soil. Dump trucks the size of houses; each carried one massive rock which they tipped in front of excavators, which in turn placed them precisely in the sea defences. They passed a hoarding that proclaimed the project to be *The Creation of a Deep Water Harbour: a gift from the Government of Japan to the Republic of Gamasi*: Paul considered this to be an extremely generous gift.

As they entered the outskirts of the city, the volume of traffic forced the cars to slow. Pressing in on either side of the road were stalls and open fronted shops with dusty goods piled outside. He glimpsed narrow side alleys of tin roofed shacks. Close packed humanity: near naked big-eyed children, wizened old people, crippled beggars, street vendors and porters pushing overloaded bicycles. Weaving amongst them were the dogs, slack nipples or testicles swinging under sharp ribbed bodies.

Paul had witnessed poverty before through the back windows of a car. Over ten years ago when Mom and Dad had decided to drive to Florida rather than fly. The journey took them through Mississippi and Alabama. But it had been a quaint tumble-down-shack, All-American sort of poverty, somehow easier to accept. You felt that the grizzled black men sitting under their porches were all working on soul numbers for their next album.

Their Mercedes stopped with a lurch that propelled him towards the Russian couple on the opposite seat. He saved himself by grabbing the man's knees. Blushing, he mumbled an apology, and then busied himself craning for a view as to why they had halted. The Russian grunted acknowledgement then resumed his high volume, guttural conversation with the girl. They both scared Paul; the man was menacing and the girl oozed sexuality. There appeared to have been a minor accident involving the first car. Bundles of reeds were spread across the road. Suddenly an old white Land Rover slid to a halt next to their cavalcade and six uniformed men sprang out and began to strike anyone within reach of their long black batons. Paul could not tell whether they were police or army, but under their assault the bystanders hurriedly cleared the road and they moved forward again. He glimpsed a collapsed cart, the side of the mule impaled on a shattered wooden shaft, it stood patiently as its blood drained onto the road. Paul, whose whole life was ritualised electronic violence, shuddered.

Johan Koeffe sat in the third car and watched as the police struck out randomly at the people in the street. His first time in a third world country and he was horrified. He had travelled and worked all over Europe, but this was so different. The dirt, the poverty, the casual violence and the people's acceptance of all three.

He thought back to his home village near Düsseldorf, everything so clean and organised. As the road blockage was being cleared, he stared at two small boys sitting on a low wall; about the same age as his sons, maybe ten or eleven it was difficult to tell. Barefoot, matchstick legs in threadbare shorts, arms draped over each other's bare shoulders, they returned his stare, faces emotionless. Johan in air-conditioned comfort, only feet away, felt as if he was on a different planet.

The cars surged forward and the boys disappeared from view and his life. He shook his head, but they were imprinted on his retina, like a flashbulb in the dark. To clear their image he focussed on his fellow passengers. His boss sat next to him listening to the Goffs' advice on how to obtain an Elephant shooting permit in Zimbabwe.

The road was widening, the surface smoother and then a surreal sight. In the centre of Kamba, surrounded by green lawns and high iron railings, sat a medieval castle. Open mouthed he nudged Wolfgang Schmidt.

The Goffs followed their gaze. "Bloody hell, it's Balmoral," brayed Fiona.

They pressed against the windows as the replica of Her Majesty Queen Elizabeth's Scottish home passed by, to be replaced by other grand properties half hidden behind massive gates and high, wire topped walls.

Then the faded colonial splendour of the Hotel Ambassador. The cars swept through the open gates and pulled up in the shade of its arched portico. Uniformed porters sprang forward to open the doors. The manager emerged, a towering figure in full tribal costume, his richly embroidered robe trailing the ground. Sweeping off his fur trimmed pillbox hat, he greeted each guest in turn, then ushered the party into the vast edifice of dark hardwood and tropical plants that was the main foyer. They passed through a phalanx of minions in white shirts and black trousers, who dispensed cold drinks and keys from silver trays. The manager stood rocklike in the centre and directed the flow using a staggering range of languages. Changing effortlessly from German to English, to Russian and back again.

Michael Bray and Lorna Karrol followed the liveried porter as he crossed the cavernous hall and entered their suite. Mike was steeling himself for his big revelation. The minute this guy leaves I'll tell her, he promised himself. He waited and without realising his hand went under his hair to stroke the scar.

The rooms were models of Victorian excess. Their heavy drapes would not have been out of place in a theatre and the bed could have accommodated a harem. The porter busied himself adjusting the air conditioning whilst Mike fumbled for a small denomination note. As soon as the door closed Mike turned to see Lorna standing on the far side of the bed, holding his gaze, she shrugged off her safari shirt.

He swallowed, his eyes drawn to the thrust of her breasts, "Lorna there's something we need to talk about."

Lorna pouted as she unclasped her waistband and with a wriggle of her hips, trousers slipped to the floor. Naked she knelt on the bed, "Can it wait?"

Mike looked down on the curve of her back and the lift of her buttocks. Lorna slowly moved to his side of the bed, he stared mesmerised by the swing of her breasts as she shifted balance onto one hand and began to unbutton his fly.

He cleared his throat, "Well it is rather ..." She took his tip gently between her teeth, his voice broke, "... but yeh, I guess it can wait."

Wolfgang Schmidt carefully removed all his clothes, laid a large white bath towel on the floor and begun his 100 sit-ups.

Lindy moaned in mock passion as Vladimir Serovec pummelled her finely toned buttocks into the bed cover. She stared over his broad hairy shoulder at the ornate cornice, her vision blurred by the energy of his thrusting. Such had been his urgency that he had not bothered to undress her, the moment they were in their room he had drawn her to him. He had lifted the hem of her skirt around her waist with one hand, pulled aside the front of her thong with the other and entered her. For once the moaning was easy as she was in pain. The front of the thin material was trapped between them, cutting into her clitoris, but Lindy did not complain.

Paul Henning tugged on the braided cord and drew the heavy drapes. Surfing the TV channels, he glimpsed the distinctive profile of Burt Reynolds., *The Gumball Rally* he sighed and slumped into an easy chair.

Johan Koeffe sat on the edge of the bed and listened to his home telephone ringing distantly through the background of line interference. At last it was picked up, "Hi son, are you missing your dad?"

Robert Goff lovingly stroked the smooth contours of his Parker Hale. He stood legs braced in front of the tall window. Slowly he lowered the barrel until it rested against one of the stained timber mullions. He squinted through the telescopic sights at a taxi driver dozing outside the hotel gates. With minor movements he brought the cross hairs onto the man's ear. He steadied his breathing, gently caressed the trigger. With a sharp explosion of air from his pursed lips, he mimicked a shot.

Fiona looked up from her armchair on the far side of the room and raised an amused eyebrow. "Get 'im Rob?"

He turned and smiled boyishly, "'Course I did Fee."

In a nearby house McRae lay naked on top of his damp bed, his stump throbbing. The rent was very cheap, but he wished he had paid the extra for air conditioning. His thoughts drifted to his latest group. Usual fucking nightmare mix of madmen and sad bastards. The Germans are usually ok, disciplined nation. Especially the older guy, born 50 years too late that one, can picture him strutting around in his SS gear all peaked cap and jodhpurs. Not so sure about the younger one, but once he gets the taste for it, he'll be fine.

I could really do without those upper class twats. People like Mr and Mrs Fucking-Goff buggered the army for me; you've only to look at 'em to hate 'em. He elevated his damaged leg and inspected the inflamed, scarred flesh. But I guess they'll be no trouble once I've got 'em trained. They're tough though, nothing can test a human like the British public school system; army basic training's a piece of piss compared with what the upper classes expect from their little kids. And the killing will come as second nature to 'em; that lot've been killing pheasants and peasants for a thousand years.

That Russian, there's something ... fire in his eyes. A hard bastard. I've seen his type before – though not too often, thank Christ. His lassie knows her job, even if it is spent on her back.

Then there's fat boy. Could do with a couple of years in the marines. Then McRae shook his head. No wouldn't make any difference; that guy's flawed, you can see it a mile off. If I'm lucky he'll piss off home in a couple of days.

No worries about the other Yank though, that guy could make it anywhere, a winner, a survivor, dump that bugger in the Ritz or prison, he'll sort it. Sorted himself a top shag as well. That's one tasty bit of beaver he's got. McRae fondled his sweaty genitals. Saved you until last Miss Lorna Karrol. He smiled, I think ten minutes of you and me all alone, is just what the doctor ordered!

5

Cedric Farringdon, Her Majesty's Consul to the Republic of Gamasi read the secure communication slip just placed upon his desk. He pressed his intercom, "Ah Joyce, see if you can round up Jonathon please."

Jonathon Forbes, Trade Attaché arrived five minutes later as his boss was re-reading the communiqué from London. The Consul peered over his half moon glasses at the young man, "Ever heard of tantalum?"

The attaché frowned in concentration and took a guess, "Southern Goa Sir?"

"No it's stuff, not a place. Very valuable stuff it appears." He waved the slip of paper, "Soon be on par with gold at the present rate. When refined from tantalite ore, it's used in the manufacture of mobile phones, computers..." He referred again to a document, "pagers, surgical equipment, aircraft engines, loads of things that require good heat and electric conductibility, combined with resistance to corrosion and a high melting point."

"Fascinating, Sir."

"Don't be facetious Jonathon. Majority of the stuff is mined around this part of the world, but in areas belonging to our more ... unstable ... neighbours."

"Think I see where we're going. Does London want us to check if there's any in Gamasi?"

"Appears they've already done it; do you remember about six months ago that team doing the mineral survey?"

Jonathon Forbes frowned again, "The Australians?"

His boss shook his head, "Seems not, actually they were our chaps."

"Bloody good actors then."

"Bloody good surveyors too. They found loads of the stuff, tantalite, deep in the forest north of here."

Forbes pondered, "going to change things a bit, once news gets out. Maybe President Amutu will be able to live in the style to which he would like to be accustomed."

"Yes that's our problem, mustn't get out ... not until we're ready that is. First thing in the morning I want you to have a meet with whoever is Amutu's Minister for Trade this week and get a mineral trade agreement signed and sealed."

"One problem immediately comes to mind Sir. When Amutu realises how big this is he'll blow us out and go to the highest bidder - probably some of our far eastern friends."

"True Jonathon, but one can only do ones best in these situations. Can't send in the gun ships any more."

Forbes turned to go, leaving the Consul to his thoughts of simpler times.

"Ah Jonathon, one more thing. London has already dispatched a field officer, and I quote, *just in case the situation warrants it.* So we have a spook in Gamasi, for our very own personal use."

"That's nice Sir. And how do we contact our James Bond?"

Cedric Farringdon replaced his reading glasses. "Staying at the Ambassador, arriving this afternoon, name of..." he focussed on his paper, "Goff."

6

It was mid morning of the first day of their holiday and Lorna was wondering why the group, minus the Russian girl, was sitting in the lounge listening to one of the strangest welcome meetings ever devised by a holiday company. Not only was the content more akin to indoctrination, but the holiday rep. was resplendent in full dress military uniform, complete with a chest full of medals. Even without his uniform, General Gboja would be a striking figure. Immensely tall and powerful, only protruding teeth and ancient acne scars marred his dramatic appearance.

The first part of his talk was unscripted and interesting. With broad, square hands the General pointed to enlarged photos on the pin boards arranged behind him. He described, in Lorna's opinion rather excessive detail, Gamasi's flora and fauna. The common theme was that most species were designed to kill or disable human beings. Lorna thought that considering what humans had done to Africa's flora and fauna this seemed eminently fair. Strangely General Gboja was under the impression that she intended to spend her holiday crawling around in the forest, instead of reading by the pool and cavorting in bed with Mike, as planned.

After coffee and a very good selection of biscuits, the General launched into *The History of Gamasi*. This started pleasantly enough with a view of the idyllic tribal lifestyle of the central African hunter-gatherer. Gboja had a talent for oratory.

Suddenly Lorna was snatched away from her minute inspection of a damaged finger nail by his thundering, and no doubt justified, tirade against the slave trade. Amidst much scowling and arm waving, he described in vivid and nauseating detail the conditions of capture and shipment of his ancestors. No smallest detail of human waste or disease was omitted. She noticed the German pair, cowering in the front seats being sprayed liberally with spittle. Lorna felt that *Thomas Cook* was probably not a retirement career option for the General.

The next subject for his invective was the British Colonial period. It appeared the noble people of Gamasi had been crushed under the imperialist tennis shoe for over 100 years. These foreign parasites had bled them of their natural resources and apart from the roads, railways, airport, sewers, fresh water, electric, hospitals, schools, administrative and legal systems, had given nothing in return.

Amidst a fine spray of saliva the tempo built to encompass, *The ceaseless efforts of his country's heroic armed forces to combat the enemy within: that terrorist rabble of the insurrectionist minority groups*. It appeared that all Stalinist excesses were as nothing compared to this enemy: murder, robbery, rapine and arson were their daily fare.

Lorna watched two thin gardeners in brown coveralls making desultory stabs at the weeds in the jungle garden outside the lounge window. Then something in the talk caught her attention: she wasn't sure, but thought the General had just thanked Xtreme Tours and their guests, *for their invaluable assistance in combating our terrorist threat*, what did he mean?

The meeting was coming to a close without a question and answer session. McRae dragged himself out of his chair in the far corner, well out of spittle range. He thanked the General, who nodded in acknowledgement whilst wiping his chin with a large white handkerchief. As the guests arose and stretched, McRae announced the *Sights of Kamba Tour* after lunch. The group filed off towards the restaurant.

Lorna took Mike's hand, "What did he mean at the end about our help with their terrorist problem?"

Mike hesitated, "I guess our tourist dollars must help, but it's more than that..."

Robert Goff grasped Mike's elbow as he stroked his hidden scar. "Bloody hell, makes you ashamed to be British doesn't it," he guffawed.

Mike turned from Lorna, "I'm not."

Unabashed, Robert shrugged, "Yah, but you're one of us really, sort of cousins." He leaned forward and flashed his boyish grin at Lorna, "you know, different branches of the same family."

"That's jolly nice," responded Lorna.

As they ate their chicken and rice Lorna returned to the subject, "What did he mean in the lecture about *assisting with their terrorist threat?*"

Mike nodded his thanks to the waiter as he topped up their beers, "Well we're supposed to help them put down the threat. Weren't you listening to the General?"

Lorna's loaded fork paused halfway between her mouth and plate, "Sort of, but I still don't get it."

He fiddled with his glass, "We help put down the terrorists … you know..."

Lorna shook her head, "No Mike I don't know. Back home we reluctantly put down our old family dog, but never a terrorist. Please explain."

"Well, we go out on patrol and … assist the local troops … they've got a big problem, you heard what the General just said."

"They're not the only ones! What sort of *assist* … carrying stuff?"

Mike made a face, "no, more than that, we're here to fight terrorism."

Lorna stared at her plate and silently shifted rice for a minute; Mike fidgeted. She looked up, "Right, so this disparate bunch of weirdoes are all here to fight terrorism?"

"Yes … well not only for that, it is a very beautiful country..."

"Oh I see. So as a break from sightseeing, they shoot a few locals?"

"No, not really … well obviously some are local, but the local guys are all mixed up with foreign backed troops."

Lorna opened her eyes in mock alarm, "No surely not! Wouldn't it be unethical to bring in foreign assistance?"

"Ok you can mock, but this is something that has to be done. You just heard what the General said."

Lorna's eyes were hard and she hissed, "Mike please stop quoting that idiot in the Gilbert and Sullivan uniform. Do you honestly trust and believe that guy?"

"He's their top anti-terrorist co-ordinator; it says so in the holiday…"

"Mike that guy is a nightclub bouncer … alright so tell me where he won those medals? I must have missed all the international conflicts that Gamasi has been involved in!" Bray just returned her stare in silence. "Ok, I'll tell you where I think he got that chest full of medals … off the fucking internet." Lorna's voice was becoming strident and people at the neighbouring tables stopped eating and looked their way.

The headwaiter appeared, "Everything ok, Sir? Madam?"

Mike flashed him a smile, "Yes thanks." He stared pleadingly at Lorna and spread his hands in supplication, "Look let's go outside and talk this through."

As they walked in the garden Mike tried to take Lorna's hand. She snatched it away and folded her arms, "Now I see what all the guns were about. I assumed they were for culling game."

Mike had gathered his thoughts and stroked under his hair, "Lorna, I believe this is one of the most important things we can do. Terrorism threatens us all, it's too easy just to stand by and let those bastards…"

"Mike don't you DARE lecture ME on terrorism," she took some deep breaths and then continued quietly, "Now please tell me exactly what this…OUR holiday is all about?"

"I've just said; we are attached to patrols and assist in actions against known terrorist groups, as required."

"What's this *WE*, you're not assuming I'm going…"

"No, no, just the shooters in the group."

"Oh I see, just the shooters, how nice. Mike they're a bunch of fucking loonies, ok rich loonies, but loonies none the less."

Bray nodded, "well I guess it would attract the more oddball..."

Lorna viscously plucked a large leaf as she walked and dismembered it, "and this country's armed forces really need this bunch of ... of ... oddballs?"

"They're very poor, right near the bottom of world's rich list, the money's gotta help."

Lorna gave hollow laugh, "Ok, take that fat nerdy West Coast guy, Herring or Henning. He's going on jungle patrol with you?"

Mike nodded, "Not with me, but I guess someone's got him."

"Mike, no one would want that sad, clumsy bastard on their table tennis team!"

Bray shrugged, "Maybe he's better than he looks."

Lorna just stared in disbelief, "Ok, so tell me, how did you volunteer for this bold adventure?"

Mike furrowed his brow, "Well that's the weird part..."

Lorna snorted an interruption, "I think not, but carry on."

Mike ignored the comment, "one day, I got a call..."

"Really? Not from God I assume! Was it the White House?"

"Look you can make fun of this, but to me it's deadly serious."

Lorna stopped, blocking the path, her eyes blazing, "Oh Mike I'm SO sorry, I never realised it was serious. I never realised it was SERIOUS finding you're on vacation with a fucking schoolboy psychopath ... and not just your common or garden psychopath, but one who thinks he can present it to you as ... as some sort of honourable crusade. Look Mike, I didn't buy all that War on Terrorism crap back in the States and I sure as hell don't buy it here!"

The group sat outside the front door of the Ambassador hotel in the same three air-conditioned Mercedes that had ferried them from the airport. The first and second cars had local guides; McRae in the third was accompanying the Germans and Bray, who at this moment could not be found. Johan Koeffe looked out of the tinted glass at McRae in the reception trying to track down the New Yorker and his pretty girlfriend. Wolfgang Schmidt sat in the opposite corner exuding irritation: Schmidt detested tardiness. With a shrug the courier returned and in a waft of humid air, slid in the front next to their driver. The cortege swept away without the missing couple.

Their first stop was the towering wrought iron gates outside the Presidential palace; the copy of the Scottish castle at Balmoral. Four sentries stood in the shade, automatic weapons swinging loosely, staring at the group. The passengers in the first two cars alighted and stood listening to their guides. McRae showed no inclination to leave the air-conditioned comfort.

"Shall we join the others?" asked Schmidt.

The Scotsman shrugged, "You can if you want."

The Germans sat in silence and stared at the manicured lawns and flowerbeds.

McRae's answer to Johan's enquiry about the history of the building was a gruff, "you're having dinner with the wee man tomorrow night, and best you ask him yourself."

Schmidt hissed in disgust, this was not how a guided tour should be conducted, "I assume you have no great respect for President Amutu?"

McRae didn't bother to turn around, "I guess anyone who can stop this bunch exploding and at the same time line his pockets, can't be that stupid."

"What bunch?"

"The Gamasis: they all hate each other."

The Germans exchanged glances. "Why do they hate each other?" asked Johan.

McRae sighed; this was too much like work, "Look the population's around five million divided into three tribal groups, plus a few mixed races you can't really classify. The Christians and the Muslims hate each other, but who they both hate most is the minority Animists. Take Joseph here," he nodded to their driver, who waved a languid hand, "he's a Fasa, same as the President. They make up nearly half the population, they're Christian and get all the best jobs." Joseph flashed them a dazzling smile and nodded vigorous confirmation. "The second biggest group is the Muslims. Then there are about twenty percent Animists, who live in the jungle eating fruit and monkeys, like they've done for a million of years."

Schmidt frowned, "So apart from the resentment over jobs, what is the problem?"

McRae shrugged, "Search me; I guess people just like to hate." The Scotsman stared silently as the two local guides, standing outside in the blistering heat waving and pointing at the imposing stone façade. Suddenly he had an idea, "Of course there is the cannibalism thing. Not so long ago the Animists used to eat the others." He considered his statement, "though obviously not fast enough if they're a minority."

After a tour of several buildings that were relics of the British colonial period, now housing various government departments, they pulled up outside the art deco facade of the Amutu Free Hospital. Not waiting for McRae, Schmidt and Koeffe joined the others as their guides herded them through the main entrance. They were honoured as the Minister for Health awaited them; a sweating, obese man fronting an escort of young male assistants.

The visitors were ushered into a pristine children's ward where immaculate nurses in starched 1950's style uniforms, complete with winged hats, were mopping the brows of apparently healthy, doe eyed children. Each child was tucked tightly into the rows of snowy white beds.

A grey haired consultant in white coat and looped stethoscope appeared and solemnly shook each visitors' hand. The Minister nodded, chins wobbling as the consultant explained how, but for the help of their benefactor, President Amutu, this hospital could not function. But even the great man's generosity was not enough and any of these patients could die, (he swept an arm to encompass all the silently suffering ranks,) if more help was not forthcoming. The doctor led the group, pausing at the foot each bed. Impressively, without reference to notes he detailed the ailments of each patient, most seemed very serious, but fortunately curable.

The Minister and his bevy of clerks followed closely behind, all transfixed by the Russian girl's jiggling buttocks and expanse of shapely legs and thighs under her micro skirt. Due to the height of her heels, she walked using Serovec's arm for support. There was an audible intake of breath when she leant forward to stroke the tight curls of one of the tiny patients. Their circuit of the ward slowly returned them to the door, where in impassioned tones the consultant pleaded for their financial assistance. Behind them the Minister's assistants gathered, clutching extremely tax effective covenant forms, all conveniently drafted with every visitor's details. Everyone declined the forms. Lindy, the Russian temptress, after much pouting and arm tugging, persuaded Serovec to withdraw a thick wad of 100 dollar bills and peel off a number, which he handed to the fawning politician.

The plump young American then created problems by offering his credit card.

Johan Koeffe took the opportunity to ask for the toilets. He was led by one of the clerks through a maze of corridors to a freshly painted suite. Johan guessed by the explosive noises from a nearby cubicle that his young guide's needs had been greater than his. After washing his hands he set off alone to find the group.

Taking a wrong turn he became increasingly aware of the distant sound of many voices and a nauseating smell. At the end of the corridor was a pair of battered doors, as he approached the stench was catching in his throat and the noise was louder. Far behind him a door banged followed by the sound of running. Johan really did not want to see what was behind the doors, but found himself reaching forward. The runner was approaching and shouting in some African language.

He pushed against the hinge and realised the noise was not conversation, it was moaning. The smell hit him and he felt the brash in his throat, heralding vomit. Packed tightly along both walls were foetid mattresses, on each lay an emaciated body, wrapped in stained rags. Some on their backs, eyes closed, mouths agape, not moving. Some rolled and groaned.

As he stood at the door, he felt a hand on his shoulder pulling him back, it was the young clerk, "Sir, sir, no go in there, very dangerous."

Johan turned, taking deep breaths, he fought his heaving stomach as he was led back down the corridor. In shock, his English deserted him, he searched for the right words, "What … what is that room?"

The clerk gabbled, eyes wide in fear, "No good for visitors, very bad illnesses sir, people die all the time."

7

10.30 Friday morning after breakfast the group was back in the lounge for the *Ideological Discussion.* Lindy the Russian girl was the only one missing, but she was never around early.

McRae's introduction of today's lecturer was not effusive.

Mr Milton Keats looked like he had been assembled from the top and bottom halves of two different human beings. In a white shirt and plain tie, above the waist he looked normal, but below he ballooned. Tightly encased in dark trousers, his hips and buttocks were enormous, the group watched in fascination as he waddled up to join McRae at the front.

Lorna found her eyes drooping, yesterday General Gboja had just been boring, now Mr Milton Keats sent you to sleep. *The Enemy at our Door* was delivered in well-modulated English, but clearly for the one-hundredth time. It would appear that under the guiding hand of their beloved President, Gamasi was a model of democratic liberalism: but what stood between the country and an idyllic future were the efforts of the terrorist forces lurking in the forest to the north of the capital. Led by non Gamasis with massive foreign funding, they recruited the young and gullible with lies and false promises. Terrorist excesses, of rape, murder, robbery and arson were described in detail: Lorna wondered sleepily at what point a certain level of these crimes, became an excess.

She thought about last night, the atmosphere between her and Mike, their first night together they had not made love. They had slept rigid back to rigid back, hoping not even to touch. The evening had also been a strain, the terrible Goff couple had joined them at their table and Mike had chatted as if he hadn't got a care in the world. After dinner the National Heritage Dancers had cavorted around the restaurant for far too long, illustrating the *Ethnic Diversity of Gamasi,* their drums

THE BIG GAME

had given her a headache and she had gone to bed early, first putting on a long tee shirt.

As Mr Keats droned to a conclusion, McRae summoned the mid morning refreshments. At the coffee pot, Lorna found herself next to her plump fellow American who was sweating, despite the air conditioning. She felt she should make conversation, "You can hardly believe what Man can do to Man."

Paul Henning nodded, "Yeah sure," he frowned, "no ginger creams today."

Lorna looked at the selection of biscuits, "No? Isn't life a bitch?"

Paul grunted, then brightened, "Hey, they've got jaffa cakes though."

She wandered off to watch Milton Keats from a distance as he worked on inflating his abdomen with chocolate wholemeals.

They resumed their seats for a question and answer session.

First was Wolfgang Schmidt, "Who is funding the terrorists?"

Milton Keats had answered this one many times: it seemed that his country did not enjoy good relations with either of its neighbours, both harbouring ambitions to absorb Gamasi.

"But they are both poor countries, how can they afford to maintain this support?"

Mr Keats adopted a worldly wise air, "Sir, not all nations have a government like Gamasi, they spend money that should rightly go to the people, for improper use."

Next the Russian Serovec asked about the terrorist's weaponry. Mr Keats claimed little knowledge and referred him to Sergeant McRae, or General Gboja who would be conducting their afternoon session.

As if back in the classroom, Robert Goff's arm shot up, "Have they got a leader, these chaps?"

Keats hesitated, "Yes, his name is Churu, he was a Colonel in our army until he turned to treason."

"What treason?"

Again the moment to weigh his response, "He tried to make a revolution. Needless to say it failed."

Mike Bray this time, "How many are we up against?" Lorna noted the use of the word *we*, the first time anyone in the group had acknowledged that Churu and friends were their enemy as well. She shot him a withering glance.

"It is difficult to say, they claim thousands, but in reality it is only hundreds. They're badly trained, many of very low intelligence, young people and women."

Lorna bristled and spoke for the first time, "I'm surprised your army hasn't beaten them then, as they're only women and young people!"

Keats looked surprised, this was not in his script, "It will not be long," his smile took in the whole group, "with the help of our foreign friends."

***

Aggression Assessment was not a one hundred percent success. Paul Henning had discharged his weapon into the Gaiety Ballroom's mirrored disco ball. As soon as the American unpacked his new rifle, it was obvious he was unfamiliar with firearms. General Gboja allocated one of his training corporals to help. Despite being a non live round session, Mr Henning was the first in the group to have a confirmed hit.

As hotel maintenance staff treated the injured mirror ball, McRae checked each shooter's ability. He assessed them as they stripped, cleaned, re-assembled and went through their loading and jamming routines. The rest of the group displayed an impressive familiarity with their weapons.

If Paul Henning was at the bottom of the heap, then Vasyl Serovec was most definitely at the top. The Russian's World War Two rifle was like an extension of his body, his fingers a blur as he went through his routines, eyes closed as he loaded blanks and cleared imaginary jams. McRae was the proud holder of the Royal Marines "Sniper First Class" badge – the equivalent of an Oscar in the world of snipers, but he had never seen anyone equal to this Russian.

The Scotsman did not believe that women should be allowed to handle guns, but was grudgingly impressed with the ease and fluidity with which Fiona Goff handled her Parker Hale rifle.

Assessment over, McRae reminded his group that they would be collected at 18.30hrs in the foyer for dinner with President Amutu.

8

It definitely moved this time. David Churu watched as the board gently see-sawed above him. The weight of water had lifted the far end and it was in perfect balance. As the water continued to drip, its next move would be towards him. The bruising to the bones of his ear canals ached.

Long ago he had ceased fighting, realising it was pointless. If it had just been his hair then he believed he could have torn it out by the roots, but the ear tubes held his skull exactly in place under the nails.

He thought about his four children and his beautiful Sita. How would they survive without him? Assuming they were still alive, like many predators Amutu killed the offspring of any challengers.

Time stood still, David had no idea how many hours he had been listening to the drip of water above him. Suddenly a new idea occurred to him, supposing this was all just a psychological technique and the board was fixed to stop just short of his eyes?

9

Lorna had expected to hate President Amutu and was rather irritated to find that she could not help but like him. She watched the short, bearded man as he circulated the high ceilinged reception room, putting each guest at his ease.
I guess he's just a good politician, she thought, but his ready smile and apparent interest in others was disarming. In his dark, well-cut suit, he would have blended into any city institution. When she was introduced, his handshake had been firm with just the hint of a bow. He displayed an impressive knowledge of New York and gave a very brief description of his various visits. This was not the self-obsessed dictator she had conjured up. He questioned her about her job and family, then listened attentively to her replies.

Large barn size doors were thrown open at the end of the room and the guests were summoned to dinner. Glittering in the candlelight from ornate candelabra, the table and settings were magnificent. Immaculate white-coated footmen held their chairs as they were seated in accordance with little white name cards in silver holders. President Amutu sat at the head of the table flanked by Lorna and Fiona Goff, their respective partners beside them. The conversation and fine wines flowed freely throughout the excellent meal.

Fiona Goff persuaded Amutu to explain the reasons for building his replica castle. "When I was a student in England I used my vacations to travel throughout the British Isles. I fell in love with your ancient architecture, hence my little bit of it here in Gamasi."

Lorna could not resist, "You live in great style Sir."

The President's laugh was deep and booming for such a short man, "Ahah Ms Karrol, or may I call you Lorna?" He smiled his thanks at her permission, "I detect a loaded comment. I guess you've seen the poverty in my country and feel that I should live in a mud hut?"

Lorna blushed at his directness, "Well all this," with a sweep of her hand she indicated the dark panelled walls, paintings and sumptuous table, "this luxury, seems at odds with how many of your people live."

Amutu nodded, "You are right, but like your own President," his smile included Fiona Goff, "and of course Fiona's own Royal Family, I don't own any of this. I merely serve the people and hold all this..." he searched for the word, "opulence, in their trust, this is the shop window for Gamasi. Would you prefer me to attract investment and entertain foreign representatives sitting cross legged in a hut?"

Fiona Goff intervened, "I think the problem is the disparity in lifestyles, between them and you."

Amutu paused, then chuckled, "if I may say so, I think both you ladies look, but do not see. Within a few hundred metres of both your Buckingham Palace and the White House are homeless people living on the streets."

"You have no homeless in your country then?" asked Lorna.

"Here no one needs be homeless, anyone is free to go into the forest and build themselves a house out of the natural materials and grow food to live." He raised a quizzical eyebrow, "I think we all know what would happen to your homeless people if they tried to do that in the United States, or England."

Mike intervened, sensing the conversation was straying beyond the bounds of polite dinner party conversation, "Are you married Mr President?"

Amutu smiled at Bray, "For my sins Michael, I have three wives, as allowed in the Koran.

Bray looked surprised, "But I read somewhere that you're a Christian."

"I was brought up a Catholic, but now I embrace the three religions of my people, Christianity, Islam and Animism."

Lorna frowned, "Isn't that difficult?"

"Easier than you might think. When you look at the core of each you realise that all three believe in the same thing, it's just the interpretation that is different. I take the best from each." He chuckled, "although I frequently question whether my three marriages was one of the best aspects of Islam. Each of my wives is from one of our religions."

Robert Goff had broken off his conversation with Paul Henning, "President has your Catholic wife got reservations?"

Amutu considered for a moment and a fleeting look of sadness passed over his face, "Much of life is compromise, but she is a wise lady and understands."

Lorna held Amutu's eye, "It's a pity they couldn't be here tonight."

He brightened and again the rumbling laugh, "If they had, we would never have got a word in sideways."

Robert Goff again, "Sorry we're breaking all the rules here, talking of politics and religion.

"Mr Goff, as some famous person once said, everything in life is politics - and religion is everything in life, if we ban those two, we speak of nothing." Throughout dessert and coffee they stayed on neutral subjects; their homes, work and families.

Lorna began to suspect that she had misjudged Fiona Goff: the brainless aristocrat could just be a facade. Behind it she caught glimpses of a very bright young woman. They're a strange couple, so alike, but not compatible. Shiny new wedding rings, so it could even be their honeymoon, but there was no sexual frisson between them. I've never seen them so much as hold hands; maybe that's the British upper classes for you. Perhaps Fiona's playing a part, but why? Do they have arranged marriages over there? One thing I'm sure about is that Robert's just what he seems – a brainless gun nerd! As they moved back into the reception room Lorna stayed close to Fiona Goff and the President. She wanted her suspicions confirmed.

It did not take long. Fiona mentioned an Amnesty International report, not normal light reading in British stately homes, "If I may be allowed to return to politics President?"

Amutu nodded his encouragement to the English woman, "Please do Fiona, it would be unreasonable to invite your help in resolving one of my country's problems and then to impose limits."

Lorna noted this was the first reference to the reason they were in Gamasi. She was unready for what came next.

The English woman held the politician's gaze, awaiting the reaction to her next words, "Amnesty allege that innocent people die here, at the hands of your government."

Amutu remained silent for some seconds, then dropped his eyes and examined the floor, deep in thought. Lorna could sense Mike and Robert's concern at the question, they both shuffled but said nothing.

"Before I respond Fiona, may I ask you a question? she gave her approval with a slight nod, "Why did you come to my country?"

There was no hesitation, "I was invited and I believe in what we're here to do."

Again the examination of the floor, then he looked up and met both women's eyes, "I see that you're also interested Lorna?" He ignored their partners, focussing only on the women. Lorna nodded; he was calm, giving no hint as to his reaction to this direct questioning.

The seconds passed and then with a deep breath, he reached a decision, "yes this is true, sadly my government has been responsible for the deaths of innocent people." His answer was also a challenge, no excuses, no qualification, he stared silently at the women. His words hung in the air, Amutu let the silence and eye contact work for him.

Lorna broke it, "But you're a humane man, how can you allow this?"

"Same as you do," he responded.

All semblance of deference fast receding, Lorna blurted, "But I don't, I've never had anything to do with the deaths of innocent..."

Strangely his laughter lines deepened, he was smiling at her, "Oh yes you do Lorna, every day," he included his questioner, "you as well Fiona. "Let us examine the first few years of this century. Do you know how many thousands of innocents in Afghanistan and Iraq you've killed?"

Lorna felt Mike's hand on her arm, but she could not stop, "That's nothing to do with me. I actively opposed the wars in..."

Suddenly they glimpsed the power of the small black man in front of them. He raised his voice by just a few decibels, his eyes blazed and with a cutting motion of his hand silenced her, "You can fool many people Lorna, but never fool yourself. You salve your conscience by saying that you never voted for them, but you countenance a government that imprisons without trial and tortures prisoners of war." Lorna was shaking and sensing her distress Amutu became urbane once more and included all four guests, "My friends, there are many things in my country that displease me, but we are a new nation, only half a century old. Every year, bit by bit, things here get better … when you return home in a few days will you be able to look around and say the same thing?"

He half turned and surveyed the rest of the group, "And now you must forgive me, I have been neglecting my other guests." With a slight bow he went to join the Germans and Russians.

The limousines arrived and President Amutu stood at the door to bid them farewell.

When he came to Lorna he held her hand between both of his and smiled at her, "it was good to meet you Lorna," she smiled back and thanked him. He released her hand and started to move away; suddenly he turned back as if a thought had just occurred to him.

He addressed Lorna and Fiona, "Please forgive my presumption but a piece of advice for you both as we will probably not meet again. Always be very careful when planting your Union flag and your Stars and Stripes on the moral high ground, you may find it is not firm enough to support them."

10

David instinctively closed his eyes as the nail dropped towards him. It stopped, resting gently on his eyelid, the tip pressing on the soft skin.

Another drip of water fell into the bowl above. How much did one drip weigh? The pressure on his eye felt no different, how many drips would it take to pierce the skin?

11

"Lorna it's just a firing range!" Mike had stood at the end of the bed and stared at her propped up on the pillows. Eventually she had given her blessing to his morning trip and now had to reconcile how she felt about the whole holiday. Time at the pool was the order of the day.

Paul Henning lay on his stomach in the sun, or the prone position as Sergeant McRae called it. He had the distinct feeling that over a quarter of a million dollars should buy you more respect than the Scotsman was presently showing him. It was as if he was a conscripted rookie, the soldier hadn't yet sworn at him, but he sensed it was not far off.

McRae focussed his binoculars on the cardboard outline of a charging infantryman one hundred metres away – it was unmarked, "Ok laddie, let's go through our procedures again." Paul was sweating in all his new equipment. Ear protectors, eye patch, elbow and shoulder pads, he drew the brim of his baseball cap closer to his nose.

"First, shuffle yourself around until you're comfortable and your whole body is in line with the target." Paul wriggled his plump body deeper into the dirt. "Good, now wrap that sling tightly around your left arm – and draw your weapon snugly into your shoulder, comfortable?" Henning nodded. "Now this time you're going to take up the pressure on that trigger then gently squeeze. Ready?" A grunt from Henning. "Three breaths, hold your breath, drop onto the target, squeeze."

McRae focused back on the target, there was a hole just on the edge of the figure's right hip, "Congratulations laddie, you've spoilt his pants."

THE BIG GAME

Late morning and the sun was searing. Lorna stood naked in the bedroom and applied a liberal covering of high factor oil before trying on her new black bikini. She examined her image in the full-length mirror and decided that it fitted as well here, as it had in the store back home. She turned, raised up on her toes and craned around to check her behind, maybe a bit brief but looking good, so what the hell! Throwing all her stuff into a beach bag and knotting a sarong around her waist she headed for the pool.

The sun and heat hit her as she walked onto the patio, the stones scorched her bare feet so she chose a lounger under a thatched umbrella. The pool boy spread a towel for her and the waiter brought a cold drink. She adjusted her bikini, pulled the peak of her cap down low over her eyes, brought up her book to ward off potential conversation and settled down to think.

What I've got to sort out is how I feel about this whole situation. At first it just seemed mad, but the deeper I get, it begins to make a bit more sense. These guerrilla forces pose a terrible threat to the population, that's if I believe everything these government guys say, which I guess I don't, not one hundred percent anyway.

That General Gboja's a bit spooky, Milton Keats is rather sweet and I think President Amutu is ok, but one person's terrorist is another's freedom fighter. Anyway whatever the rights and wrongs here, its Mike's involvement I've got to get my head around.

She sipped her drink and watched two old ladies swimming together, heads slowly progressing down the pool like a pair of grey seals.

I think Mike genuinely believes in this terrorist thing, which in my mind means he's stupid. So the big question is, do I want to screw a stupid guy even if he's amusing and got a great body? But just maybe it's me being stupid! I've not known Mike long, but you get a feeling about people and I'm sure he's a good guy. But why does a good guy volunteer to shoot people?

The new material was flossing her ass, so she shifted onto her front, reversed her baseball cap and rested on a forearm. I know what I'll do, as soon as he gets back from the firing range I'll talk it over with him. And this time no shouting or sulking, just calm reasoned discussion.

The beer bottle exploded against the wall. Mike put his hands over his head to ward off the shards of glass, if he had not ducked it would have hit him full in the face. Lorna was groping one handed in the mini-bar for more missiles as she shouted at him, "So if they'd been Eskimos we'd be tearing around the fucking North Pole behind a pack of ... of ... those big wolf-dog ... things?"

"Look I know it's my problem, but..." he was not quick enough to avoid the Schweppes tonic which hit him harmlessly mid chest. The gentle impact seemed to madden Lorna even more and she followed up with a volley of mineral water, Coca Cola and spirit miniatures, scoring only a disappointing fifty percent.

"Your problem? Your problem? You fucking pathetic moron. It ceased to be your problem as soon as you decided to come here and murder people. From that moment it became everyone's problem. Everyone who comes near you ... including me!"

The man in reception sensed that the pretty American woman was far from happy; in fact she emitted an air of contained fury. Luckily they had spare rooms and he swiped her credit card as she waited tensely the other side of his counter. He summoned a porter to collect her bags from the room she had shared with Mr Bray and with a sigh of relief watched her stride off to the elevator. She had asked for the mobile phone number for the representative of Xtreme Tours and after rummaging through the office, he dispatched a bellboy to her new room with it written on a sheet of hotel paper.

Mike was still collecting missiles from under the bed when she returned to their room and delivered the speech she had rehearsed in the elevator, (no more husky/wolf-dog moments this time!) "Please go to the bar, or wherever, while I pack."

He moved beseechingly towards her, "Look Lorna, can't we talk about this?"

She did not look at him, but dragged her case over to the wardrobe, "No thanks, I've always tried to avoid talking to psychopaths."

Mike's further attempts were met with a stony silence, so he banged out of the door nearly colliding with her porter waiting outside.

Lorna heard him apologise and shouted her advice to the porter through the half open door, "Don't get in his way, he might shoot you." She finished packing, checked the room one last time, and then invited the porter in to take her case.

***

McRae shut off his phone, sank back in his bar chair and released his breath in a long sigh. Bloody hell, why do they bring women along? They're always trouble. There're plenty of cheap local girls who try harder and give you no shit. He took a long pull on his beer bottle and thought about the conversation he had just had with The American Beauty. She wanted to return home as soon as possible, what could he arrange? He had told her the truth about scheduled flights into Kamba – there weren't any. It wasn't the tourist season, so no chance of a spare seat with one of their flights. She had asked if there were any light aircraft for charter.

"Well there's Hansie, a South African with a Cessna, he always hanging around town. Very difficult guy to track down though," he told her thoughtfully, "could be up country somewhere, but if he turns up, he'll be your man."

He had described the road option if she was feeling lucky; she had wisely refused. The simple answer was to wait until Wednesday week when all the madmen got flown back in Amutu's jet. Of course there could be another option that he had failed to mention, a spare seat on one of the commercial flights that were always in and out of Kamba. He pondered his reason for omitting that bit of information and laughed to himself; you never know what can happen in eleven days here, she might even get bored and fancy a bit of rough: a ruggedly handsome, one legged, Scotsman for example!

His phone rang – it was her again. He grinned, "So quickly?"

"Mr McRae it's Lorna again, I've been thinking, is there another hotel I could move to?"

He smiled, "I wouldn't recommend it, the Ambassador's the only one that doesn't include cockroaches."

"Ok, but please let me know as soon as you manage to track down that South African."

"I'll be right on his case Lorna … oh and could you do me a favour as well?"

She sounded surprised, "sure, if I can."

He smiled at the wall, "forget the Mr McRae, its Tom."

"Ok … thanks Tom."

McRae gently closed his mobile phone and grinned. You're welcome. I'm always available to a maiden in distress.

A sun-tanned man in a khaki vest turned around on his barstool and in a broad South African accent called across the room to McRae, "Another beer Tom?"

McRae upended his bottle, "That's exceedingly nice of you Hansie."

The South African spun back to the bar and shouted at the owner, "Hey George, more beers down this end."

12

David Churu stopped screaming as he fought the vomit reflex. The waves of agony as the weight of water had driven the nail through his left eyelid and retina were gradually reducing in intensity.

Despite the pain and shaking he knew if he vomited when pinned on his back it would all be over. But why cling onto life? I know they'll kill me soon after the second nail pierces, so why hang on? If I suffocate on my vomit it'll all be over in minutes. He teetered on the brink of choking, but still kept desperately swallowing the saliva that flooded his mouth.

He felt the friction of the nail as it drove slowly down through his eyelid. The slightest movement helped its passage and he tried to control his shivering. He could not judge how deep it had penetrated his eye, he just knew it was in there working its way into his head.

Then cutting through the pain and nausea, a thought - maybe they had miscalculated and the first nail would lodge in the bone at the back of his left eye socket before the second one pierced his right.

Moments later he received the answer. The gentle touch of the second nail just teasing his other eyelid.

13

Jonathon Forbes sat outside the Minister for Trade's office and examined the life size marble statue of Queen Victoria at the head of the stairs. Strange that they never removed her after independence, he thought. The only change was to the dedication on the base. It now read, *From Her Royal Highness To The People Of The...* then someone had stuck a long rectangular piece of faded cardboard with the words *Republic of Gamasi* written in black felt tip pen over the final words. No doubt it says Reunion Coast underneath, thought Jonathon.

The door opened and a clerk ushered the Englishman into the Minister's office. All the trappings of colonialism remained, but the new incumbent did not favour filing as all around the walls of the vast room were stacked dusty, yellowing bundles of paper, each secured with brown string.

Standing to one side the clerk announced Jonathon in the ringing tones of a toastmaster, "Mr Jonathon Forbes, the British Attaché for Trade."

The Minister, a clean-shaven, unmemorable man of middle height, dressed in a creased grey suit, came around his desk and they shook hands.

The Minister was new to the job and despite meeting him at an official function, Jonathon could not recall his previous incarnation. He played safe, "Good to meet you again Minister, and congratulations on your new post."

"Thank you Mr Forbes," he indicated a chair opposite his desk. After tea and pleasantries had been exchanged, the Minister got down to business. "As you know, we have received documents from a British company relating to mineral extraction rights."

The Englishman hesitated as if searching his memory, "Ah yes, my office received a copy. Have to admit I only scanned it, but they seem pretty standard terms – percentages etc."

The minister referred to a fax. Even upside down Jonathon recognised the notepaper of a venerable firm of London based commercial lawyers. He made a mental note that he went to school with one of their very junior partners. "It would seem so," the Minister tapped his file, "and you consider this mineral company trustworthy?"

Forbes adopted an expression of mild shock, "Oh most certainly. Please be assured if we had even the slightest doubts as to their probity, they would not have progressed this far. We place a very high value on the continued goodwill that exists between our Governments."

The African nodded, and then drummed his fingers on his desktop in thought, "What interests us is the timing."

Forbes looked confused, "Timing Minister?"

"Yes timing. It is some 50 years since our countries went our separate ways."

"We prefer to think of it merely as a revision of roles, rather than a separation."

The Minister smiled, "As you wish Mr Forbes, but it is still 50 years since independence and in all that time no interest has been shown in our mineral rights."

Forbes shrugged and adopted a deferential tone, "An unforgivable oversight, but with my department's help, one that will soon be redressed."

"But we still find this timing interesting." Jonathon thought he knew the reason for the *we*; he sensed Amutu's influence. The Minister continued, "Interesting in that it follows an Australian mineral survey."

Forbes looked surprised, "Really? Is there an Australian company interested in a similar agreement?"

"No, not that we know of."

Again the slight shrug, "Then I would assume it's a coincidence. Although we are all Commonwealth partners, we no longer have any control over our Australian friends."

The Minister paused and studied the diplomat, "Maybe Mr Forbes, but I'm always very suspicious of coincidences."

As soon as the door closed behind Jonathan Forbes, the Minister picked up his phone, "I need a list of all Australian mineral companies – yes now, as quickly as you can."

***

Lorna had continental breakfast sent up to her room, which had a view over the front lawns. Exactly at ten o'clock she was standing at her window. At five minutes past the hour a convoy of four army Land Rovers swept down the drive. Her heart sank as she scanned the occupants; she could clearly see Mike's profile in the back of the lead vehicle as it accelerated out of the gates. "You bastard," she breathed as tears welled up in her eyes, "I hoped you'd change your mind at the last minute."

It had been a sleepless night. He kept knocking on her door until nearby residents complained to the reception. Then the phone calls started until she unplugged the receiver. Finally, some time in the middle of the night she had heard him slide a note under her door. The single sheet of hotel paper still lay crumpled in the corner where she had thrown it. Unrepentant, pig headed, the letter could have been from a different person than the one she thought she knew. It had even contained a misquote: *For evil to flourish, it only requires good people to do nothing.* Sanctimonious shit!

Lorna had spotted McRae and fat Paul in the second Land Rover, so she dialled his mobile from the bedside phone. McRae had to shout above the engine noise and drumming of stones under the chassis, "'Fraid not, no sign of Hansie yet. I tried all his usual places last night. I even took a run out to the airfield, but his plane was missing."

THE BIG GAME

"Thanks a lot for all your trouble Mr Mc ... Tom, you'll have to let me know what I owe you."

He grinned out of the window, "Don't worry about it. But tell you what, I've just had an idea. Where'll you be tonight?"

"I've nothing planned, so here at the hotel I guess."

"I'll be round about eight then, meet you in the front bar."

Lorna hesitated, she did not want to meet Mike, "Could we make it somewhere else?"

"Sure, I'll pick you up and we can go for a Chinese up the road."

Much to Paul Henning's surprise the Scotsman grinned at him as he closed his phone.

"Nice one Yankee Doodle, got a hot date tonight, now I've got to come up with a plan!" He rubbed his hands, "and now my friend, let's bag us a few bunnies."

Henning smiled weakly in return. He thought he preferred McRae when he was morose.

Lorna chose her usual corner away from the pool under the thatched sunshade. She ordered a cold drink then laid down on her stomach and made a pillow with her arms. She desperately needed to catch up on her sleep.

She had no idea how long she had been sleeping, but she woke to someone gently nudging her shoulder. She opened her eyes and focussed on a pair of lightly tanned, finely muscled woman's legs. Her gaze moved upwards and she noticed rows of round dark bruises on both inner thighs. Gathering her thoughts, Lorna rolled over and realised it was the Russian woman.

In guttural English the woman said, "You sleep too long." Lorna was confused; did this girl think she was the Sleep Police? Even more confusing the Russian then began to pull down her minute orange bikini bottom, "I got this only yesterday!"

Lorna slipped on her dark glasses and it all made sense, "Oh I see, you got burnt."

"Yes, the sun, it gets through this things," she indicated the thatch above with a toss of her short tousled hair. "I watch you. It is time you are turning over."

Lorna looked at her watch lying next to her shoes and realised she had been asleep for two hours, "Yes, thanks a lot, I was stupid."

"No stupid, only tired, " Lindy laughed throatily, "I guess maybe your man like mine, very strong in bed."

Lorna was horrified, "no no, not at all, well yes ... but not any more..."

The Russian looked concerned, "that is a problem, in my room I have some tablets that will help him."

Lorna started laughing, the other woman smiled, "I make the joke?"

Lorna sat up and took Lindy's hand, "No, I'm sorry, I wasn't laughing at you, it's just ... oh I can't explain..."and then she realised she was crying.

At that moment the waiter arrived and the Russian woman took control. She ordered them both fresh drinks. Brought over her bag and fished out tissues which she handed to Lorna. Pulled another lounger into the shade of the thatch, then sat and sipped her drink until the American settled herself.

Lorna touched the tissues to the corners of her eyes, "I'm sorry, I didn't mean to do that."

Lindy shrugged, "That's ok. You want talk?"

Lorna paused, "I don't know ... not yet. But let's talk about other stuff."

The Russian smiled at her, "Other stuffs are good."

Soon they were perched on high stools in the imitation beach bar, sipping Cuba Libres through straws. "But I didn't even know you spoke English?"

"Why should you? We never have talk."

Lorna felt guilty, she had dismissed this woman as a rich man's brainless tart, "Where did you learn it?"

"I start in school. Russian schools are good, maybe best in world. But also I speak French, Spanish and some Danish … if you speak Danish you understand Swedish and Norwegian."

Lorna was amazed, "My God, you are right about Russian schools."

Lindy laughed, "No I only learn English in school. The others I learn from UN."

"I see … is Ewan your partner, the man you're here with?"

The Russian frowned, "No his name is Vasyl. I am saying UN … the United Nations."

Lorna was confused, "I didn't know the United Nations did education."

Lindy roared with laughter, then wiped her eyes with a carefully manicured hand, "Lorna now it is you that make the joke. UN Peacekeepers, I fuck the Peacekeepers, they give me money and teach me their languages. More languages I learn, more money I get."

For once Lorna was speechless.

"That is past, for two years I'm just with Vasyl."

"Are you married?"

"Vasyl is, but not to me. He has fat wife and five fat children. In Moscow he is a very big businessman. He gives me money and a beautiful apartment. These days I fuck no other man."

Lorna ordered two more drinks and signed the tab. She poked the ice with her straw and thought about her next question, "And are you happy Lindy?"

The other woman considered her answer, "It is ok, but my life has a big sadness."

Lorna felt the melancholy in her tone, "What's that?"

The Russian searched for the right words, "From four years old to sixteen I do gymnastics, every day for many hours. I was good, very good, but not good enough. When they make my country's team I am not one." She paused reliving the memory, then brightened and grinned sideways at Lorna, "So I say fuck you committee, I go to Bosnia and work for United Nations. For five years I do this work And now I am twenty three years old, very rich and on holiday in Africa."

14

The dripping water was building the pressure on David Churu's right eyelid. Despite the agony in his left eye all his attention was focussed on his right; when would the nail burst through the skin and enter his remaining eyeball? Would the next drip be the one? Or the second? Or the third? Through the pain he was aware of two pairs of footsteps approaching, they stopped just short of his body.

President Amutu looked thoughtfully down at the man, at the puddle of excrement and urine between his open thighs. He dropped onto his haunches and squinted under the scaffold board, closely inspected the compression of the remaining eyelid. The skin was gradually whitening and stretched tight around the point of the nail, it was about to let go. What would be first, would the skin break down on its own, or would more water be needed?

Amutu studied the mouth of the pipe as another drip began to form. A perfect pear shape, it swelled, gathering weight, straining against its own surface tension as the bottom fattened. He thought it strange how something so small and insignificant could have such an influence on two mens' futures. It's not the object, it's the situation that makes the difference. What a difference it would make if this small globe of water fell anywhere else on the planet.

It separated and fell.

Halfway through its journey into the bowl he reached out and intercepted it with his cupped hand. He stared at the water in his palm as it traced his life line; then he switched his gaze to the naked man shivering on the floor inches from him.

Once more he examined the mouth of the pipe: again the underside was changing shape, slowly forming a convex bulge as a new drip was born.

15

The four Land Rovers stopped at a cross roads about ten miles north of Kamba just in sight of the jungle. An old British army truck with a canvas top was parked just off the road. McRae and the Gamasi corporals and privates walked over and spoke to a large group of soldiers squatting in its shade around a small fire.

Mike Bray sat and wondered what the hell he was doing here when he should be back at the hotel trying to talk Lorna round. *Not that my talking has been too successful to date! If she wasn't so unreasonable I could split my time, part doing this and part chilling out at the hotel or beach. But she's got it in her mind that I'm some gun-crazed madman. All I want to do is help these guys; and maybe lay a ghost at the same time.* As he thought, he rubbed the long scar hidden under his hairline.

McRae listened to the group and made notes of the latest intelligence on rebel movements. He was pleased to hear that there was lots of local activity, saving the need for gruelling trips up country. There were handshakes all round and then the soldiers piled back into their truck and roared off towards Kamba for some welcome R & R. McRae decided on his displacements. It was a small group so he had a private, or a corporal for each shooter, leaving him spare. Much better than some weeks, when he had two shooters to each instructor. *It's that bloody Gboja's fault; keen enough on the dollars, but doesn't want to release the manpower.*

After a brief discussion, the Goffs were dispatched north with their private driving and a corporal sitting next to him. Next the Germans headed off on the western road in a cloud of dust. The soldiers allocated to Mike Bray and Vasyl Serovec climbed aboard their Land Rover and they bounced off towards the east.

Paul Henning sat in the rear of his vehicle and watched with trepidation as the rest of the party disappeared. His guts were gurgling and he felt another spasm coming on. He stared at McRae chatting with the two remaining soldiers; occasionally they would point or wave their arms. At one point he saw McRae indicate with a nod of his head either the vehicle or him, both Africans turned around and stared, then laughed.

The pressure was building, so with his buttocks tightly clenched Paul hobbled over to McRae. Despite the pain his mouth watered at the smell of the barbeque and he glanced into the glowing embers. Although the flesh was blackened and the limbs distorted it was the unmistakable shape of a child. Mouth open he stood transfixed, his bowels forgotten. He stared at the clawed hands and his horrified gaze moved down to the feet. With dread he focussed on the face, the empty eye socket under a heavy brow, the long canine teeth exposed in a silent scream.

McRae broke into his reverie, "What do you want laddie?"

Henning stuttered, "What's that?"

The Scotsman followed his gaze, "Bush meat, their breakfast. What do you want?"

"Tissues … would you have any tissues?"

The Scotsman looked at him as if he had just crawled out from under a stone, "no."

Paul took a deep breath, "I need to crap."

"So use leaves, that's what God made 'em for."

The American scooted into a clump of bushes and dropped his new safari pants just before the world fell out of his ass. When the spasms subsided he looked around for suitable leaves, all he could see were long thin blades of dry grass. He made a pad and cleaned himself as best he could. He sniffed his fingers: they smelled of shit.

The soldiers and McRae were waiting for him in the vehicle. Paul hurried over, grabbed his bottle and poured torrents of water over both hands as he scrubbed them. He was interrupted by McRae's shout as he leaned out of the window, "What the fuck are you doing?"

Paul looked up to see three faces staring at him in disbelief, "Washing," he replied.

"Well fucking don't, in future the only washing you'll do is in your room." McRae pointed to the pool of wet earth at the Californian's feet, "Out here laddie, that's the difference between life and death"

As they set off on the northern road, Paul was seething; he summoned up his courage and prayed his voice would not shake. He cleared his throat, "What's with the Crocodile Dundee act McRae. We're only half hour from the city, I bet there's a gas station with a Coke machine just up the road." Silence … McRae didn't even acknowledge he had spoken.

After ten minutes they pulled off the road and the older soldier spoke at length into a radio in an African language. Paul sat miserably in the back next to McRae. His ass itched like crazy; there must have been some sort of powder in the dry grass. They drove on again and after another few miles turned onto an unmade track. Paul felt another spasm deep run through his guts. They ground forward at little more than a walking pace with foliage growing closer either side. Paul felt a build up of gas and risked a fart, immediately he knew he had made the wrong decision. As their Land Rover crawled in and out of the deep ruts Paul slid around in his shit.

After a few minutes McRae glanced at the American and sniffed, "Are you ok?"

Paul stared straight ahead and mumbled, "I think we'd better go back."

The Scotsman frowned, "You what?"

Paul cleared his throat, gathered himself and spoke louder, "Mr McRae, please remember that I'm the guest here and I want to go back to my hotel," his last words held just the hint of a tremor.

McRae nodded, "Ok laddie, if that's what you want."

Paul was on a roll, "And another thing, please stop calling me laddie."

"Ok Mr Henning sir." McRae leaned forward and tapped the driver on the shoulder, "Turn around as soon as you can; laddie here has shat himself."

***

Lorna came out of the cyber booth and was surprised to see Paul Henning walking up to the reception desk. She had just emailed friends and family a much edited version of the truth. She saw no point in mentioning the bad news, namely she was marooned in a banana republic with a psychopath and that the only good news was she had made friends with a Russian prostitute: better by far to stick to details of the weather and hotel.

Concerned that Mike had also returned early, she sidled up to the American just as he leant conspiratorially close to the receptionist. "Have you got a drug store?"

The young African's eyes grew huge as he stammered, "No, no sir, we have nothing like that here, this is a top class hotel, no have no drugs here."

Lorna quickly intervened and smiled at the terrified man behind the desk, "It's ok, leave this to me." She guided Paul away from the desk, noticing that he shrunk away from her light touch upon his arm. "Look Paul … it is Paul isn't it?" he nodded. "This place used to be British, so I guess they call a drug store a chemists, or maybe a pharmacy. Anyway, what do you need?"

Henning looked embarrassed. He rarely made eye contact, but now he inspected his trainers, "I've gotten a stomach bug," he mumbled.

Lorna commiserated, "…But hey no problem, you know that Russian girl Lindy?" Paul made a grunting noise which Lorna took to be assent, "Well she's got every drug known to man, let's go see her."

They walked together towards the pool. "Is all the group back?" she had to strain to hear his response.

"No just me ... you know ... the stomach thing."

Lindy was sitting in their usual corner under the thatched umbrella. To ensure a seamless tan she had just dispensed with the top of her bikini and the tiny bottom was dangerously low. As they arrived she was applying oil liberally to her breasts. Paul Henning became engrossed in a large palm tree to their left in the jungle garden.

"Lindy, Paul has a bit of a problem."

The Russian flashed him a dazzling smile, "hi Paul, sorry about that." The American made a rasping noise deep in his throat and examined the palm tree even more closely as Lorna explained. Lindy rummaged in her bag and produced a foil strip of diarrhoea pills. She held them out to Henning, "Here Paul, these will correct you."

Now the Californian had a new problem, he wanted to take the pills without looking at their owner. He shifted his gaze from tree to the flagstones at his feet and shuffled sideways like a crab towards the sound of her voice. With eyes averted he reached out, palm upwards. He waited, but Lindy did not place the strip in his hand, she just sat on the lounger holding the strip six inches in front of her breasts, smiling. The seconds dragged by and Paul was forced to look up; he grabbed the pills and with a strangled, "Thanks" nearly ran into the hotel.

The first thing that Lorna noticed as she searched for her room key was the corner of a white envelope poking under the door. Her heart sank, whatever Mike had written she knew that it would never work. She dumped her pool stuff on the bed and retrieved the envelope from the carpet. Turning it over she realised it was not hotel paper; the embossed logo was familiar, but she could not place it. Inside was a single sheet of official Presidential paper. She scanned the brief hand written note; President Amutu had invited her to dinner.

Lying naked on the bed, Lorna re-read it twice more. At the bottom he had put his direct number with a request to ring him and arrange a convenient day and time. She smiled as she read the words in brackets under his signature, *Charles Amutu - President.*

She reached for the phone and tapped in Lindy's room number, "Guess what? The President has asked me for a date!"

"Russian or American?"

"Neither. This one, President Charles Amutu."

For a moment the distinctive throaty laugh was the only response, then, "When?"

"Anytime, it's up to me."

"Maybe you will soon be First Lady of Gamasi."

"The Fourth is the best I could hope for. Anyway what do you think I should do?"

Lindy misunderstood, "Don't fuck him on the first date."

"No, no, I mean do you think I should accept?"

Again the laugh, "how often do you get asked out by a president? Are you mad? You are young, single and sexy, of course you go."

Lorna rang the direct number and Amutu picked up. Minutes later she had arranged her first date with a head of state for seven thirty the next evening.

***

It was as good as a day off and McRae rarely got one of those. By one o'clock he was in George's bar with all his drinking mates. He told Hansie the pilot about his abortive morning trip.

The South African scented business, "Do you think he might want flying back to Accra? Be the usual drink in it for you."

The Scotsman considered the question. The commission was tempting, "Possibly, I'll talk to him when he's a wee bit better; you wouldn't want him shitting in your plane, be a long trip." He guessed that Paul Henning would be taking no further active part, so Tom McRae could have himself a nice little holiday. There's no way I'll let Hansie ship out the fat man; if my American Beauty got to hear about the flight all my little holiday plans would fall apart. He grinned to himself. No way Jose, Ms Lorna Karrol is a very important part of my holiday plans!

By six o'clock the drink and heat had gone to McRae's head. He stumbled as he stood up to leave. George called to him, "You're off early Tom."

The Scotsman tapped his nose, "Got a hot date at eight."

His friends laughed. Someone shouted, "If it's that fat bitch, you'll be back here by half past."

McRae shook his head, "no no, it's a new one, a real classy bit of vag!"

***

Lorna walked into the foyer at exactly eight, praying that Mike would not be around. There was no sign of him, but McRae was leaning on the reception counter. He was the smartest she had ever seen him, cleanly shaven and wearing freshly pressed shirt and trousers, even his shoes were polished. They walked out of the front door and the Scotsman handed her into the first taxi in the queue. He slid in next to her and even his overpowering aftershave could not disguise the strong smell of drink.

The Chinese restaurant was only two minutes away. The décor and menu were the same as everywhere in the world, with the exception of China. It soon became obvious to Lorna that not only was McRae drunk, but that they had vastly different perceptions of this meal. McRae was flirting clumsily and she realised that this was her big opportunity to find out what Xtreme Tours was all about.

"Wine or beer?" he asked her.

"Neither thanks, I think I'll just have a Coke."

McRae shook his head, "Bad decision, they always put ice in it, made with the local water."

Lorna smiled at the waiter, "A cold can of coke and a glass please, no ice."

The Scotsman opted for beer and wine, "Just in case you change your mind."

They ordered their meal.

As Lorna poured her Coke, she asked about his job. "So how long have you been doing this Tom?" she assumed correctly that his favourite subject was Tom McRae, little further prompting was required.

"About eighteen months, a group every two weeks, apart from during the rains."

Although Lorna knew very little, she thought it would be more rewarding if she let McRae think she knew all about the holidays, "Are Xtreme good to work for?"

He laughed, "They pay me a thousand dollars a shooter, that's good enough for me."

She frowned, "It's so long since Mike booked I can't remember much about them."

"Don't ask me darling, never met 'em. Couple of years ago I caught up with an old mate at a reunion; he's doing the same thing for them in the Far East. Gave me a mobile number of this guy, sounded like a Rupert..."

She frowned, "Do you mean his name was Rupert?"

McRae chuckled, "No he was *a Rupert*, an officer, an English army officer. Anyway, soon afterwards a parcel came for me, ticket to Accra, all the clothes, some cash up front to set me up ... and I'm still here. Every month my money gets paid in England and I live here for f ... next to nothing. Here in Kamba I can live like a lord on just my tip money"

THE BIG GAME

Lorna looked puzzled, "What I don't understand is why a government would want them, these parties I mean. Why do they want them charging around shooting people?"

The soldier laughed, "The money love, quarter of a million dollars a shooter. Look yours is a small party, but some are twelve, once I had fifteen. That's the best part of four million dollars, granted Amutu doesn't get all of it, the Rupert at Xtreme must take a chunk, and then there's my oner."

"You mean that they each pay quarter of a million dollars for their holiday?"

Through the fog of alcohol McRae began to sense that something was not quite right, he burped into his fist, "'Scuse me … didn't your guy tell you all this?"

Lorna thought quickly, "No it was my birthday treat, a surprise."

McRae considered this possibility and was satisfied. He raised his glass and tapped it against Lorna's, "Well happy birthday love." With difficulty he returned to the thread of his conversation, "Obviously your man didn't pay a quarter mill for you; it's just flights and expenses for a shooter's guest.'" McRae drifted off and seemed to be speaking to himself, "But maybe now it's not just the money, it was at first. Now the Xtremers are really racking up the kills. Maybe we're getting better at finding the buggers, or maybe there's more of 'em. These days Gboja and friends actually seem to expect results from us, to begin with we were just a joke. But think about it… top marksmen with top weapons, they've got to get results."

Lorna did think about it as their main course arrived. McRae ordered more beer and Lorna another Coke. "Sure you won't have a proper drink?"

Lorna refused and prompted him again, "Are all the groups like this?"

"No two are the same. Like I said, this is a small one. It's mostly Yanks, sorry Americans and Arabs, some Japanese and Chinese. My mate in the Far East says some of his are all Japs, you know, corporate groups, Christ knows who's running their companies while they're all running around in the jungle."

"But how do people find Xtreme? I can't imagine they advertise in the Sunday papers."

McRae gathered his thoughts, "From what guests have told me it's all done by invitation. Most of 'em have been on game hunting tours, stuff like that. Maybe it's from the shooting mags, I don't really know: think you can buy lists of names can't you?"

Lorna nodded, "I see. Anyway Tom, what's your idea about how I can get home?"

The sudden change of subject unsettled him for a moment, "Oh yeh," he concentrated with an effort, "my idea wasn't to get you home, just out of the Ambassador."

"Well that would be a start. Have you found a good alternative?"

"My place, you could stay with me," he hurried on quickly, "I've a spare room. It's not smart, but there'd be no chance you'd run into your man."

Lorna smiled, "That's a very nice offer Tom, but..."

"It's no trouble," he waved at the remains of the meal, "as soon as we're done, we can grab a cab and I'll show you around."

"No really Tom, I would prefer to stay where I am. Mike's out all day and so it's not a big deal and hopefully I'll soon be on my way to Accra."

McRae shrugged, "It's up to you, but the offer's there."

"Yes and thanks a lot. Talking of Accra, did you have any luck with your pilot friend?"

16

David Churu had become so used to timing the drips that he could judge them to the second. Now two were long overdue; had the pair standing next to him switched off the tap? Even without the weight of extra water the pressure of second nail was building as his skin broke down. It was compressing his eyeball, it felt like the other just before it pierced, he could only be seconds from total blindness. He croaked, his voice had disappeared through lack of water and screaming. He tried to call out to the unseen spectators beside him.

President Amutu was deep in thought as he stared down at the tiny trace of water in the centre of his right palm, now hardly more than a patch of dampness. He changed focus to the mouth of the pipe. The new drip was nearly ready to fall. As it separated he reached out his other hand and caught it just above the metal bowl.

From below the scaffold board he heard a rasping sound: the movement of saliva over parched vocal chords. He checked underneath; the very tip of the nail was now hidden in the eyelid. He looked from palm to palm. Then as if he were weighing the traces of water in each he performed a small juggling movement, left and right, left and right, left and right. He stood up and wiped both hands on the seat on his beautifully tailored suit. Seconds ticked by as he stared down at the prone figure, then he nodded to himself as if he had come to a decision.

President Charles Amutu reached forward and scooped a large handful of water out of the bowl and slung it against the far wall. He turned and walked out of the door. Over his shoulder he called to the man in the expensive shoes, "Release him."

17

As they set out for their second day in the jungle, Mike Bray thought over his conversation a few minutes ago with McRae in the foyer. The Scotsman had said that yesterday was unique in that not one of the group had even seen a target. The unusual number of rebel movements reported by the government patrols, had resulted in nothing. Mike hoped for better luck today.

The first part of their journey was always easy thanks to the Japanese Government, a fact that the traveller was reminded of every few kilometres. They had donated a broad, surfaced highway that was cutting a swathe all the way from the new harbour to deep into the rainforest. Some of the trucks roaring in both directions were carrying fuel and construction materials, but the majority were stacked high with massive hardwood tree trunks destined for Japanese living rooms.

The old army truck was again waiting at the crossroads. The three eight man patrols were grouped around its tail smoking. The drivers stayed with the guests as their corporals were briefed. Primed with the latest intelligence, the Land Rovers set off to the north, west and east.

Mike thought about the Russian next to him. He knew that Vasyl spoke some English, but was a man of very few words. Throughout yesterday he had only responded to Mike's, "Good morning" and "See you later." Admittedly their pursuit did not lend itself to gossip, but during both journeys Mike's attempts at conversation had only met with grunts and nods.

THE BIG GAME

After travelling north for ten minutes they pulled onto a rough track and bumped along for a further five before parking in a small clearing. There were four Government soldiers sitting on a fallen log, they stood up to greet the arrivals as they climbed out of the Land Rover. The patrol commander, a tall thin corporal with impressive facial scars, spoke rapidly to their own lance corporal. As soon as their driver had disabled the 4x4's engine they set off into the jungle, collecting on their way another four patrol members who had been on watch deep amongst the trees. The commander placed Serovec fourth in line, then two more soldiers and himself between the Russian and the American.

The heat and humidity were intense and Mike envied Serovec's shaven head as he felt the sweat soaking his hair. He wiped his face and neck and considered a change of hairstyle. He reached up and stroked the long white scar hidden under his hairline. Perhaps not, everyone will want to know about the scar. Their progress slowed as the jungle became denser. Every few minutes they would halt and the patrol would listen carefully, before moving off again in Indian file. There was such a variety of bird and animal sounds that Mike did not know what they were listening for. Suddenly they stopped and stood motionless for five minutes. The tall scarred commander turned and made the clenched fist *stone* sign. Mike had no idea why and with difficulty resisted the temptation to make the *paper* sign back.

After half an hour the ground started to slope downwards. At the next stop Serovec and Bray were paired off with their original driver and guide who acted as their spotters. After much whispering and pointing the rest of the patrol moved off, leaving the four on their own. The lance corporal took Mike by the arm and crouching down they moved forward down the slope. Serovec and their driver slipped off to their left.

77

Progress now was very slow. On hands and knees, trying to keep his rifle dry and clean, Mike followed the boots of the soldier ahead. The earth and rotting leaves were full of moisture; every plant shed its droplets onto him as he inched forward.

The corporal stopped and rolled onto his side and beckoned. Mike peered through the foliage, straight ahead was a large pool fed by a stream. Fifty metres away on the far side of the water, he gradually discerned the circular shapes of three man-made shelters. They had been formed by bending branches then weaving in broad leaves. The corporal's face was only inches from his; he placed his finger to his lips for silence. He then pointed to Mike's rifle and mimed pulling the trigger. Although there was no target the American slowly moved his weapon into the firing position, then reached under his hair and stroked the scar.

Mike slowly checked his watch again; they had been lying watching the shelters for over four hours. Brightly coloured birds came to drink. Fish broke the smooth surface of the water as they snatched insects, but the encampment remained silent. He had no idea if there were rebels there, or if they were waiting for them to return. The afternoon sun was filtering through the canopy and his clothes were as wet as if he had showered in them. He watched a large centipede approaching over a dead leaf. Using his body hair for grip it climbed up and over his forearm, slid down the other side and carried on its journey. Mike turned his head to see if the corporal next to him was asleep. The man met his eyes and held up one finger.

Mike nodded without knowing why. What's he telling me … One what? One minute? One hour? One rebel?

Suddenly there was movement from the middle shelter; a bare-chested young man in combat trousers crawled out and stretched hugely as if he had just woken up. He drank deeply from a battered plastic bottle. Another young man half emerged from the same shelter; but sat down in the doorway and examined his right foot. Then an older man levered himself out of the low doorway by the using the top of the sitter's head as a prop. The young man grinned and took a swipe at the other's back as he walked away.

The corporal tapped Mike's arm, mimed drinking from a bottle, then pointed and raised his thumb. Mike felt his chest tighten and his stomach cramp. This is it, all the waiting is over. The moment I've been planning for so long has finally arrived. One last touch of the scar, he eased off the safety catch and shuffled his rifle into position. At six times magnification the target's face filled the sight; the man had an acne problem. On his forehead there was a fresh pustule straining to erupt. It's all so right, this has to be ordained, he's even got the acne. A ghost of a smile stole over Mike's face, well I've a perfect cure for that my friend, he brought the cross hairs exactly onto the mound of pus where it stretched the skin.

The corporal was holding up his hand, he cupped his other and blew into it making a high whooping sound. Mike tucked his rifle butt into his shoulder and caressed the trigger. The volcano of pus moved as the young man drank, Mike followed it with the cross hairs. The corporal dropped his hand in a cutting motion.

Mike fired. The target snapped back, a fine pink mist fountained from the back of his head as the impact threw him off his feet. At the same moment the older man crashed over as Serovec shot him. Mike was already dropping his sights down towards the sitter in the doorway, but just as he aimed the man was flung backwards by the Russian's second shot.

There was movement from the other two shelters as shiny black bodies erupted from the interiors. They were holding weapons, rubbing sleep from their eyes as they tried to focus on their attackers. Mike swivelled onto the new targets. But this isn't right ... their chests aren't right, they look like boys ... but they've got breasts. His sights focussed on a figure that was bringing a Kalashnikov into the firing position, very short hair, small thin body, but below a blue bead necklace were budding breasts. As his finger froze on the trigger, the girl's head was thrown backwards as if she had been hit with an invisible baseball bat.

Throwing aside his rifle, Mike began to scramble to his feet, he was shouting. "NO STOP, STOP, THIS ISN'T RIGHT!" The hours of immobility had stiffened his muscles and he fell forward. The corporal grabbed his shirt and forced him into the ground.

Automatic fire mowed down the rebels as they stumbled around half asleep on the edge of the pool. The eight man patrol broke out of the tree line just up stream, they stood legs braced in the water and raked the encampment. One tall slim girl dived and swam underwater towards where he lay. In the chaos Mike was sure none of the patrol had spotted her, only small vee shaped ripples marked her passage under the mirror surface of the pool. She surfaced half way across bright white teeth sparkling as she gulped in air, facing him; he could see her eyes blinking and wide open in terror, droplets of water cascading off her tight black curls. He realised he was shouting at her, pleading with her to swim faster. Then it was as if an invisible hand half lifted out of the water, her arms flew backwards as Serovec's bullet exploded in her skull.

***

It was nearly six thirty and Lorna still hadn't showered. Her problem was she still did not know what to wear for dinner with a president. After trying on everything she had brought, she decided they were all too short or showed too much top. When packing in New York, what had seemed suitable for a romantic holiday with Mike now seemed suggestive.

She rushed down to the hotel shop and checked their ethnic range. There was a lightweight silky gown in an elaborate silver and white pattern. The high collar and hem that swept the floor seemed eminently restrained. She bought it and ran back to her room.

Freshly showered, she decided there was no time to do her hair so she would have to wear it up. As she sat naked on the bath towel putting on her makeup, the phone rang. It was the reception informing her that the President's car had arrived. The gown fitted perfectly, no time for underwear, no one will ever know! Slipping on her favourite heels, she grabbed her bag and headed for the lift. As soon as it whined to a halt she spotted Mike's back as he read something on the reception counter. Lorna hit the button for the first floor and after an agonising delay; it reluctantly shuddered upwards once more.

"Oh my God!" she exclaimed as she slid back the lift doors. The whole landing wall opposite was a full-length mirror; silhouetted against the light from the lift it looked like she was naked, I'll have to change. She glanced at her watch, no time; just have to be careful of the light.

She ran down the single flight of stairs and at the bottom peered around the corner. Mike still had his back to her, but now he was speaking to the younger German. The problem was she would have to pass within six feet of him to get to the front door. She could see the limousine parked outside, its driver leaning against the trunk. All Lorna had to do was walk the fifty feet from the base of the stairs without Mike turning around.

Shoes! He would hear her heels on the tiled floor and automatically look. She slipped them off and with her bag in one hand and shoes in the other launched herself into the foyer. Halfway across the German spotted her.

He nodded and smiled, "Good evening." Mike automatically turned.

Lorna's nod included them both. "Good evening." she replied. She felt their eyes on her back as the chauffeur held the car door open.

Mike stared, mouth slightly open as Lorna got into the Presidential limousine. What the hell is going on? he asked himself.

***

81

Lorna was shown to Amutu's private dining room by a white-jacketed footman. The President was dressed in a casual cream shirt and light brown trousers. He took her hand and kissed her lightly on each cheek. Such was his charisma Lorna no longer noticed that he was some two inches shorter than her. "You look beautiful Lorna. I'm pleased you could come"

"Thank you…" she searched for a proper title.

"Charles please," he grinned, "I much prefer it to Charlie as they used to call me at university in England. Would you care for a drink before we eat, A little champagne perhaps?"

They chatted about America and England whilst sipping an excellent dry vintage. It was a hot and humid evening, but the air conditioning made the room pleasantly cool. Again Lorna was beguiled by Amutu's relaxed and witty personality. The only aspect she found slightly disconcerting was his habit of letting his gaze stray to her breasts. Get real Mr President, she thought, I bet all your wives are better endowed. The footman asked Amutu if they were ready to eat and before sitting down Lorna visited the toilet. As soon as she looked in the mirror she understood Amutu's fascination with her chest. The air conditioning was too high and her nipples were plainly visible through the thin material. In horror Lorna rummaged through her bag. I know you're in here. At last she found two sticking plasters and scooping her dress under her armpits she stuck them over her nipples.

When she returned to the dining room Amutu was deep in a whispered conversation with his footman. As soon as Lorna appeared he raised his hand in dismissal. He would think about this news later, but why would the Australian government deny any knowledge of a mineral survey in his country? It was an intriguing development.

During their main course Lorna realised she was missing a lifetime's opportunity. This is probably my only chance to ask a head of state about how it all works: the nature of power. Ok he isn't a world leader, but he must understand the system. She looked at the bottle as their glasses were topped up and realised it was nearly finished, mostly by Amutu. Lorna steered the conversation towards Charles Amutu, the man and his philosophies.

"...One of the most important things to remember in my job is that you can have no friends; never forget Brutus."

Lorna made a face, "That's very sad."

Again the ready smile, "Not as sad as starving and living in a hut." He waved a hand to encompass the whole room, "it's the price I pay for all this."

"Then do you assume everyone to be your enemy?" He considered the question for some seconds, "Not exactly my enemy, but I consider all my countrymen to be competitors." He thumped the arms of his dining chair, "Competitors for this chair."

"Then you have no real enemies at this time?"

He laughed his big laugh, it rumbled forth from his barrel chest, "Oh yes very many. But although I'm never able to choose my friends, I always try to choose my enemies very carefully."

Lorna frowned, "I don't understand."

He rolled a silver napkin ring, deep in thought, she got the idea that he was deciding how much to say. Eventually he gave a little nod, "I'll explain. Last night I chose a new enemy. It was a difficult decision, but I believe he was the best choice. Not my equal, but a good man and a good leader."

"That doesn't make sense, why would you choose a good leader as your enemy?"

He smiled, "I disagree Lorna, it makes perfect sense. Only a fool wants a fool for his enemy. I know this guy very well. It's essential that I know exactly how he thinks. I know his strengths, but more importantly I know his weaknesses."

Amutu paused and placed the napkin ring exactly in the centre of his cutlery. "It also tidies my life. I've chosen someone good enough to unite all my enemies under one banner, but not good enough to win this chair."

18

David Churu was aware of at least three pairs of footsteps approaching and then the clank of a galvanised bucket on the concrete near his feet. He screamed as they raised the scaffold board, wrenching the nail out of the remains of his left eye: not a real scream, his screams had now become just dry rasping. There was movement either side of his head and he felt the pegs in his ears turning, they were withdrawing. Then the sound of a knife being removed from its sheath.

A hand grabbed the front of his hair, pulling his head forward against the grip of the glue. He felt a blade being inserted in the gap between his neck and the floor. There was a sawing sound, starting at the base of his neck as the knife was dragged up the back of his head. Roughly, he was hacked free. The straps were removed from his wrists and ankles, but he was too weak to move.

They lifted him under his arms and supported him in a sitting position. David heard the familiar ripping sound of adhesive tape being unreeled. Again fingers locked in his hair and the tape wound quickly around his head and over his eyes. There was a scrape of the bucket on concrete and the overpowering smell of warm water and disinfectant as someone threw the contents into his crotch.

He could feel a man each side of him, but without a word being exchanged they pulled him upright and bare feet trailing, dragged him out of the room.

19

Lorna repositioned all the pillows against the headboard and climbed back into bed. Deep in thought, she sipped her coffee. *How else can I escape this place? I could ask someone other than McRae. Ok he's sleazy, but I guess he knows more than most westerners about Gamasi. I wonder if it's worth trying to contact that pilot guy myself?*

Her bedside phone rang: she immediately recognised the guttural, "Good morning."

"Hi Lindy, you're awake early."

The Russian woman chuckled, "I am awake for many hours, waiting for you to tell me of your date. I was not sure you come back."

"I took your advice, I was back here before midnight. And before you ask, Charles was a perfect gentleman."

"Aha, so it is Charles now? I want you to tell me all that is happened."

Lorna laughed, "I will, if you'll come with me to the airport this morning."

"You are leaving?"

"Not yet, I just want to find a man there."

Lindy paused, "now I am interested. I will come. At what time?"

"…How does this Amutu know you and Mike have big problem?" Lindy was quizzing Lorna as they were being driven to the airport.

"That's the strange thing. He seemed to know that we had split. I don't think much happens in Gamasi that he doesn't know about."

"Do you have more dates?"

Lorna considered the question as they swung through the airfield gates, "He asked me, so I guess it depends how I get on now with this pilot guy." The taxi stopped and they stared at the odd assortment of small aircraft parked near the government hanger. During the drive from town Lorna had explained her mission.

Lindy shrivelled her nose up at the planes, "I do not trust these machines."

Lorna was inclined to agree, "Perhaps he's not here."

Nothing had changed outside the hanger since the Xtremers first arrived. The five guys were still lounging in their plastic chairs surrounded by a cloud of smoke. They stared as the women got out of their taxi.

Lorna smiled at them, "Would you guys know where I can find a pilot who would take me to Accra?"

At least two of them spoke English and a short discussion ensued. They then considered the question in silence for a few seconds. At last the tallest one spoke, "Hansie the South African guy, he will."

"Is he around?" Two heads turned to the group of light aircraft. The spokesman shook his head, "His plane is over there, but no Hansie.

"Any idea where I can find him?"

Both linguists looked at one another blankly, then consulted their colleagues. The shorter one had an idea, "Don't know where he lives, but he hangs out in a bar in town."

"Any idea which bar?" This appeared to be a tough question; finally they narrowed it down to three. The taxi driver was summoned and he was familiar with them all.

Lindy volunteered to check out each bar when they pulled up outside. The last one they visited was George's and after less than a minute she reappeared at the door and gave Lorna, who was waiting outside in the taxi, the thumbs up. As Lorna entered Lindy was already seated at a table drinking from a bottle of beer. Two men were seated opposite her; one was

Tom McRae. The Russian girl grinned and pointed, "This is Hansie the pilot."

Lorna looked hard at McRae as she sat down, "So you tracked him down then Tom?"

"Just this minute found him, I was about to ask him about your flight."

Lorna noticed the pilot opened his mouth then flinched as McRae kicked his ankle. "Well now I can do it myself thanks. Hansie, can you fly me to Accra airport?"

"No problem, when do you want to go?"

"As soon as possible. How much will it be?"

Hansie stared at the ceiling and calculated, "Eighteen hundred US should cover it, in cash."

Lorna frowned, "Cash could be a problem."

"Sorry, but it's the only way I work."

Lorna was pensive on the drive back to their hotel, "Looks like I've a bit of organising to do," she said to Lindy when they were back in the Ambassador's foyer.

Lindy headed for the pool and Lorna for the cyber booth near the reception. She was surprised to see Paul Henning's plump figure slumped in the seat. As she waited she noticed that Henning was searching for flights back to the United States from Northwest Africa. Eventually he finished, as he got up she spoke to him, "Hi Paul, I think we might both be after the same thing."

He looked startled, "What do you mean?"

"I'm trying to get home, how about you?"

"Yeah, but getting to Accra is the problem." He nodded towards the reception, "They say there's no easy way to get there, even by road. Guess I'll have to wait until next week when this ... this vacation's over."

"That's more than a week, for less than a thousand bucks each I can get us out of here."

20

The following morning the mood was very different in each of the three Land Rovers.

In the lead vehicle Mike Bray felt slightly sick as he fingered the scar under his hair; while Vasyl Serovec was hoping for an even more successful day. In the second, Johan Koeffe was still in shock and wondered how long he could continue. Wolfgang Schmidt was quietly confident that he could repeat, or even improve on yesterday's tally. In the final one Robert Goff hoped that today he would beat both the Russian's and the older German's total. Fiona meanwhile, was thinking about how she could get out of any further trips.

The trio approached the cross roads and the old army truck was parked up as normal, with soldiers squatting in its shade. Serovec sat next to the open window, his rifle cradled in his lap. He craned forward sharply as his driver began to slow, then hit the man's shoulder and shouted, "DRIVE ON, GO, GO!" Confused, he continued to brake so Serovec brought up his gun and jammed the muzzle hard into the back of the driver's neck; again shouting, "GO, GO!" The Land Rover was nearly stationary, but the driver got the message and floored the throttle, it jolted, coughed and then surged forward again. Now the corporal next to him was also screaming in Fasa at the driver, as he desperately grabbed gears.

The group behind the stationary truck exploded into activity, bringing up and aiming their weapons at the Land Rovers. The following drivers hit their throttles and in a hail of bullets and dust followed the leader as he threw his vehicle onto the east road away from the truck. The Xtremers, cringing in the foot wells, were showered with splinters of glass as their windows shattered. Bullets whined overhead, there were the deafening percussions of lead on interior as each Land Rover was strafed.

Within seconds they outdistanced the firing but the last 4x4 containing the Goffs had taken fire into both rear tyres and was crabbing down the road as its driver fought desperately for control. Their corporal shouted into his radio and the Germans' car slewed to a halt ahead of them. Back at the cross roads the army truck lurched into view, billowing exhaust smoke and dust as it set off in pursuit.

Both soldiers and the Goffs abandoned their vehicle in the centre of the road and raced for the Germans' Land Rover twenty metres ahead of them. Even as they ripped open the rear tailgate and threw themselves into rear, the driver was gunning his engine. Rear door flapping open, they careered off again; all four panting in a tangled heap of arms and legs in the luggage space. They stared through the open back door as the army truck drove at full speed into their wrecked Land Rover, flicking it off the road like a toy. Robert Goff looked bereft, "Our rifles are in there!"

Fiona shrugged, "There wasn't time."

In the leading 4x4 Mike yelled at Serovec above the roar of the engine and howl of wind hitting them through the shattered glass, "What's happening?"

The Russian shouted one word, "Rebels!"

Re-entering Kamba from the east, both badly damaged vehicles pulled up outside the Ambassador Hotel. The shaken group alighted and inspected the rear of the Land Rovers. The spare wheels bolted to the back doors had probably saved their lives as they were peppered with bullet marks. They agreed to meet in the bar after returning to their rooms to change and dump their guns.

McRae was still there drinking strong coffee, just as they had him left less than an hour ago.

Mike Bray handed Serovec a large beer, "How did you know they weren't the real patrols?"

The Russian hesitantly selected his words, "The bodies are wrong today, they want to look sleeping, but I see they are very awake. Today they do not smoke. They all hold weapons ready, before today many weapons still in truck."

Mike offered his hand, "Thanks, you saved our lives."

Serovec enveloped the American in a numbing grip, "No problem, but first I save my life."

Robert Goff and Germans also thanked him and shook his hand warmly.

McRae sipped his coffee and thought over this morning's events. The rebels are getting more confident if they ambushed the intelligence patrols, and then hijacked their truck. They've never been that close to the capital before; could be time to ask London for a transfer!

Un-noticed amongst the general conversation, Fiona Goff slipped out of the front door and walked briskly down the drive. She approached the first taxi in the queue and gave him the name of the smartest restaurant in Kamba.

***

Lindy looked up at her American friend as she arrived at the sun loungers. "Good morning Lorna," she checked her watch, "Or good afternoon! You are late up today."

Lorna dropped onto the lounger next to the Russian girl, "I was out with Paul Henning."

Lindy pulled her sun glasses above her forehead and grinned widely, "Then you are both surprising me. Lorna soon there will be no men left."

Lorna laughed, "No you misunderstand. This morning I went with Paul to that bar we visited yesterday. Then on to the airport. Hansie wasn't at either place, so I left messages at both telling him we've got the cash and want out of here as soon as possible."

"That is sad, I will miss you."

Lorna laid a hand on the girl's arm, "I'll miss you to, I've enjoyed your company. Anyway I saw your man in the bar, so you won't miss me today."

"What here? Back already?"

"Yup, it's strange, gotta be some sort of problem. It looked like all of them including Mike and my Scottish friend. They're all in the bar getting drunk."

Lindy shrugged, "Then for sure I will be working this afternoon."

Lorna settled back and opened her book, nothing to do now but wait for Hansie to contact me. Might as well try and enjoy the rest of my vacation, even if Mike isn't far away. I hope he doesn't decide to take a swim!

One other thing distracted her from her book and kept niggling her. Something she had witnessed that morning just did not make sense. Across the road from George's bar, just up the street, there had been a smart looking establishment with seats and tables under a striped awning. As they had driven passed, she had seen Fiona Goff climb out of a taxi to be met by a good looking young white man. At the time she had wondered what Fiona was doing in the city rather than hunting. It was possible that the man was just a friend, but how likely was that in Kamba? And why meet him in there instead of at the hotel?

21

David Churu assumed he was in the boot of a car. He had been forced into a restricted space which stank of petrol. Every few seconds part of his body was bounced against sharp projections as they drove fast along an unmade road. He groaned as the circulation returned to his hands and feet. The floor tilted as they drove off the road and stopped.

A welcome flood of fresh air engulfed him as the boot lid opened. Hands grabbed him under his knees and armpits, he was lifted clear of the car and carried a few steps. Together the hands released him to drop him onto damp earth, then silence. He tensed, waiting for the sound of a cocking weapon or the press of steel against his head, but nothing.

He listened for the sound of running water. If he was on the river bank why hadn't they slung him straight in? His arms and legs were free, but knew he hadn't got the strength to swim. The joke about Amutu's opposition came back to haunt him … was this their macabre idea of a joke? Was he surrounded by crocodiles? Were both men waiting for the show to start? He flinched at the thought of jaws about to tear into his flesh … two car doors slammed. The roar of an engine and the sound of tyres disappearing. He lay still, was it a trap? Were there other men still standing next to him? He was too weak to care and he found his consciousness sliding away.

As soon as the car was out of sight, a section of scrub at the edge of the forest rose up and approached the road. It was five soldiers festooned in small branches and leaves. They grouped around the body and one shone a shielded maglite.

"Dead corporal?"

Another whispered, "No he's breathing." He pulled a matt black commando dagger from a sheath taped to his Bergen, slid the blade under the tape around David Churu's head and sliced it through. There was a collective intake of breath. Despite the collapsed eyelid, the crust of dirt and aqueous fluid they all recognised him. "It's the Colonel."

The corporal took control. He checked David's airways and rubbed water over his parched lips and mouth. "Ki, get medics here quickly," he turned to another, "We'll stay with him, Mo, you bring the captain."

22

Cedric Farringdon was seated behind his desk at the Embassy when Jonathon Forbes stuck his head round the door. "Joyce said you might spare me a few minutes Sir."

The British consul waved his attaché to a chair, "I'm expecting a call shortly, but carry on. Is it about that ... tantalising stuff?"

The younger man smiled, "tantalite Sir. No, not about that. The mineral agreement was all signed, sealed and passed up the line. I would expect their company people to be arriving shortly. No, this is just a couple of things I thought you should know about."

"Fire away then."

"Firstly, as you know we have a chap who's very pally with the rebels." Farringdon nodded. "Well he's been in touch and it appears that Colonel Churu has reappeared."

The Consul frowned, "Thought he was dead?"

"Appears not, very much alive and ready to come out of the closet and challenge Amutu."

"That could be a nuisance. In your opinion Jonathon, is he actually anti-Brit?"

Forbes considered his answer, "There's not a simple answer really. I don't think he's anti or pro anyone. I've met him a few times at functions etc, but I can't really work out where he's coming from. At the risk of boring you Sir, I'll quickly go over what I can remember of the man." Farringdon nodded and the younger man searched his memory. "Born in Uganda, Asian father and Ugandan mother, educated at the Elton International School here in Kamba, then Cambridge. After Uni, officer training at Sandhurst; where I believe he acquitted himself with distinction. Came back and was one of Amutu's bright boys ... until recently that is!"

THE BIG GAME

Farringdon's eyes crinkled, "Maybe an unguarded word was dropped to Amutu that Churu was being a naughty boy?"

Forbes half smiled, "I really wouldn't know Sir."

"And you have another matter Jonathon?"

"Related subject really. You recall that London's placed one of their spooks, name of Goff, in the Ambassador Hotel?"

Farringdon nodded, "Yes, terribly kind of them."

"We recently had a chat. Apparently Goff's been charging around in the jungle and believes the rebels are getting stronger and closer by the day."

"I see, well, I'll leave you to monitor that Jonathon, but please keep me up to speed."

The attaché sensed his dismissal. He arose and headed for the door, the Consul stopped him on the threshold. Forbes turned to see the Cedric Farringdon deep in thought. Over steepled fingers he asked, "In your view Jonathon, would HMG be better served by Amutu, or Churu?"

"Oh, Amutu without a doubt Sir. He may have the occasional flirt with the opposition, but at the end of the day he understands and respects the system. I get the feeling Churu would be a loose cannon"

"Better do all you can to keep Amutu in his job then Jonathon."

"I'll do my very best Sir."

***

In the shade of the plastic tarpaulin, a ring of faces looked down on David Churu as he lay on the camp bed. His left eye was covered in a pad of bright white gauze. Despite the water his voice still croaked, "If all is in place, go ahead."

The large man in battle dress kneeling next to his right arm protested, "We would rather wait for you Sir."

Churu's voice gained strength, "it will be at least a week before I'm fit. You cannot afford a false start, it could wreck everything. Are you confident … everything is ready?"

95

The big man responded quickly, "Yes everything is just as you planned."

Churu nodded, "Then it's on. That's an order Major Beyla." He softened his voice, "Remember we're just individuals, the Revolution is greater than all of us."

***

Lorna put down her book and glanced at the green figures of her digital alarm clock. It was one thirty two in the morning and she was exhausted. Every hour she had rung down to the reception and every time they had confirmed there had been no call from Hansie the pilot. If there was no call, she would be stuck another day in Gamasi. She was feeling desperate, supposing one of the other staff has left a note in my pigeon hole, maybe he hasn't bothered to check? Before I go to bed I'm going down to look for myself.

When the lift arrived at the ground floor she looked over to the bar just to make sure the rest of the group had gone. Apart from Fiona Goff they had all been in there from late morning until at least midnight, promising some sore heads tomorrow. In the dimmed lights all she could see was McRae's shaven head drooping over the back of a chair: it looked like he wouldn't make it home tonight. The night porter, a patient man who had spoken to her less than a minute before, confirmed there was still no message. As he spoke she glanced into the box with her room number on; it was empty.

Lorna was at an Independence Day cookout at her parent's old house. She watched the fireworks and chewed on the uncooked frog burger that her old maths teacher, Mr Ferris, had just handed her ... She rolled over and rubbed her eyes. Although she was now completely awake the sound of fireworks continued.

Then she realised it was small arms fire and coming from an area very close to the Ambassador Hotel. She lay in the dark and listened, it's definitely the crackle of guns and close, very close. Her clock was showing three zero seven, she switched on the bedside light and dialled the reception, the phone rang unanswered.

Throwing on her dressing gown she padded to the window and pulled aside the heavy drapes. Standing right next to the glass she could now hear distant firing, but could not work out where it was coming from. There was no sign of life in the road, but that could be usual at three o'clock. She opened the window. Now the sounds came from all around the city, single shots then return bursts of automatic fire. She realised this was no military exercise, but full scale street fighting. Shutting the window, she went back to the phone, as the reception number rang unanswered her bedside light went off. In the dim glow of the emergency lighting she struggled into her safari suit.

Out in the corridor a door banged back on its hinges, shaking the plaster as it struck the wall. Heavy footsteps were running towards her room. She breathed out as they passed her door and continued on to the far end, another door slammed in the distance. Her bedside phone rang; it was Mike, despite recent events she was relieved.

"Have you heard the firing?" he asked.

Her voice trembled, "Yes, what's happening?"

"I don't know, do you want me to come down?" Lorna despised her weakness, but found herself inviting him. The phone rang again as soon as it touched the rest.

It was Lindy, "Are you ok?"

Lorna replied, "Yes, Mike's coming. Do you know what's happening?"

In the background she could hear shouted Russian. Lindy translated, "Vasyl says ... to stay on top of the window."

Lorna was confused, "I don't understand ... what does he mean?"

The Russian girl cursed, "No, no, he is saying ... to stay away from ... the window" There was a knock on her door. Holding the phone in one hand, Lorna squinted through the spy hole; in the gloom she could make out a fully dressed Mike flanked by both the Germans. She let them in and was startled when she saw they were carrying five rifle cases and boxes of ammunition. Mike caught her look, "We didn't want to leave them in our rooms." Returning to the phone she told Lindy about her visitors.

The situation was straining the Russian girl's English, "Vasyl and I will soon be arrivals," she said and rang off. The guests in the rooms either side of Lorna were leaving. She heard their doors slam and then the sound of running feet. Wolfgang and Johan were standing either side of the window, now above the sound of small arms were regular heavier detonations.

Wolfgang looked back into the room, "Mortars," he said.

"What the hell is going on?" she could not keep the tremor out of her voice.

Mike pulled a face, "Looks like someone's started a war."

***

Cedric Farringdon stood at his bedroom window in his Paisley pattern pyjamas. Beyond the Embassy compound he could glimpse the occasional muzzle flash, mortar and RPG detonations made his window shake.

Below, in the garden, Royal Marines had taken up their allotted position around the perimeter wall. Bloody hell, this is all we need, he thought. And they promised me somewhere in the Caribbean.

23

The distant sound of combat made David Churu curse in frustration at his weakness. *Two years in the planning and here I am lying in bed.* An approaching pair of headlights threw moving shadows of trees onto the tarpaulin stretched above his head and then the roar of a hard driven Land Rover. It bumped to a halt a few metres away, the headlights bore into his bivouac. The twin beams cast profiles of injured men as they were helped to the makeshift medical tent next door.

Passengers unloaded, the driver ducked under the plastic sheet. In a half crouch he saluted, "Progress report from the Major Sir." He ticked off the points on his fingers. "We've taken control of the electric, the water, the airfield, the TV and radio station, as well as the main police station and the telephone exchange. But there's strong resistance at the President's palace and the army HQ."

"Did we take the choppers at the airfield?"

"Not sure Sir, but I haven't seen any sign of them."

Churu nodded, "How's it going at the docks?"

The driver looked crestfallen, "I'm not sure Sir, Major Beyla didn't say."

"Well, carry on and thank you."

David lay and worried. He was relieved that some objectives had been secured. But the three helicopters would create havoc at first light if they had not been disabled. The dock area was one of their prime objectives, as it held the stocks of food and fuel, plus the source of support if the Government troops held out. David pulled a face, *what am I thinking of, my whole plan is based on surprise. I always knew if it came to protracted combat, vastly outnumbered and outgunned, we can't win.*

"You're forgetting Paul Henning!" Lorna pointed out.

The group had been discussing how to contact McRae and the young Goff couple. Serovec was half concealed by the drapes, leaning against the window frame. Rifle cradled in his arms, he stared out into the night. Up until that point he had taken no active part in their conversation. Without turning he said, "It is good to forget him."

Lorna looked at the Russian, "What do you mean Vasyl?"

For a moment he did not reply. Still staring into the distance he replied, "He is weak man ... man with problem."

Lindy spoke in rapid Russian to her partner, he did not reply just gave a hint of a shrug. She turned to the others, "I explain, Vasyl believe it is good for Henning stay in his room ... until we are know what is happened."

Lorna bristled, "Well I disagree Lindy, Paul will be terrified on his own." Serovec said something else in Russian, but Lindy did not interpret.

"Does anyone know his room number?" asked Johan. He had been ringing the Goffs' room for some minutes, but they had not responded. Lorna gave Johan the number and he dialled. After a few minutes he shook his head and held out the handset, "I am not sure it's working."

Mike, Johan and Wolfgang decided to go in search of the missing members of the group.

Deserted and only lit by faint emergency bulbs the stairs and corridors were eerie. Mike felt rather melodramatic walking down a hotel hallway holding his rifle, but Wolfgang had insisted they all took loaded guns. Over his shoulder Mike said to Johan, "What I don't get is where are the staff ... and all the other guests."

"There were not many other guests."

"Sure, but it's still kinda weird not to see anyone."

Wolfgang added, "The staff arrive each morning in minibuses, I see them when I am doing early running. When the shooting began there would only be night staff."

Despite banging loudly on the Goff's door they got no response.

Paul Henning's room was next. On the third knock there was a muffled response, "Who is it?"

Mike replied, "It's Mike, Wolfgang and Johan. You ok?"

"Yeah, what's happening out there?"

"We're not sure, but it's not good. Can you open the door?"

There was the sound of a heavy object being dragged across the floor and Henning opened the door a few inches. He owlishly inspected the three armed men for some seconds and then reluctantly ushered them in. He was bare foot and dressed in a baggy bright yellow tee shirt and very long matching shorts. Mike was unsure whether this was sleep or day attire; he took a guess, "do you want to get dressed and join us on the next floor?" Henning looked confused, but after ripping the label off a pair of new tennis socks he pulled them on, followed by white trainers. He finished off with a floppy white sunhat over his thinning hair. As they prepared to go Wolfgang asked Paul where his gun was. The American opened the wardrobe and pointed to the gun case. "Better bring it," said Mike, "and any ammo."

Henning picked up the case as if it was red hot. With a small sigh Wolfgang went over to the wardrobe and dragged out six large cases of ammunition, "Is this all you have?"

Mike wondered for a moment if Wolfgang had made a joke. Paul did not make eye contact with the tall German, but seemed to channel all his responses via Mike, "The guy I bought this from said it would be plenty." Because of the weight they slung their rifles over their backs and carried a case of ammunition in each hand. Paul followed behind with just his gun case, held at arm's length.

When Paul Henning walked into Lorna's room, Vasyl slowly studied from head to foot the yellow and white apparition glowing in the middle of the room. He raised an eyebrow at Lindy who was lounging on the bed filing a nail, then returned to his vigil without comment.

Mike peered out of the window; the situation looked unchanged. Still the continuous small arms fire and an occasional heavier detonation, but they seemed no closer. He nodded to the dark city, "I wonder where McRae lives."

Suddenly a thought occurred to Lorna, "He could be downstairs. About two hours ago he was asleep in the bar and he didn't look like he was going anywhere." They considered her point.

"No person could sleep through this. Especially not an old soldier," said Johan emphatically.

Johan was wrong. When both he and Wolfgang peered around the corner at the base of the stairs, they spotted McRae across the dark, deserted reception area. Slumped in an easy chair near the bar just as Lorna had seen him at one thirty. Head tipped back, mouth wide open, he was snoring loudly. The Germans walked over and stood in front of him. Wolfgang nudged the soldier's boot. McRae grunted and opened his eyes; he lifted his head and with great difficulty focussed on the two men in front of him. Silently he took in their weapons and then stared around the dimly lit bar. Then he heard the sound of distant gunfire. "What's ... I was dreaming..." He coughed, rubbed his face and started again, "What's going on, who's shooting?" Through the mist of alcohol, his instincts began to work. With a struggle he pulled himself upright and stood with his head cocked on one side, suddenly alert and listening. Wolfgang briefed the Scotsman on the little they knew of the situation.

McRae nodded, "I guess you're right. Fucking rebels have kicked off. We should be ok, they're a bloody joke." He gathered his thoughts, "Better get ourselves organised though." He limped up the stairs following the Germans. His head thumped at every step.

McRae convened a meeting. As the room was getting crowded, Mike and both women sat on the bed. Henning sat at the desk. Both Germans and Serovec stood near the window.

The Scotsman took the easy chair, "First thing to remember is this isn't the only time the government has had this sort of problem. Every five years or so these mad buggers try to kick out Mr Amutu."

"Do you think we're in any danger?" asked Lorna.

McRae considered the question, "not at the moment, judging from what I can see out of the window."

"But if the fighting gets closer?"

McRae rubbed his head and took another drink of water. He needed coffee, but there was no way to heat the water. "What you have to keep in mind is that this isn't a proper war. Even if the rebels were to win," he raised a hand to forestall Lorna's interruption, "I'm not saying they will, I'm just saying that in the very unlikely event of them beating the Government forces … well, they would want to keep the old Ambassador Hotel undamaged. They want the foreign money just as much as Amutu. And that means looking after foreign visitors as well, namely you lot."

Wolfgang made a point, "Perhaps they will have no choice. If either army enters this hotel, then the other will have to fight to get them out." They all agreed.

McRae concurred, "Yes, you're right." He looked at Serovec who was still half hidden behind the drapes and raised his voice pointedly. "So if the fighting starts to get close, we will just have to make sure none of them get into the hotel." He Russian looked over and nodded to indicate he understood his brief. "And now let's go and look for that young couple," grunted McRae.

The Germans loaded their pair of spare rifles and handed one to McRae. As he acquainted himself with the Walther he grinned to himself, can't believe this, I was planning to get into Lorna Karrol's room, but was hoping for a bit more privacy! Scotsman in the lead, Mike and the Germans set off again in search of Robert and Fiona Goff.

Robert and Fiona were comfortably perched on the edge of the hotel roof with their feet wedged against the parapet. "Warm enough Fee?" asked Robert.

Fiona gave a small shiver, "Bit chilly, but dawn's coming up, so it'll soon warm up." They were both dressed in their green hunting clothes and each holding a pair of binoculars. Fiona brought hers up to her eyes and pointed, "I think the Gamasis over there are dropping back a bit."

Robert adjusted his lens and inspected a deep scuffmark on the toe of his brown leather boot. He was rather annoyed as he had recently bought them in London at a very exclusive gentleman's outfitters, "I think that damned staircase has actually cut the leather!"

Fiona threw him a withering glance, "Rob they're outdoor, all weather boots, you must expect a bit of damage."

Robert shrugged, "guess so, but still bloody irritating." He lifted his gaze from his boot and with long slim fingers spun the adjuster, "What did you say?"

"I said, I think the Gamasis over at three o'clock are dropping back."

Robert focussed on that sector, "Not being picky Fee, but I guess they're all Gamasis."

"Yah, 'spose you're right. I meant Government chaps as opposed to rebels."

They both tensed at the sound of footsteps on the metal staircase that lead to their vantage point from the roof hatch. Fiona indicated the large brick chimneystack and they both quickly scrambled behind its bulk.

Mike Bray raised his head above the ridge of the roof. He called to his colleagues, "Nice view of the city, but no sign of the Goffs."

"Morning!"

Mike nearly lost his grip on the ladder in surprise when the English couple shouted from behind him. He turned to see them both leaning against a huge chimneystack.

"Hi," he answered, "we've been looking all over for you."

Robert gave his braying laugh, "Sorry, jolly thoughtless of us. We come up here most mornings to watch the sunrise. Fantastic view don't you think?"

Mike came up the last few steps, "Sure, but rather marred by that war down there."

The Goffs both nodded. "Terrible business," agreed Fiona. They greeted Johan and Wolfgang who had joined Mike, whilst McRae elected to remain in the roof space below.

When asked his opinion, Robert Goff seemed to think of the fighting in terms of a rugby match. "I would say it's pretty even at the moment. Neither side's making much impression, though Fiona was just saying that Amutu's team seem to be losing ground over there." He pointed and then checked with the binoculars, "Yes you're right Fee." He lifted the strap from around his neck and handed the binoculars to Mike Bray. "A few minutes ago the reds were holed up at that water truck, now they are nearly down to the cross roads."

Mike focussed on the tiny figures firing from behind a car about a quarter of a mile away, "Why do you think they're Communists?"

Robert looked confused so Fiona answered the question, "Oh no, we call them reds because they're in the east sector in front of us, they all wear red armbands. On your left they wear white, yellow to our right and if you go to the side of the roof behind us you'll see the blues."

Johan was using Fiona's binoculars, he spoke to Wolfgang in German, "Yes, the rebels don't have any uniforms, just a coloured band at the top of each arm." He apologised to the others, "I am sorry, but I do not know all the English words."

Fiona laughed, and then replied in fluent German, "That is no problem, when I become excited I sometimes lose all the words as well."

Johan and Wolfgang stared at her in amazement. "You speak German!" exclaimed Wolfgang.

"A little," she replied in that language.

105

Ten people in Lorna's room were too many for comfort. The sun was up and without air conditioning it was becoming unbearably hot. The action had started only six hours ago and already McRae's grip on the group was slipping. Lorna leaned back against the headboard and watched as three potential leaders began to make their presence felt. Wolfgang Schmidt, Vasyl Serovec and Mike Bray were like three lions sizing each other up. The veneer of courtesy remained, they still played lip service to democratic decisions, but the cracks were appearing. At the moment, her money was on the German.

After a lengthy discussion and a show of hands it was decided to monitor progress of the street fighting from the roof. They divided themselves into two shifts with five people in each; a shift equalled a two-hour watch whilst the other rested. They also decided to move their base from Lorna's room to the executive suite on the top floor. Shift one was first for lookout duty. Headed by Wolfgang, they filed out of the sweltering room, followed by Johan, the Goffs and a very reluctant Paul Henning.

Shift two agreed to spend the next two hours collecting supplies. There were sixty-five rooms each with a mini bar, every one needed to be emptied of their small bottles of water. Lorna, Lindy and Serovec were not interested in leading, so Mike and McRae tossed a coin; Mike won.

They made their way down the stairs to the reception in search of the passkeys. Conveniently they were clearly labelled and on top of the manager's desk. Lindy, Lorna and Vasyl were dispatched with the keys and large canvas laundry bags to raid every room. McRae and Mike disappeared into the kitchens to see what else they could find.

Entering her first room, Lorna stared at the disordered bed where last night's occupants had slept, the unwashed coffee cups and discarded bath towels on the floor. As they met back in the hall Lorna said to Lindy, "Isn't it strange that all the guests got out so quickly. Where did they all go? Why are we the only ones left behind?"

The Russian girl nodded and frowned, "I also have been thinking this. Maybe they know what was happening."

Vasyl was going ahead unlocking the doors and pushing them open for the women to enter. Lorna's next mini bar was just inside the door on the right. As she bent to open the tiny fridge door she glanced at the bed and froze. Under the bedclothes was the distinct shape of two pairs of feet. As she straightened and began to apologise she saw the dark halos of blood around both heads. For a moment it was as if the world had stopped and then she started to scream.

24

The fear of defeat lay heavy on David Churu's mind. Every hour the volume of firing grew less, which was his most dreaded scenario. He was either winning or losing, but he had no idea which. If it had remained constant he would have known that neither side had gained supremacy.

He cursed the lack of information and then felt guilty, every man and woman was needed to bring down Amutu. They couldn't spare even one to keep him informed.

It was after mid-day and despite the thick canopy, the sun was making patterns on the tarpaulin above David's head. He was worried. The sounds of battle had nearly disappeared, reduced to just rare bursts. The only chance his people ever had was if the Government forces collapsed quickly.

It was now nine hours since they had launched the attack. He heard the distant whine of a small motorbike. The rider stopped close to his bivouac and entered,

"Message from the Major Sir."

David nodded; the next words would seal his fate.

"All objectives apart from the Presidential palace secured Colonel."

David grinned, "Including the army HQ?"

"They surrendered about an hour ago Sir."

David swallowed and felt the prickle of tears behind his good eye. When he trusted his voice he asked, "What's happening at the palace?"

"It's surrounded Sir, but until we have consolidated and disarmed all the surrendered troops the Major has decided to delay a final attack."

The Colonel nodded again, "Please convey my congratulations to Major Beyla."

***

The door slammed back against its spring as Vasyl burst into the room, his rifle panning back and forth. He took in the situation at a glance and shouted in Russian. Lorna was clutching two bottles of water and staring at the bodies as Lindy ran into the room, but now her screams had become huge gasping sobs. Lindy enveloped Lorna in her arms and gently turned her away from the bed. Serovec inspected the victims. A plump middle-aged black couple; they both had a neat bullet hole in the centre of the forehead. He checked their temperatures by slipping his hand into their armpits. He poked his finger into the man's congealed blood and thoughtfully rubbed it between thumb and forefinger; then wiped his fingers on the pillow. Turning, he guided both women back into the corridor.

Lorna was now sobbing quietly with her head on the Russian girl's shoulder. Vasyl made a face at Lindy and taking the passkeys out of the opposite door he opened up the next room and went in. He was inside for only a few seconds, he held up two fingers to Lindy when he re-appeared. She stroked Lorna's hair and watched her partner as he progressed down the corridor. As he came out of each room he either shook his head, or held up one or two fingers, each time he had more small bottles of water stuffed in his pockets. Slowly he worked his way back towards them, at one point grinning and holding up three fingers.

The corridor completed he stood and opened a small bag of peanuts and said in Russian, "Their killers are long gone, they were killed around six hours ago … but it's difficult to tell in this heat."

Lindy indicated Lorna, "We had better get her upstairs."

Serovec emptied the nuts down his throat in one. He shouldered the laundry bag of water and they headed for the stairs.

McRae and Mike Bray were pushing a rubber wheeled trolley full of tinned food towards the bottom of the stairs. Lorna was still too upset to speak, so Lindy updated them. Vasyl interrupted her description of the rooms, "Not all guests is dead. Many escape." Mike asked how he knew they had got away.

The Russian shrugged as if it was obvious, "Empty beds, bags gone."

McRae asked for details of the shootings. Vasyl's face betrayed no emotion, just an analysis of events, "Two, maybe three shooters, very good, only one bullet in each body, small handguns with…" He spoke in rapid Russian to Lindy, she supplied the word. "…With silencers."

When they got to the top floor, McRae and Mike Bray went up the roof ladder to tell the watchers on the roof the new development. As the streets below were quiet, they held their meeting by the hatch so they could still watch the front of the hotel. On the roof there was a slight breeze, but the sun was now fully up.

Wolfgang Schmidt wiped perspiration from his face, "Very soon the bodies will smell."

Mike Bray glanced at Fiona, but she appeared unmoved by the prospect of sharing a hotel with rotting, fly blown corpses.

Robert Goff spoke, "There's no way of telling how long we'll be holed up in this place."

McRae nodded, "At least there's no problem with food or water. The kitchen stores are stacked and there's loads of bottled water."

"How long will the water last?" asked Johan.

McRae scratched his head, "Ten people … more than a month … and then enough beer and spirits for another."

The Scotsman chuckled, "Or a week if we have a party."

No one acknowledged his humour as they stared silently down at the city below. The only source of intense firing came from the direction of the Presidential palace. The top of the Balmoral castle tower was just visible in the distance.

Paul Henning spoke for the first time from the shade of the chimney, his voice broke mid sentence, "Surely our governments ... you know ... they've embassies ... they've gotta get us out of here."

Fiona Goff took a slug of water from her bottle, "There's a British one." She tapped a bulky satellite phone, "Not got a lot of battery left, but I'll give them a call and see what they know." The Goffs walked a little way away from the group.

Vasyl had been studying the street below whilst the others talked, the brim of his cap pulled low over his eyes. He hissed to draw their attention. In the distance a small convoy of half tracked personnel carriers and light tanks was approaching.

"Shit," breathed McRae, "looks like things are hotting up."

Serovec raised his rifle and sighted on the vehicles. He slowly traversed from the first vehicle to the last, "No government marks," he grunted.

Mike frowned, "Does that mean they're in rebel hands?" The Russian did not answer.

McRae was scanning the vehicles through one of the German's rifle sights replied, "Must do. They don't want to take friendly fire, as soon as they capture 'em they'd blank out the Gamasi flag."

They all watched as the three tanks and one armoured carrier passed the hotel gates and bounced on towards the sounds of shooting. The two remaining carriers swivelled to a stop, one blocking the Ambassador's entrance and one the exit. At an unseen signal the rear doors burst open and eight soldiers emerged from each. They quickly deployed around the gates and vehicles. Both vehicle commanders' heads and shoulders poked out of the roof hatches as they examined the hotel through binoculars. Simultaneously the group on the roof dropped down behind the stone parapet, then in a line peered over the edge.

Despite the distance from the rebels, Mike Bray found himself whispering to McRae who was only the other side of Schmidt, "What shall we do?" The soldier did not answer.

Serovec on Mike's right answered for him, "nothing ... we wait."

At the main gates and on the roof, no one moved. Paul Henning's tremulous voice broke the silence, "Do they know we're up here?"

McRae glanced towards the questioner. All he could see was the new soles of Henning's trainers and the yellow bulge of his stomach as he lay flat on his back in the gully behind the parapet, "Don't think so, they're concentrating on the ground..."

Plucked from between Bray and McRae as if punched in the face, Wolfgang Schmidt crashed back against the roof tiles.

"What the fuck!" shouted Bray.

They turned in horror as the German slid slowly back down the angle of the roof to rest in the gully against their legs. A long smear of blood, bone and grey pulp traced his progress down the tiles. They shuffled away from him. He lay snoring, bubbles of blood pumping out of his nose in time with his breathing. There was a neat hole where his bottom lip joined the point of his chin, but a fist size hole ripped out behind his left ear.

Johan knelt and stared at his boss, "What can we do?"

McRae hissed at him, "Keep down."

Mike grabbed Johan, forced him below the parapet and hissed in his ear, "Nothing ... we can't do anything."

In shock, Johan grabbed Schmidt's wrist as if to take his pulse, "He's alive, we must help ... we can't just..."

A voice came to them from the far side of the roof; it was Fiona Goff, "What's happening?"

McRae shouted, "Stay where you are and stay down. Wolfgang's been hit!"

The Goffs quietly absorbed the information. "Is he bad?" called Robert.

McRae looked down at Schmidt. Blood foamed from his nostrils at every laboured breath. "Yes," was his simple reply.

THE BIG GAME

Serovec began to dismantle a section of roof by inserting his stubby fingers into the gap where the roof tiles joined the gully, Serovec. Bray and McRae watched him in bewilderment.

"What the hell are you doing?" asked Mike.

Serovec indicated the front of the hotel with his head and smiled, "I go kill him."

It was the first time Mike had seen him smile, "Who?"

The Russian tossed aside another tile, "The sniper." He nodded upwards to the exposed roof hatch, "Now he want for us to go there."

Enough tiles had now been removed from between the timbers to accept his stocky frame. Serovec handed his rifle to McRae, "I will return to room," he said, then lowered himself into the roof space. They stared into the gloom at his upturned face, then handed him down his weapon.

On hands and knees, they turned back to Wolfgang Schmidt. Johan Koeffe was hunched near his head and Paul Henning was crouched by his feet. Schmidt still snored and bubbled.

Henning dragged his eyes off Wolfgang's face and looked at Koeffe pleadingly, "Why can't he die?"

Lindy glanced at her watch, they had waited long enough. Lorna was perched on the edge of the settee, clutching her glass. The Russian pointed above her head, "Its time we took over from the guys up there, will you be ok?"

Lorna had stopped shaking and just felt numb. She gulped the remains of the large brandy Lindy had forced upon her and it had made her feel better. She nodded, "sure, I'll be ok, It'll be better up there in the fresh air away from all those..." she tailed off at the thought of the couple lying in bed three floors below. With a determined toss of her head she stood up and forced a smile, "Lead on."

At the end of the corridor, they went out of the door marked *staff only* and onto the steel stairway that gave access to the roof. When they arrived at the stair head Lindy pushed against the warped timber door that lead onto the roof, it was stuck. She turned to Lorna who was two steps below her, "Can you help?"

Lorna joined her on the top tread and together they shouldered the door. It flew open, crashed back against the chimney stack and Lorna stepped out. Five figures were huddled below her in the gully, in unison they shouted, "GET BACK!!!" Puzzled, she looked down at them as something tugged her hair, then smacked into the door frame behind her head. She felt herself being dragged backwards as Lindy hauled on her shirt. They both crashed into the wall and then clung onto the banister to prevent them tumbling down the metal staircase. Imprinted on Lorna's mind was the image on the roof; Wolfgang laying in the gully with Johan, Mike and Paul crouched round him.

She stared at Lindy, "What's happening?"

"Shooting, it nearly hit you."

Lorna ran her fingers under her hair, but could feel nothing. She looked in horror at the Russian girl, "Was that a bullet?" Before she could reply they both tensed at the sound of the door being opened at the base of the staircase. There was no escape onto the roof and now there was someone below them, they clung together in silence.

"LINDY," the shout was clearly Vasyl Serovec. There followed an exchange in rapid, high volume Russian. Tugged down the stairs, the sight that met Lorna at the bottom was bizarre. Serovec was hanging upside down out of the ceiling hatch at the base of the staircase, with his rifle suspended above his head.

When they reached him he handed the weapon to Lindy, then with impressive agility for someone of his age and bulk, swung lightly out of the access hatch and dropped to the floor.

Lorna followed dumbly as they had another rapid exchange during the short walk to their room. Hurriedly Serovec made up a small bag of bottled water and snack food, gathered up his

THE BIG GAME

rifle and left. Lorna felt like a small child; events and conversations were happening around her that she could not understand; she was also very afraid. This isn't like me she told herself, what's happened to that tough New Yorker?

As Vasyl disappeared she pleaded for an update, "I saw Wolfgang, I think he's hurt."

Lindy nodded, "Yes, he is very bad." She chose her words, "Soon he will be dead."

Lorna felt herself begin to panic again, she took deep breaths and poured herself another brandy, "There must be First Aid stuff around ... we could go up there again and throw it to them."

The Russian shook her head. "No good, he has big hole," she indicated with her open fingers a section at the back of her head. Lorna could think of nothing to say. Lindy continued, "and Vasyl, he has gone for a snooper."

"What's that? Do you mean a snoop around?"

"I don't think so ... a snooper ... a soldier who can shoot from far away."

Despite everything Lorna found herself smiling, "Oh a sniper, not a snooper."

Lindy frowned, "I am sure I know this snooper word, what is a snooper?"

Lorna could not believe what was happening. Minutes ago she had nearly been shot, in the next door room were rotting corpses and she was now giving an English language lesson. "It's someone who looks at people ... when they shouldn't."

Lindy considered the answer, "Do you mean when they are without their clothes?"

Despite everything, Lorna found herself beginning to laugh, "No not naked ... please Lindy another time?"

Lindy smiled, "Ok, he's gone to kill the snooper ... sniper and the others are making holes in the roof so they can also come here."

25

David Churu struggled to raise himself on one arm. He felt weaker than a baby, but he owed it to the big man crouching on his haunches next to the camp bed. He offered his hand, "Nat, I congratulate you on behalf of our people. It would not have happened without you."

Major Nathaniel Beyla smiled broadly and shook his old friend's hand, "Thank you David, we couldn't have done it without your planning. Anyway, we haven't finished the job yet."

Churu nodded, he felt the lump in his throat, he was afraid to ask the next question because he knew the answer. He coughed and ploughed on, "And any news of Sita, or the boys?"

The Major lowered his eyes, "Not yet I'm afraid, but everyone is looking."

Churu did not trust his voice, "Ok. What's happening with Amutu?"

"He is still holed up in the palace; all his guards who were elsewhere when we launched the attack have fallen back there. We are just containing them at present."

Churu considered the situation, "When you are ready Nat, hit them hard, we don't want them breaking out."

"Will do Sir, I'm bringing up all the armour we have captured and tonight we will pound them."

"Good. One last thing, as soon as you can spare a driver I need to get into Kamba. I'm going mad just laying here."

Major Beyla frowned, "Is that wise Sir?"

David Churu laughed, "Probably not, but it's what I want."

***

Using the passkeys Vasyl Serovec went into every fourth floor room on the front of the hotel. In each one he shuffled along the wall until his right shoulder was next to the window frame. Using a broom he had found in a cleaning cupboard, he smashed two or three panes in each window, and then carefully knocked out the remaining shards.

During his visits he calculated that room 415 must be next to the chimneystack. He let himself in again and ignoring the dead couple in bed, he tapped and checked the shape of the walls to confirm his decision. With his back to the closed door he stared out of the window. The whole office block opposite the hotel could be seen with only slight positional adjustments. He swept the woman's cosmetics off the dressing table onto the floor and dragged it over to the door. He returned for the chair and placed it exactly between the door and dressing table. Sitting down he rested his rifle on the mirror supports and traversed the office windows opposite. He paused his sights on each one in turn, then grunted with satisfaction.

Re-locking the door he set off back to the roof again to arrange a decoy.

McRae watched in disbelief as Paul Henning hung from the rafters afraid to drop the last few feet into the roof space, "There's no hurry laddie, you can hang around there as long as you like."

Robert and Fiona Goff had completed their hole in the tiles on the far side of the roof and he could see the thin Englishman's legs appear as he prepared to climb down.

Serovec approached from the access hatch, "Is Schmidt dead?"

McRae sensed Johan bristling beside him, "Yes," he replied.

The Russian nodded, "I need him now."

They all looked confused and wondered if it was a translation problem. Serovec returned their stares in irritation, "You must hold him up."

No one understood. McRae spoke first, "I don't understand ... hold him up?"

"Yes, I have to spot the sniper."

Mike Bray broke the stunned silence, "Are you suggesting we use Wolfgang as a target?"

Serovec was unmoved, "Yes."

Johan stared in amazement, unsure he had fully understood, "You want the sniper to shoot at Wolfgang?"

Serovec nodded, "Correct ... he is dead."

Mike Bray intervened, "Look Vasyl, you can't do that ... Wolfgang is one of us."

The Goffs had now joined the four men. Paul Henning was standing under the hole checking his hands for splinters. Johan was just staring in silence.

Serovec shrugged, there was no hint of expression on his face, "It will not hurt him ... and maybe save lives."

Fiona interrupted and directed her question at McRae, "Tom, this can't be right, there must be another way?"

"We could make a dummy..."

The Russian tutted in irritation, "It will be too long time, we have dummy up there..."

Johan rushed towards the Russian shouting, "You do not say my friend is a dummy...a dummy that you can use..."

Mike Bray and McRae each grasped the German's arms to restrain him. Serovec did not move, just looked quizzically at his potential attacker. He then turned on his heel and called over his shoulder as he headed for the roof hatch, "No problem, I will arrange."

Johan Koeffe and Mike Bray were struggling to assist Paul Henning to drop down from the hatch whilst McRae leaned on a rafter and watched. Robert and Fiona Goff were in the stairwell below, each steadying one of his large white trainers.

The service door behind them opened and Serovec re-appeared, he had a middle aged man's pyjama clad body drooped over his shoulder in a fireman's lift. Seeing his access to the roof blocked the Russian dumped the body in the corner, turned around and went out again. Paul Henning peered between his legs at the corpse slumped beneath him. He saw the bullet hole in the forehead gave a strangled cry and let go of the hatch. In the small stairwell Robert and Fiona had no escape as Paul dropped on top of them. Disengaging themselves from the corpse and the American, they struggled to their feet. Henning's scream as he inadvertently touched a cold bare foot was deafening in the small space.

Serovec re-appeared with three lengths of heavy drape cord knotted together. Ignoring the winded Henning and Goffs he threaded the cord under the dead man's armpits and offered the other end up to the row of faces framed in the roof hatch. Reluctantly the three men hauled the dead hotel guest up to the hatch and then McRae and Bray grasped his arms and pulled him into the roof space.

The Russian synchronised his watch with McRae's, "Take him to the chimney. In exactly ten minutes lift him up, I will be ready."

Back in room 415 Serovec made his preparations. First he went into the bathroom and collected damp bath and hand towels. He folded the bath towel and placed it on the polished wooden surface of the dressing table. The hand towel was doubled and draped over the point where the mirror pivoted.

He settled himself comfortably in the chair and shuffled his feet into the carpet until he was satisfied. After swivelling his watch to the inside of his wrist, he picked up his rifle.

Carefully placing the front of the stock on the mirror support, he positioned his left elbow on the bath towel, making minute adjustments until it felt exactly right. Resting his cheek on the stock he squinted through the 4 power sights, the office windows 300 metres away sprang clearly into view.

He traversed the top floor where he calculated the shot must have come from. As he did not know which way Schmidt was facing when shot, it was pointless making guesses from the entry and exit wounds.

Instinct told him that his man was behind one the six central windows. They were the windows he would have chosen, immediately opposite the centre of the Hotel Ambassador, immediately opposite the chimneystack where McRae was now crouching with his "dummy".

Serovec knew that his opponent was good. Exactly as he had done, all the top floor windows had been broken giving no clue as to where the shot had come from.

Waiting just like him, deep in the shade at the back of one of those rooms, was the sniper. He checked his watch, three minutes to go. He went through his routine, tensing and releasing his arm and shoulder muscles, deep controlled breathing, pulse rate down.

It was Afghanistan all over again; only now grey concrete instead of rock, an African instead of Mujahadin. The still humid air was perfect, no need to shoot off target to allow for the wind, not hot enough for distortion. He eased a competition grade 7.62mm round into the chamber.

By change of focus only, he watched the second hands on his watch approach the ten minutes deadline. He respected McRae; he would raise the body right on time.

Ten seconds to go, five seconds and he blinked rapidly to lubricate his eyes; he would not blink again until after the shot. He focussed on his favourite window and took up the pressure on his trigger.

The muzzle flash was from the window next door, he was too late.

Serovec moved and waited, another flash, he fired, aiming at the source of light, his shot within fractions of a second of his opponent's. He sprang onto his feet, kicking the chair back against the door. His hand a blur as he worked the bolt, pumping in new rounds then back onto the trigger.

Moving randomly around the room, aiming-firing, aiming-firing into the window opposite, knowing that if the other man was alive he would be doing the same. When he had emptied all five rounds in his magazine he pressed his back against the front wall, panting. There had been no return fire.

As Vasyl Serovec leant against the wall gathering his breath he stared at the couple in the bed, their small third eyes stared blindly at the ceiling.

***

Cedric Farringdon jumped as his desk light came back on. Electric's back on again, he thought. There was a gentle tap and his trade attaché poked his head around the door.

The Consul indicated a chair, "Take a seat Jonathon. What news from the front?"

"Appears things are going badly for Amutu sir."

Farringdon made a face. "Bugger. How badly? Can he pull something out of the bag?"

"Well, I wouldn't write him off yet. He's holed up in the palace with most of his Presidential Guard. The rest of the army has gone over to the rebels. Plus the navy and air force of course, but that only means one patrol boat and three helicopters."

"How many has he got in his personal guard?"

"Around five hundred men. They're top soldiers, all hand picked, well armed, fight to the death etc."

Farringdon nodded slowly as he digested the information, "Do you think they could break out and turn it around?"

"Possible sir. If they counter attack and make a good showing, I'm pretty sure the army will change sides again."

The Consul glanced at his watch, "Give Colonel Churu his due; he's done a bloody good job in less than fifteen hours."

Jonathon Forbes nodded, "I hear it wasn't Churu though, it was all led by a guy called Beyla. He was one of the Colonel's buddies."

Farringdon raised an eyebrow, *was* one of the Colonel's buddies? Power struggle already amongst our rebels? "Do we know anything about this new man? Where his sympathies lie etc?"

121

"I'm afraid not, but once it's safe to venture abroad I'll find out."

Farringdon smiled ruefully, "Well the electric's back on, that's always a good sign."

Forbes rose from his chair. The Consul held up his hand, "Just one more thing. London's a bit concerned about Goff … you remember? Their spook, or should I say our spook? Last heard of under siege at the Ambassador Hotel."

"Yes Sir. We got a satfone call a few hours ago, all seemed ok then. Sitting on the roof watching the fireworks with all the other guests … all the live ones that is..."

The Consul nearly shouted, "Live ones? Is the Ambassador under attack?

"Not at all. But it appears that last night the rebels bumped off all the Amutu sympathisers in their beds and then scarpered."

"You sometimes worry me Jonathon.

"Sorry Sir."

Farringdon picked up a secure communication slip and quickly re-read it. "Fiona and Robert Goff. Seems they've got friends in very high places, Buck House even! No clue as to why our man would bring his wife on a mission?"

Jonathon Forbes allowed himself a small smile, "I understand that Robert Goff is on holiday and Fiona is actually his sister."

Cedric Farringdon shook his head, "His sister? Bloody hell Jonathon, no wonder London's in a flap! That family has had enough scandal to last them a century."

"Oh no, nothing improper. It's just London's cover story to get someone on the ground. And I should point out Sir that it is Fiona Goff, not Robert who's the spook. Her brother just helps run the family estates."

Farringdon snorted, "Are you telling me our agent's a woman?"

"Exactly Sir."

"My God, what next? Please hold the war our secret agent is pre-menstrual!"

"I understand the ladies acquitted themselves rather well in that field during the Second World War Sir."

The Consul grunted, "True enough Jonathon ... and when you think about it, women were designed for espionage!"

***

Fiona Goff slid another chicken into the oven and once again thanked the god of kitchens for bottled gas.

"Much smaller than the chaps at home," pointed out Robert as he handed her the final stringy bird, tidily tucked up in foil.

"Yah, but we've done one per person." She called to Lindy, who was only just visible on the far side of the room, "How's it going?"

The Russian girl was ladling beans from a huge catering tin into a massive pot, "Ok, I will make them hot in one hour."

Lorna sighed and looked at the huge mound of potatoes between her and Paul Henning. She had only peeled a few and already she was bored, maybe this is what I need at the end of a day like today, a repetitive familiar job. She glanced at the Californian in the candlelight; it did not look as if he had ever peeled a potato before.

He worked in silence, slowly and precisely, each one a work of art. Fiona and Lindy came over to help and the heap began to shrink. Paul was still on his third potato, so they dispatched him to prepare a huge pot of boiling water.

Fiona looked at the other two women, "Good to see the old stereotypes are alive and well. We're down here cooking while the men are playing cowboys and Indians on the roof."

Lorna laughed and it felt good. It had been a very long day.

26

Colonel David Churu sat in the passenger seat of the Land Rover; it was hard to find the energy to hold himself upright. Major Beyla stood by his open window as they both stared at the dark outline of the Presidential palace in the distance. "Are you confident we can hold the Presidential Guard if they break out?"

Beyla paused and glanced at the driver. He swapped to English, "Not really, at the moment it's a stand off. They don't know how strong we are, but even though we outnumber them four to one I doubt we could cope with an organised counter attack."

"How about bringing up the old army units, to stiffen our people?"

Major Beyla shook his head, "You know my feelings on that. I don't think we can trust them. Not yet, they changed colours only a few hours ago, what's to stop them doing it again?" For a few minutes they both considered the situation in silence. Then Beyla continued, "And we both know if we try a frontal attack it will fail."

David spoke, "Our big problem is the only people who know all the tricks built into that place are both in there … General Gboja and Amutu himself. The only thing we are sure of is that the ground floor is impregnable."

The Major nodded, thinking back over the cloak of secrecy that had surrounded the palace's construction contract. The use of a French company and all foreign workers, the thousands of tons of concrete and steel reinforcing for no obvious reason. The millions of dollars of aid money that was supposed to fund schools and hospitals that had gone into the castle in front of them.

THE BIG GAME

The Colonel was thinking about the investigations they had carried out during the coup planning. The big question mark had always been the Palace. It had soon become obvious that the garden *features* were tank traps and heavily fortified bunkers. Bunkers that were equipped with heavy machine guns, manned by highly trained troops. Inside his fortress Amutu will have enough food and water for weeks.

"We have a problem Nat and it's the one thing I hoped wouldn't happen. Amutu holed up and probably tomorrow Gboja will launch his counter attack."

"We'll be ready for him Sir."

The Major and the Colonel parted, but after a few metres David Churu's driver reversed back. "One more thing Nat. I forgot to ask you about those foreign shooters in the Ambassador, what's the situation?"

"Just as you instructed Sir. They are contained in the hotel."

"Any attempts to escape?"

"Not yet. I'll soon have some more specialists free that I can send up there."

"Good, they're not a priority, but if and when you can spare some snipers send them along." David smiled, "We must make sure our foreign hunters get their monies worth from their sniping holiday."

***

It was ten o'clock and Lorna felt her eyes drooping. The combination of food, heat and stress was having its effect. Keeping well back from the window she looked out over the city. The gunfire had ceased hours ago and it seemed as if the Ambassador was the only major building without electricity.

Serovec and Henning were on roof shift with infrared scopes watching the troops below. Just before dusk the sixteen soldiers from the front gates, had split into pairs and spaced themselves at regular intervals around the hotel perimeter.

Lindy was dozing on one of the mattresses they had dragged into the suite.

McRae, Johan Koeffe, the Goffs and Mike Bray were sitting in a circle on the floor like a group of hippies. They were arguing about the next course of action.

Robert Goff believed they should negotiate, "I know they were rebels this morning, but now it looks like they're the people in charge. They may not even realise we're foreign nationals."

Fiona disagreed, "No Rob, I think they're very aware of who we are. Look at the way they came in and shot all those guests in the rooms around us. They must have been working to a plan and that plan involved keeping us alive." They all considered her point.

Johan broke the silence, "But what about Wolfgang? That was not an accident."

"You're both right," said Mike, "There's something here we're missing."

Robert fiddled with the satellite phone, "If only we could charge this damn thing it would be so simple to find out."

"We'll just have to go out and ask those guys at the gate what's happening," suggested McRae. They all stared at the Scotsman.

"Are you volunteering?" asked Mike.

McRae nodded, "No problem, in the morning I'll go out the front door under a white flag."

***

David Churu lay on a camp bed in a side room at REV-HQ, as they had renamed the old government building. He could not sleep, despite his weakness and the painkillers. There were squads out looking for Sita and his sons and every time footsteps approached his door he thought it was news.

He closed his good eye and re-ran his conversation with Nat Beyla. There was no answer to the palace problem. In all his months of painstaking planning it was the one element that he could never resolve. That palace had nearly bankrupted his country, swallowing foreign aid ... suddenly he was struck by an idea ... foreign aid.

The Japanese Government projects; the harbour and highway into the interior. Officially these would allow modern deep draught vessels into Gamasi and help it compete in world markets. The real reason was so Japanese companies could remove all Gamasi's tropical hardwood from her remaining rainforest; aid linked to logging contracts was the way it all worked. Gathering his breath he called the sentry outside his door.

Within five minutes Major Beyla was at his bedside. "Nat I want you to round up all workers who drive heavy tracked machinery. Take them to the harbour and highway sites and bring all the earth moving equipment; at gun point if necessary"

Beyla frowned, "Will do Sir, but may I ask why?"

Colonel Churu grinned, "You may Nat; tonight we are going to build a memorial; a permanent memorial to ex President Charles Amutu..."

27

As Major Beyla completed his officer and NCO briefing it became difficult for him to make his voice heard. The ground three hundred metres from the Presidential Palace shook beneath his feet as the night was filled with the sound of approaching heavy tracks.

The crawlers had been diverted from the construction of logging roads. Their massive hardened blades could force a two-lane road through all but the densest forest. Their drivers perched high above the road, were dwarfed by the machines they controlled.

The engineers feverishly strapped perforated steel plates around the cabs whilst the NCOs instructed each driver. One by one they moved off to their allotted sector. Platoons of troops formed up behind the three light tanks, which set off for their respective stations.

The crawler allocated to the front of the Palace belched a plume of smoke skywards as it roared forward with Major Nathaniel Beyla and his staff running close behind. Up ahead the sound of shooting intensified as the Presidential Guard spotted the attack. Breathing hard, Beyla picked out the distinctive crackles of heavy and light machine guns, interspersed with the detonation of rockets and grenades.

When a few metres from the tall perimeter fence, the crawler driver lowered the earth mover's blade and drove straight through without a change in pace. The steel and brickwork supports were mashed under its tracks. He continued to lower the blade and dug into the carefully tended front lawn, gauging and rolling a six metre wide mass of soil and shrubs ahead of him.

Next to arrive were the dump trucks, each packed with huge boulders intended to hold back Atlantic storms. They spun around outside the Palace gardens and sat waiting, gently rocking on their massive ribbed tyres.

Then the excavators appeared like lumbering dinosaurs, toothed buckets swaying high above the houses. Their engines strained at maximum revolutions, more used to sedate trundling around the harbour site, this was probably the longest journey they had ever completed.

David Churu's plan was working. Every time the crawlers reversed, they left the earth banks a little closer to the palace, immediately the next contingent of infantry would dash forward to crouch behind it. Using the fresh cover they would pour fire into the Palace and its support bunkers.

Again and again, each time at a slightly different angle, the crawlers roared forward driving more tonnes of earth before them. Gradually the gaps in the ring got smaller until it encircled the whole Palace.

The NCOs blew sharp blasts on their whistles to warn their troops. The dump trucks reversed at full speed, running their rear wheels up onto the summit of the ring of earth ring. With bullets ricocheting off their metalwork, they rocked to a halt and jettisoned their loads of rock over the lip. Then with their empty bucks still towering in the air they roared back to the harbour to re-load.

Dawn was approaching and the Presidential Guards were moving to vantage points in the upper Palace rooms and on the roof. The strengthening light was improving the aim on both sides and casualties rose.

The crawlers were heavily targeted and there were constant delays as replacements drivers slid into the hottest seats in Gamasi. Despite the casualties, the machines were steadily approaching the perimeter line of bunkers and the excavators were ordered into the fray. For safety, the excavator drivers tucked their machines close behind the earth bank. Spotters radioed them directions from distant vantage points. Straining to hear the voices in their headphones, the operators tried to scoop earth against each bunker's exit door. In the tumult of battle it wasn't working and the excavator buckets flailed blindly around, one second grazing the reinforced concrete roofs and the next ineffectually pressing mounds of earth against blank walls.

Beyla abandoned the effort and ordered the operators to shelter behind their machines and wait to be recalled.

The Guards began to abandon the bunkers and fall back to the Palace. Despite being supported by a hail of covering fire from their colleagues in the roof, only half survived the dash.

The earth ring rose steadily higher as it approached the Palace. The rebel soldiers scrambled and slid in the loose soil as the angle of their bank got steeper. Now the rim was level with the second floor windows and both sides maintained a withering fire only twenty-five metres apart. Still the fully laden dump trucks, with tyres scrabbling for grip, reversed up the earth bank. They teetered near the top, as they sent their rocks tumbling down the other side to crash against the Palace walls.

Major Beyla decided it was time to bring back the excavators. At his signal the operators crawled cautiously behind their controls once more. As soon as their infantry support formed close behind them, they moved up against the ring once more. This time their lack of accuracy did not matter and like drunken boxers they flailed and pounded their massive loading buckets against the Palace walls. At every point the structure began to crack, the upper stories collapsing. Amidst showers of dust, roof tiles, and bricks Presidential guards tumbled down onto their fellows below.

On every side the crawlers continued to drive massive walls of earth up the slopes. At the summit, they curled it over to join the huge rocks and collapsed building materials that had once been a castle. Fearing their imminent entrapment, groups of Guards began to storm up the moving banks into the closing ring of guns. The few that made it over the lip were hacked down on the other slope by the waiting rebels.

THE BIG GAME

They stared at the massive mound of fresh earth. The earthmovers continued to crawl over it as the surveyor and his assistant sought perfection from every angle. David Churu reached out of the Land Rover window and shook Major Beyla's hand, "Once again Nat, you've managed to achieve the impossible."

"A good plan helps Sir."

The Colonel smiled acknowledgement, "Are you sure he's in there?"

They both knew to whom he was referring, "He didn't escape, we're sure of that."

David stared at the mound and talking to himself said, "Buried alive, it's a bad way to die but you deserve it Charles Amutu. Now you have a few hours to think." He turned back to the Major, "How long will they last?"

Beyla made a face, "I guess they've already suffocated."

"We must think what to erect there," Colonel Churu nodded to the top of the hill, his single eye misted, "To remind us of all the disappeared."

***

The old man dragged back the threadbare rug that covered most of the floor of his one room hovel. The sound of the battle coming from the Palace a quarter of a mile away was intensifying. He hefted his spade and began to scrape at the compacted earth in the centre of the floor. Gradually a half metre square emerged and wheezing with effort he began to dig all around the edge.

Ten minutes of hard scraping exposed a joint all the way around and after straightening his back and resting on the handle for a few minutes, he stabbed the edge of the spade into the lip. With all the power in his frail shoulders he levered back and gradually a rusty steel plate began to rise from its seat. With the toe of his ancient army boot he slid a timber

131

wedge into the gap and started to work on the opposite side. With the plate laid to one side, the old man sat back in his one rickety chair and waited.

The muffled sounds of battle echoed up from the hole, along with sporadic gusts of musty air. Then in the distance, a crawling and dragging; it stopped just below the floor and a pained grunt heralded the sweating face of General Gboja. He wiggled his broad shoulders through the small space and crawled out. After greeting the old man, he knelt and accepted a large white bundle from someone following. Reaching down once more like a magician into his hat, he plucked forth a pretty black woman. As she stood and brushed the dust from her hands, the General half pulled the stocky, bearded figure of President Amutu out of the hole.

The President forestalled the old man's shaky salute by clasping both of his hands warmly.

Gboja lay on the floor once more and reached deep into the tunnel and tugged sharply on a rope. In the distance came the sound of a dull explosion and the rumbling of bricks, a gust of hot air and dust billowed out of the hole and made them all cough and close their eyes. With slim delicate fingers the woman un-knotted the sheet that held their bundle and separated the contents.

Gboja stripped to his shorts and dressed quickly in the bright white clothing and hat of a devout Muslim. The old man held up a flyblown mirror as the General applied theatrical adhesive to his face. Behind Gboja's back, President Amutu and the woman were casting aside their dusty coveralls and donning full black burkhas and veils. General Gboja gave one final check to the full black beard and opened the door a crack.

They had waited for the cover of darkness as there were no streetlights, but now the road was dotted with small silent groups, all standing with their heads bowed. They could wait no longer; he beckoned to the woman and Amutu and they stepped boldly into the street.

28

They hadn't managed much sleep last night due to the sounds of battle. This morning the distinctive profile of the Presidential Palace was missing from the skyline. This fact alone lead the Xtremers to assume Amutu had been overthrown. The thought that Gamasi was now in rebel hands did nothing for their peace of mind.

Lorna lay on her mattress on the floor and thought about Charles Amutu. What had happened to him, had he survived the coup? Somehow I can't imagine him dead. He seemed too sharp, too much of a survivor. I guess he was the type of man to plan for every eventuality. Even if the crap hits the fan he would get out somehow.

She watched Mike and Tom McRae as they went out of the door in the low, crouched walk they had all adopted. We move around like a bunch of techies on stage at a concert. This is mad, we don't even know if there are any snipers out there, but as Fiona had said, "You never know for sure until it's too late."

The Mike business is not as bad as I thought it would be. I guess the other stresses sort of counteract the break up stuff. It's still kind of strange treating him like one of the gang. She analysed her feeling. It's only a few days since we couldn't get enough of each other and now he feels like a brother ... though not a favourite brother ... he's still a homicidal shit, but he seems much more shaken than I would have expected.

She studied the members of the group left in the room. McRae seems relaxed, this can't happen to him every week but he's taking it in his stride. Paul Henning seemed to have retreated into some kind of shell; he only talks when asked a question and then reluctantly.

She smiled as she watched Lindy sitting in the corner carefully painting her toenails. Johan was kneeling on the floor polishing telescopic sights with a paper towel. He seemed deeply troubled and she was unsure how much was due to the loss of his friend, or the whole situation.

In contrast, Vasyl had adapted seamlessly to his changed circumstances and had become a full time urban guerrilla. Maybe he assumes this is part of the package holiday; probably considers it excellent value for money and is planning to book for three weeks next year.

Although they're trying to hide it, Fiona and Robert are much the same, they seem to think it's all one big adventure. In fact, apart from Paul, I'm the only one on the edge of panic and I never thought I was a panic sort of person. What the hell will happen if these rebels have taken over? You read and see such terrible things. How will they treat us?
Why did I ever come on this fucking holiday?

McRae yawned hugely as he stapled the clean white pillowcase onto the broom handle. Hugging the wall he approached the front doors of the hotel.

Mike Bray peered around the base of the stairs. The rest of the group were in the suite using scopes to look through holes they had cut in the tightly drawn drapes.

The Scotsman sidled around the doorframe holding his makeshift flag in front of him. He pushed open the small side door and stepped out into the fierce early morning sun, his free arm raised high above his head.

The sudden activity at the entrance and exit gates told the watchers on the fourth floor that McRae had emerged. Each pair of soldiers had built a sand bag guard post butting onto the Gothic gateways. They peered over the top through binoculars at the flag waver limping slowly towards them.

A soldier at each post grabbed his radio and began a hurried conversation. Instructions received, one of the entrance guards lifted his weapon and rested it on the sand bag rampart.

THE BIG GAME

The group upstairs watched in silence as he tucked the gun into his shoulder and aimed towards the front door.

Lorna moaned and whispered, "Oh no, they can't!" From the window to her left she heard a smooth metallic sound as Serovec worked the bolt of his rifle, easing in a bullet. Below in the sun McRae hesitated, the flag hanging motionless above his head. A burst of automatic fire stitched across the front of the hotel shattering a line of first floor window. McRae froze, listening to the glass cascading down behind him.

Nothing happened. The marksman stared at the Scotsman over his sights as he took one tentative step backwards, then another and another until he felt the shade of the hotel canopy over his head. He turned, dropped his flag and hurried back inside the Ambassador.

"I guess they no want to talk," observed Serovec quietly from behind the curtain.

29

All the consulate staff, including local drivers and cleaners, was gathered in the large reception room. Cedric Farringdon tapped his fountain pen sharply on the cover of his diary for their attention,

"I've called you all together this evening to update you on the situation." He paused to gather his thoughts, "This afternoon we received a communiqué from the new provisional government of Gamasi. I will have to summarise the contents as a great deal is political rhetoric ... basically the Amutu Government is no more, as a number of army officers have deposed it. There will be a period, and I quote, *of some months during which martial law will be imposed, pending the establishment of an alternative form of government."*

He surveyed the assembled faces over his half moon spectacles, "we can only conjecture as to the meaning of the term *alternative form of government.* After the traumatic events of the last two days I'm sure we all consider our personal safety is of more immediate concern." The Consul glanced once more at the A4 sheet, "Well this document goes to great lengths to stress the concerns of the new authority regarding the safety and well being of both the civilian and foreign populations. These signatories are not familiar to us, but in the absence of information to the contrary, let us assume them to honourable and well-intentioned men. Though saying that, I feel that it would be wise, in the short term, to proceed cautiously. So please remain within the confines of the Consulate until otherwise instructed. In conclusion, they're transmitting a public announcement on the television in..." he glanced at his watch, "forty minutes time, at seven o'clock. Hopefully everything will become clearer then."

THE BIG GAME

Cedric Farringdon was seated in an easy chair in the far corner of his office near the dark wood cabinet that contained the television. His Trade and Military Attaches entered and were invited to sit down, "Ah Jonathon, Giles, pull up a seat over here, it should be on in a minute."

Both young men collected stiff backed chairs from the desk and sat in front of the television. The screen was filled with the image of an unknown flag, to the accompaniment of the haunting tones of an African male choir.

"Anything new from London Sir?" enquired Jonathon Forbes.

Farringdon shook his head, "No, just more and more flapping about that Goff couple. Appears they haven't been heard of for some time, despite their satellite phone." He made a face, "Seems some very high up people are concerned about them."

Giles Winton snorted, "Dangerous job she's got. Strange choice of career if you've got a family that worries."

The Consul nodded slowly, "True enough. Any changes out there Giles?"

"No Sir, our Marines say all's quiet … Ah, here we are." The music faded and a banner headline was shown across the flag: *An Introduction to the new Democratic Republic of Gamasi.*

"Ah Democratic, that's always encouraging," observed Farringdon with an ironic smile.

The flag was replaced with a view of Colonel David Churu in army fatigues sitting at a desk. The camera zoomed closer so he filled the screen from waist up.

The three men in the room examined the image.

Churu's head had been shaven and his fine African-Indian features appeared even sharper since his recent ordeal. A black eye patch gave him a piratical appearance. He spoke Fasa with subtitles in English, "It is with great joy that I confirm tonight we are at last free from the despotic rule of Charles Amutu and his henchmen. I am Colonel David Churu and I have been chosen to lead you until we have established the basis for a fair

137

and equal society. This will be a society run FOR the people and BY the people.

I know that many of you have suffered greatly under the previous regime and that many have prospered from your suffering.

I believe that apart from the architects of Amutu's regime, who will be brought to justice, we must consign all resentment and ill will to history. I am very aware this will not be easy, but we must find the strength within ourselves to achieve it. For it is ONLY in the TRUE spirit of a NEW beginning that we can move forward. Let us learn from our history, rather than be manacled to our history.

The next few months will not be easy. I know that at times you will doubt me and the transitional leadership, at times you will despair of it ever working, at times you will doubt your fellow Gamasis, at times you will even doubt yourselves: but I believe that TOGETHER we CAN and we WILL build a free and prosperous Gamasi that will be the envy of the world.

Tomorrow is the first day of our new Republic and I want you to embrace the challenge with joy and optimism, but tonight we have a duty to all those who gave their lives so we can live in freedom. All the old, the young, the servicemen and civilians who have died over the last hours, months and years, fighting Amutu's tyranny. I now ask you to unite in the first act of our new nationhood. In one hour's time, at eight o'clock, you will here hear eight shots to signal one minute's silence in honour of all our fallen brothers and sisters. Then afterwards, irrespective of race or religion, let us greet our fellow Gamasis.

I look forward to meeting you very soon on the streets of our capital. And now I return you to our new flag and national anthem."

The Colonel's face was replaced by the flag and male choir once more.

The three Englishmen exchanged looks.

The Consul spoke first, "All this flag and anthem stuff suggests that this isn't some half-arsed spur of the moment thing."

THE BIG GAME

His Military Attaché agreed, "A lot of careful planning went into the whole business. I've been reading up everything we have on our Colonel Churu and I have to admit I'm rather impressed."

Anyone arriving in Kamba that evening would have been justified in believing that Gamasi had just won the World Cup. The streets were filled with a delirious population celebrating release from a generation of fear. The crowd was densest near the Government building.

David Churu found the joy of the people infectious; he shrugged off his weakness and hugged and shook hands as the crowd mobbed him. Deep behind his smile ran a stream of sadness, he wanted to share this evening with the wife and sons that he knew he would never see again.

In a dingy side street a tall Muslim with very prominent teeth, smiled and shook every hand that was offered to him. His two short wives followed close behind with their eyes averted, their hands resolutely tucked in the sleeves of their flowing black burkhas.

***

The Xtremers sat around on their mattresses and stared at the shifting patterns on the walls made by the stuttering candles. They listened to the distant sound of celebrations and shots being fired into the air. Occasionally flares would light up the sky over the city.

Lorna sniffed, she was sure she could now detect the sickly sweet smell of human decomposition coming from the room next door.

Johan was tucked in the corner of the window inspecting their guards through a night scope, "They are still there. Some visitors have brought them drink."

McRae grunted, "That's good news. They're sure to get drunk, so maybe we can sneak out of here."

Lindy and Mike were in the hall making up a hot meal from tinned goods. Two days without refrigeration had rendered all the fresh food inedible, but they had huge stocks of catering tins.

Vasyl Serovec was somewhere in the hotel, creeping around in search of new vantage points. He was turning feral and no one was sure how much longer he would abide by the group's decision and resist shooting the soldiers around the perimeter.

Paul Henning seemed able to sleep whenever he was off shift. He had just consumed two packets of half melted chocolate biscuits and although it was early evening he was sound asleep .

Robert and Fiona had adapted well to their reduced circumstances and had found a Monopoly set. Their cries of joy and disappointment after each throw of the dice were beginning to grate on Lorna's nerves.

McRae seemed relaxed about the whole situation and apart from some inept flirting, was no problem; in fact his confident presence had a calming effect on everyone. He seemed to be turning into a far better holiday rep. than Lorna had expected.

Johan was missing his family. Earlier, when they had been on their own he had opened up to Lorna. It was as if he had bottled up all his fears and worries and they came spilling out. How he had never wanted to come on this vacation, but had been pressured by his boss, with fatal results. He was sick with worry about his wife and two young sons, they would be going mad. How could he let them know he was all right? If only they could get word to one of the Embassies.

"Xtreme Tours know we're here, they'll contact our Embassies," she consoled him.

Johan had looked sceptical, "I do not think so. I believe that Xtreme Tours will say nothing to any authorities."

THE BIG GAME

Lorna thought he had a good point. How legitimate was Xtreme? Were the authorities back home even aware they existed? She would talk to Mike about it as soon as possible. But that could be a problem. She had first been attracted by Mike's chilled out personality, but he was becoming more distracted by the hour. He did not appear to sleep and his eyes had taken on a darting, hunted look. When they first met she had noticed his mannerism of occasionally running his right hand through his thick blond hair, now he was doing it constantly.

30

The British Consul was shown into the Acting President's office. David Churu came round his desk to greet him. He ushered the diplomat into an aged leather settee near the window, placed an unmarked, slim blue folder on a low table between them and sank gratefully into the chair opposite. "Tea or coffee?" he asked.

As the cups were set out Cedric Farringdon scrutinised the new leader of Gamasi. The Colonel was far gaunter than he had looked on the television yesterday and he suspected makeup had disguised the obvious signs of exhaustion. He noted a tall slim, dignified man in his mid thirties. The mix of East African and Indian parentage had produced a striking, strong boned face. A long thin nose robbed him of classical good looks, but large intelligent eyes with sweeping lashes made up for the shortcoming. He was dressed in clean and pressed army fatigues without insignias; they hung loosely upon him, suggesting he had recently lost a great deal of weight.

David Churu acknowledged the Consul's formal congratulations with a curt nod and tapped the arms of his chair. "Thank you, but let us be honest Mr Farringdon, Her Majesty's Government would be happier if Charles Amutu was sitting here today."

Cedric Farringdon adopted his best noble, but disappointed expression, "Whilst I agree we always enjoyed very cordial relations with the ex President we had … reservations about certain aspects of his administration. We are very aware that life moves on and my government is hoping to forge equally close ties with yourself."

David Churu did not reply, just stared steadily at the diplomat as if choosing then rejecting a number of replies. As the Englishman was about to fill the silence, he answered. "Then I'm afraid your government will be sadly disappointed. I knew little of Amutu's international relationships, but what I've recently discovered, I find totally unsatisfactory."

Farringdon cleared his throat,. "Well obviously times change Colonel. The contracts that your predecessor negotiated were probably right for him at the time, but..."

Churu held up his hand, "I think you misunderstand me. I don't mean I want to get my snout deeper into your trough than that tyrant. Let me explain. Firstly, I'm only here until I have overseen a satisfactory transition to true democracy. Secondly, there will be no forging of links between your government and any individual in Gamasi. Anything that my country buys or sells will benefit each and every one of my people. No more commissions paid to overseas consultants, no more special import or export tariffs paid to third party brokers, no more split invoices paid direct into offshore bank accounts. Put simply Mr Farringdon, no more corruption."

The Consul's face was a mask of innocence, "Colonel Churu, I think you misunderstand the role that my government fulfils in the area of international..."

David Churu raised his voice, If you insist on patronising me, then I see no point in prolonging this meeting."

"I assure you no offence was intended. I only sought to stress the non-active role my Government adopts in matters commercial."

Churu fixed Farringdon with his gaze and then the lines in the corners of his eyes deepened slightly, "That Sir, is tantalite to an untruth."

For once the urbane Englishman stuttered, "I'm sorry ... but ... could you ... sorry, I didn't quite catch..."

"I said your statement was TAN-TA-LITE to an untruth." For once Cedric Farringdon, one time luminary of Winchester Debating Society was lost for words.

David Churu nodded at the blue folder that lay between them, "The survey report and mineral extraction contracts are in there. The timing is an amazing coincidence don't you think?" He smiled at the diplomat, who responded with a muted gurgling deep in his throat. Churu continued, "Should you ever meet the leaders of your survey team, suggest to them that just because a man DOES NOT speak English, does not mean he CANNOT speak English. Specifically two of their porters on the survey, who you would have until recently described as rebels. Each has an honours degree in Geology." He smiled again, "Coincidently both were gained at your excellent Durham University. Would you care for more tea Mr Farringdon?"

Cedric Farringdon was in a slight daze as he returned to his car. The meeting had not gone at all as he had envisaged. He felt that there was no truer saying than, *power corrupts and absolute power corrupts absolutely.* As the Rover weaved through the traffic he thought back over the last few minutes. They all start out idealists, assuming it's not just a negotiating stance. Give David Churu a few years and his snout will be as deep in the trough as Amutu's ever was.

Bit of a worry though was the Colonel's unwillingness to discuss the fate of the Goff couple and the other foreign nationals. But we can't let a few bloody tourists stand in the way of this tantalite business; assuming young Forbes can still pull it out of the bag! Anyway a five star hotel can't be the worst place for them to languish!

***

Lorna was distressed when the corpses started groaning and emitting long wet farts. During his most recent visit to the room they were using as HQ, Vasyl assured her this was normal behaviour for a rotting cadaver. The Russian's libido appeared unaffected by their changed circumstances; he arrived at least twice a day to summon Lindy for half hour sessions in one of the nearby rooms. Lorna guessed by the

THE BIG GAME

Russian girl's state of dishevelment upon return that these were sweaty and energetic encounters.

They now shared the hotel with millions of fat black flies, who dragged their bloated bodies lethargically through the soup-like air. The smell inside the hotel was the most difficult to cope with. The cloying sweetness caught in their throats so everyone avoided breathing deeply. Mike, Johan and Lorna were plagued by constant nausea and usually vomited any meal within quarter of an hour, followed by an hour of retching until the last vestiges of the food had been purged from their stomachs. They had developed a system that involved eating their meals sitting on the stairs leading to the roof hatch. The stench was still powerful, but a downdraft made it bearable; if it had not been for the scorching sun and sniper fire they would have lived and slept on the roof.

Their two-hour watch over, with difficulty Lorna dragged off her soaking shirt and trousers. She lay down on her damp mattress, pulled a thin sheet up to her chin and adjusted the head bags they all wore when sleeping. Lindy and she had made nine by cutting up their lightweight sarongs. Sleep was impossible without them, as clouds of flies invaded your eyes, nose and lips seeking out the salt and moisture.

Fighting the twin spasms of diarrhoea and nausea, she groaned as the first telltale heaviness announced the arrival of her period. She flapped the sheet to pass some cool air over her sweating body and caught her own feral odour. Never in her life had she been so long without washing. Her skin itched, was red and raw where her clothes rubbed and her hair lay damp and matted on the pillow.

On the other side of the room she could see Mike slumped on his mattress, arms behind his head, staring at the ceiling deep in thought. Beyond him, nearer to the window, she could see the bulk of McRae gently rising and falling in sleep, she envied the Scotsman's ability to sleep anywhere, anytime. She dozed and shifted as the damp bottom sheet clung to her body.

She was disturbed by guttural mumbling outside in the corridor, then the door slid open and Lindy padded into the room on bare feet. The Russian peeled off her wet tee shirt and light baggy trousers without embarrassment and slipped naked under a single sheet. Lorna feigned sleep and watched the other woman and considered how easily she appeared to have adapted; what experiences could have prepared a young woman for this ordeal? Why am I desperate, depressed and constantly on the verge of panic? Lindy seems to have no problem living in this heat, humidity, surrounded by rotting corpses whilst under constant threat of death!

Lorna dozed and woke, aware that people had entered the room. All the on-watch Xtremers, apart from Paul Henning, were grouped around the front window observing the troops at the perimeter. Johan fiddled with the aftershave impregnated cloth he wore over his mouth to combat the stench. Since Wolfgang's death, their watch was leaderless and with the tacit approval of the other three, Fiona Goff had adopted the role.

Fiona glanced back at Paul who was slumped in a soft chair at the back of the room. Her brother was jiggling Wolfgang's rifle, which he had adopted since the loss of theirs. "I believe it's time we took the initiative; I suggest at changeover we discuss with the others how we can escape."

Johan and her brother nodded their assent.

It was late afternoon when all nine gathered in the hotel foyer to discuss escape plans. First to speak was Tom McRae, "Our big problem is not getting out of here, but where do we go then?" His point was met with shrugs.

Fiona adopted the role of chairperson. She addressed the Scotsman, "You live here and know the area, what would you suggest?"

McRae frowned, "Correction, I lived here under Amutu's regime. I've no idea what's beyond those gates now. This new lot could be running the tightest police state in the world or a hippy commune."

Mike nodded, "You're right, but I guess we've gotta assume it's the police state."

Vasyl Serovec was lounging against a pillar. He cleared his throat, "The back gate is good, the one for trucks, only two men, in middle of night they sleep."

Johan pulled down his facemask so that his voice was clear, "I agree with Vasyl, when I was watching the rear of the hotel last night, they did not move for two hours."

Fiona nodded towards the troops grouped around each front gate, "It's preferable to facing that lot, but it sounds too easy. Why station armoured cars at the front and nothing at the back?" She turned to McRae, "What're your thoughts Tom?"

He grinned, "I guess that's woollies for you, probably no reason that would make any sense to you and me."

Lorna noted that McRae no longer seemed to resent Fiona and had unconsciously slipped into the habit of deferring to her authority.

The English woman tapped her teeth with a pencil and glanced around the faces, "I think we should go out that way tonight, shall we have a vote?"

Mike said, "I agree in principle, but we need to decide the whole plan that we're voting on. If we meet resistance, how do we react?"

Lorna spoke for the first time, "I think we must be unarmed, if it comes to a shoot-out we can't take on an army."

Robert Goff giggled, "Maybe not the whole army, but we could acquit ourselves well against the odd patrol."

Fiona shot him an irritated look, "Maybe, but we can't start a new war ... a war that we could never win..."

As one the group spun around at the sound of metallic jangling behind them. Un-noticed, Vasyl had gone behind the reception counter and was approaching them holding up a set of car keys, "The hotel has small truck; I think we use it tonight?"

Lorna and Fiona had been outvoted. When they met at 2 am, McRae was in the back of the small canvas sided truck silently taking the rifles from Mike and laying them carefully on bales of dirty laundry.

When the weapons were safely aboard, one by one they crept out of the service door and scrambled up the tailgate. Johan sat in the driver's seat and scoured the darkness ahead of him for signs of Serovec's return. Lindy sat in the front next to the German in case translation was required. Lorna and Paul sat on one side of the truck. Fiona and McRae perched on the other side, the darkness was total and they could only hear each others' breathing in the restricted space.

The large rear courtyard sloped down from the service door to a pair of corrugated steel gates about 20 metres away. Mike and Robert stood at the rear of the truck ready to start it coasting across the yard as soon as Vasyl opened the gates.

Lorna thought back to the heated dispute in the foyer the previous afternoon. The vote on not taking weapons had been defeated seven to two. The next issue was how to diffuse the threat presented by the soldiers guarding the rear gate.

Serovec and McRae favoured killing them. "Not 'cos we have anything against 'em," the Scotsman was at pains to assure the group, "it's just safer and quicker."

The Russian concurred, "We have killed many Gamasi's, two more no problem."

The pair had been outvoted on the killing by the same margin, but Lorna was unsure that Vasyl Serovec would respect the majority's wishes. Out there now in the pitch dark, as always, he was a law only unto himself.

The silence was broken by the sound of metal scraping on metal. The occupants of the truck held their breath. It was followed shortly by the low groaning of a gate hinge. Suddenly Serovec appeared right next to McRae and Mike Bray at the rear of the truck. He was carrying a small black aluminium case and despite expecting him, they jumped not having sensed his approach. The Russian placed his case on the ground and started pushing the truck, the other two joined in.

THE BIG GAME

Sitting in the front Johan felt the movement; he threw the clutch and engaged third gear. Both his and Lindy's faces glowed red as he turned on the ignition. Gravel rumbled under their wheels as they gathered speed. Johan's heart hammered as he steered forward in total darkness, desperately trying to remember where the gateway was located. Finding it impossible to judge their speed in the darkness, he hung his head out of the window and listened to the scrunch of tyres on stone.

He engaged the clutch and the engine pumped on and on without firing. Remorselessly their speed bled away until the truck humped to a stop. Throwing caution to the wind, Johan grabbed the ignition key and churned over the starter. The engine spun and spun, then slowed gradually as its battery died.

As Johan switched off they all heard the urgent sound of dozens of army boots sprinting towards them. From the front of the hotel came the high-pitched whines of two tracked vehicles as they accelerated up through the gears.

31

SURREY - ENGLAND

It was an unusually warm November morning as the civil servant alighted from the London train. He ignored the queue of waiting taxis and decided to stroll along the avenue that lead towards the town centre.

Commuter country at its best. Sky high domestic taxes ensured that the autumn leaves never dwelt long upon the pavements before being scooped up by an army of contract workers.

Short, neat hair, dark grey suit and black shoes, rolled up newspaper in one hand, plain features to the point of being featureless. If asked, not one of the people he passed that morning would ever be able to describe him. He was not bland, but blend.

The teashop décor could be summed up as old dark wood. The pair sitting in the window should not have looked out of place as they shared their origin with the timber used in all the furnishings, but they still did.

The man from London glanced up at the carved facia to confirm its name, walked in and approached the two men seated at the window table. Both were dressed for golf; one short, stocky and bearded, the other tall, broad with very protruding teeth. The suited man offered his hand and with a slight smile said, "Dr Amutu I presume?"

The short man returned his grasp and smiled back, "Sadly not *doctor*, now just plain *Mister* Amutu."

32

Lorna felt her ribs. She massaged the rifle bruises from when she had thrown herself on top of the weapons in the dark interior of the truck. Despite her colleagues' efforts to drag her aside she had managed to cling onto the laundry bales, keeping the hard steel trapped under her body. Shouting at her, McRae, Mike and Robert had tried to wrench away their guns, but she had hung on.

Sliding to a halt at the rear of the truck, the soldiers' torches had flooded the interior in harsh white light. Blinded, the Xtremers had shielded their eyes. Hands had locked onto their clothing and one by one they had been dragged backwards, forced onto the vehicle's grimy floor and their arms bound behind them with nylon ties. A soldier on each arm and leg, they had been lifted bodily off the tailboard and dropped onto the ground in a semi-circle.

It had seemed an eternity, laying face down in the hotel yard. Boots had strolled back and forth above her head during interminable radio conversations. In the diffused glow of the armoured vehicles' headlights, reflected off the back wall, Lorna's vision had been restricted to just the terrified face of Paul on one side and Fiona's on the other.

Eventually an army truck had arrived. They had been lifted up once more and slung face down onto its floor. Soldiers climbed in after them, sat on benches along each side and rested their boots on the captives' backs. Crushed together, they had bounced and jolted along at high speed. Each pothole sent them flying up and crashing back onto the timber floor. Between launchings, Lorna had managed to lift up her head and in the dim electric light scanned the mass of bodies to see if all the group were present. Bracing her feet hard against the closed tailboard, she saw Lindy on her right and Mike on her left. Craning her neck, she recognised all the others apart from Serovec. She had squirmed around to face Lindy, "Where's Vasyl?"

The Russian girl had frowned and shook her head.

After about 10 minutes the truck squealed to a halt, and then reversed a short distance. They had laid in the silence and listened to the tick of cooling steel. Then as one, they jumped as a heavy steel gates slammed shut. The short journey meant they were still somewhere in the city of Kamba.

***

Vasyl Serovec remained motionless and listened as the convoy rumbled off into the distance. Right hip and shoulder pressed hard into the space where the hotel wall and the steel gates met, he had no view into the yard.

The moment they heard the troops approaching, he had slipped from the tail of the truck into this place of hiding. From then on only sounds kept him informed of events. Right up to the moment of their departure he had expected the soldiers to launch a search of the area, or simply close the gates and reveal him standing there.

The sound of the vehicles receded until he could hear no more. Still he remained behind the gate and listened. For fifteen minutes he analysed the information reaching his ears, standing with his mouth wide open to capture even the smallest sound. He knew that a human could rarely remain immobile for that long and finally he was satisfied they had left no troops behind.

Slowly reaching out his right hand, he groped for the heavy steel hinges. As his fingertips encountered stickiness he knew he was in luck. He scooped the filthy grease plastered around the metal and carefully applied it to his face, neck and head, massaging it in evenly so not even the smallest area was exposed. Then collecting more from the bottom hinge he moved onto his hands and wrists.

Motion alerts the eye and Serovec now moved a millimetre at a time. The small aluminium case in one hand and his gun in the other; whilst looking and listening it took him over an hour to move the few steps from the cover of the gate to an old two-wheeled barrow leaning against the wall. As soon as the Russian reached his destination, he was transformed. He quickly laid his rifle and case in its timber bed and grasping both shafts, he set off briskly down the road.

***

Lorna lay on a thin red plastic mattress. Her small concrete cell had a steel door with spy hole. There was a tiled hole in the floor, beside which sat a large enamel water jug and half a roll of toilet paper. Light came from a single bulb set in the wall behind a wire grille.

She stared at the ceiling and wondered if Vasyl Serovec was still free. If so, will he bother to stick around and help us, or hot foot it to the border? She was fairly sure she knew the answer.

***

Dawn began to lighten the sky as Serovec bounced his handcart off the road onto an area of waste ground. Swiftly he gathered armfuls of the long dry grass that grew in straggling clumps and loaded them onto the barrow. Next were his boots; finding an area of fresh animal dung, he reached down and smeared them liberally before kicking about in the dust. He pulled a sack off an abandoned animal shelter and shaking it vigorously to remove the loose dirt; he draped it over his shoulders like a cloak.

When he resumed his journey there had been a dramatic change to the Russian's appearance. Gone was his active military bearing, now he shambled. A pronounced limp had developed in his right leg, his shoulders had shrunk and his back had become rounded.

As the morning light strengthened people started to appear on the streets. Sleep-blurred, no one noticed the old man pushing a barrow of forage. No one glanced into the face, half concealed under the sack he wore to ward off the remains of the night's chill.

On and on he limped until the distances between the houses became greater. Now the road ran between small plots of land, each overseen by a shack. Serovec noted the road ran east by the hint of rising sun on the horizon. He trundled around a blind corner and one hundred metres ahead a military check point blocked the road.

They had chosen their position well. The corner had allowed no warning and the straight approach gave the soldiers a clear field of fire. Huge concrete blocks had been positioned to create a tight chicane, ensuring all vehicles were forced to slow to a walking pace. Both sides of the road were flanked by shallow ditches and low concrete block walls. There was no choice, but to approach. Serovec pushed steadily on, as he assessed the situation.

Behind the blocks he could see the canvas top of a Jeep. At twenty-five metres a head became visible, chin resting on crossed forearms on top of the nearest concrete block. As the block was only one metre high the head must belong to either a midget, a child, or a man sitting down. Serovec favoured the latter option, which then created the possibility that the sentry was asleep. Distance and lack of light prevented the Russian seeing if the eyes were open.

Serovec shook the shafts as he walked so his dry grass began to slide off both sides onto the road. Painfully setting the barrow down on its legs, he limped round to gather up the fallen forage.

The sentry's eyes were heavy. He settled deeper into his folding chair; it was only the smell of coffee brewing that kept him awake. Si was the corporal in charge of their three-man unit, but in fact it was a two men and one-woman unit, the woman being his eldest daughter Lizzie.

They had just indulged in some light hearted banter; Lizzie questioning women's changing role in New Gamasi, before reluctantly agreeing to make coffee for her father and his best friend Rollo. But strictly on the basis that it was due to seniority rather than gender.

Si peered at his watch, now only half an hour until we're relieved; in less than an hour I'll be sound asleep. He smiled as he thought about Lizzie's spirited defence of her equal rights, better get that one a husband before she becomes too full of new ideas! Despite all the recent deprivations, Si felt good this morning, out here with his old friend and daughter. Fighting for a new Gamasi, but I won't be sorry to be disbanded!

Just as Rollo wandered off to the nearby clump of bushes they used as a toilet, Si discerned movement on the Kamba road ahead. In the half-light he squinted at the unusual shape as it crawled around the corner. Gradually as it approached he recognised its profile. It was a home made hand cart, knocked together out of timber and mounted on a pair of old motor bike wheels.

On it came. Suddenly its load of hay rocked precariously on the uneven road surface and began to slide off. The owner halted, carefully set down the shafts and emerged from behind his load. It was a hunched old man. With an air of resignation, he began to laboriously re-load his animal feed.

As Vasyl Serovec scraped up the armfuls of dried grass he stole sideways looks at the roadblock ahead. One adult male sentry, eyes wide open under the brim of a baseball cap, watching him closely. There was the small telltale profile of an automatic weapon beside the man's right arm. The Russian smelt the coffee and tried to imagine the situation on the other side of the concrete blocks.

Experience told him it would probably be a three man unit, possibly four ... though you never know with irregulars, there could be six of them tucked down there. Can't go back, no choice but to bluff it out.

Si stared at the old man through drooping eyelids. There's something strange about that old guy which I can't quite put my finger on...

Lizzie came up beside him, holding out his coffee. Twelve hours earlier and without that distraction he may have held the thought. He carefully accepted the boiling hot mug in his fingertips.

Before hefting the shafts once more, Serovec slid his rifle half out of the load and thumbed off the safety catch. Suddenly from behind the jeep another soldier appeared.

The angle was improving with every step, Vasyl scanned the area behind the blocks, there were still blind areas, but no signs of any more troops. The sentry was being handed very hot coffee; he could see the steam rising in the chill air. The new arrival moved with a fluid grace; he realised it was a young woman.

The front of his barrow was nearly at the first block when the woman looked up and directed a call at him. The alien words could be expressing surprise, command or greeting. The Russian kept his face averted and replied in a guttural grunt. Steering between the massive squares of concrete, just as he drew level the woman extended a slim arm to block his passage.

In one flowing movement he flipped over the barrow with his right arm. It crashed into the seated man spilling him out of his chair under a welter of dried grass and hot coffee. In a blur of movement, Serovec dropped backwards and down onto one knee, gripping his rifle in his left hand, his right seeking the trigger, he fired from the hip up into the woman's abdomen. As the bullet tore upwards through her body he realised what she had been holding in her extended hand; she had been offering him her mug.

The sentry was emerging from under the pile of grass and upended barrow, right arm stretching for his weapon on top of the block. Serovec's bullet entered his left ear and exited through the top of his skull. Fragments of bone and brain lifted off the man's baseball cap; which flew high into the air before bowling merrily down the road.

Still in a crouch, the Russian moved swiftly to the next concrete block, at the same time pumping another round into the breach. In a smooth arc, he scanned the area over the top of his scope. He detected a movement to his right just as another soldier burst out of a clump of bushes, his Kalashnikov spraying bullets. Serovec's single shot took him cleanly through the upper chest; he noted with a slight smile that as the man fell, his penis was hanging limply out of his trouser fly.

The Russian removed a pair chromium catering shears from his case and moved quickly between both male corpses. Then he stood deep in thought and stared down at the twisted body of the woman. Coming to a decision, he wiped his hands on her shirt, replaced the shears plus two small objects and clipped the lid.

33

Colonel David Churu looked at the fourteen faces ranged around the table that made up his interim cabinet. He knew at least half of them would welcome back President Amutu, but he acknowledged that at present Gamasi needed their expertise. Me and my bunch of soldiers can't drag this country out of the mire, I must use these bastards for as long as they're useful; use them just like they've used our country to line their own pockets.

David and his most trusted aid, Major Nathaniel Beyla, had rowed fiercely in private over the inclusion of any ex Amutu men. Whilst the Colonel was pragmatic, the Major was an idealist. In the end David had used a line of argument that he sensed was slightly underhand. "Look Nat if I can work with the people who murdered my family, surely you can? And I promise you it won't be for a minute longer than we have to."

The cabinet meeting had been wide ranging, but the tantalite issue had dominated. There were two schools of thought. Generally the ex Amutu contingent believed it should simply be sold to the highest bidder, whereas the new members wanted measures protecting the ecology of their country.

One issue they all agreed upon was that tantalite would transform their economy. This fact had been clearly illustrated by the international scrum that had descended upon them; every industrialised nation appeared desperate to woo the new administration.

This international feeding frenzy had reconciled David Churu to the Xtremers' break out from the Ambassador Hotel; even as they spoke an army of workers were toiling around the clock to expunge all signs of the recent siege. Every member of the former staff, including its charismatic manager, had been rounded up and set to work. Tomorrow the first groups of industrialists and moneymen were due to arrive, laden down with their much needed foreign currency.

David thought about the Xtremers and realised that the views of his colleagues should be sought. "Anyone got any feelings on what should be done with these ten foreign hunters?"

Nat Beyla raised a finger, "Nine Sir, one was shot." He hesitated, "In fact it could be only eight as another one is presently unaccounted for."

Unused to the new ways, members of the old regime assumed the foreigners had already been executed ... and if not, why not? The ex rebels suggested a range of options from ransoming to trial for murder.

David gave them all time to air their disparate opinions before restoring order, "If there's no consensus, I'll decide their fate." The matter was of little interest to the assembled members. After a show of hands, Colonel David Churu was delegated to become the arbiter of the fate of the foreign holidaymakers.

The cabinet filed out to set about their various tasks, leaving only David Churu and Nat Beyla sitting opposite one another to sort out a range of details. As they finished Nat hesitated before getting up.

Years of working together had taught David when his old friend had a problem. He shut his last file and raised his eyebrow without the eye patch, "Ok Nat, what's worrying you?"

"It's not exactly a worry ... I'm just unsure that you're the best person to handle these foreign hunters."

"Why?"

Major Beyla chose his words carefully, "A number of reasons; demands on your time being the most pressing."

"I will look on solving the problem of these foreigners as a light relief from affairs of state ... a sort of ... grounding exercise."

Beyla frowned and did not reply.

"Come on Nat, what's your real reservation?"

"It's difficult, but this task will involve you going back into Amutu's old Secret Police prison and your experiences there are still too fresh. I don't feel happy about you taking on a task that a lot of other people could do ... less essential people ... and they could do it without opening, and being influenced by, old wounds. And talking of wounds, there's strong evidence that these hunters mutilated their kills ... they mutilated your colleagues and after what you've just been through that's hard to accept!"

Churu nodded and bowed his head in thought. The seconds dragged by before he confirmed his decision, "I understand what you're saying Nat, but it's a job I want to do."

***

Vasyl Serovec remained crouched behind the concrete block, completing rhythmic sweeps of the area. He assumed it would not be long before the shooting attracted attention, but was unwilling to move until absolutely certain that there were no seasoned troops waiting for him to move out into the open.

No movements, no sounds, so he crawled over to the Jeep and slowly peered inside. The ignition switch was empty. He crawled back to the man and woman sprawled behind him. He found the keys in the man's breast pocket then examined his jacket. A worn and dirty camouflage blouson very similar to his own; the only item of interest was the blue strip of cloth tied around his bicep.

Serovec recalled that all the rebel troops wore one, so he untied it and stuffed it in his pocket. Pausing only to collect both automatic weapons, their spare ammunition and his black case, he returned to the vehicle. He insinuated himself into the front of the Jeep and laid along the front seats. Inserting keys in the ignition, he checked for neutral and after pumping the throttle with his left hand, fired it up.

Hunched over with his eyes level with the bottom of the windscreen, in a cloud of dust he spun the 4x4 around in a half circle and powered up through the gears. No bullets followed his progress and after quarter of a mile he dragged himself upright in the seat.

It was a pleasant morning containing just a hint of the heat to follow when the fresh unit arrived to relieve the roadblock. They were surprised that no one noted their approach; they shouted a ribald greeting and received no reply.

Ten miles down the road Serovec whistled his favourite passage from Radetski's March as he drove steadily eastwards away from the city.

***

David Churu shivered as he stepped into the prison once more. The smell and sounds were the same and he was drawn back to the worst hours of his life. Then he realised there was a difference: the sounds weren't the same; the groans and screams were missing. He rocked unsteadily and his driver reached forward to support his arm, "Are you ok Sir?" The Colonel nodded and breathed deeply, unable to speak as the memories of his wife's torture came flooding back.

A huge black woman in straining olive green shirt and trousers, her head enveloped in a brightly coloured bandana marched towards them. Smiling hugely, she enveloped David's hand in both of hers and in a volume that made him wince, expressed her thanks for giving the people their freedom.

This was a common reception wherever he went; even if the wheelers and dealers still reserved judgement upon their Acting President, the people made no secret of their love for him. "Our job has only just started," he returned her smile; "I hope my countrymen still like me in a years time."

Still grasping his hand she accentuated each word with a crushing squeeze "We know you're a good man, we know we can trust you because you've suffered with us."

In a very unmilitary way, David sensed a prickling behind his one good eye. He swallowed and cleared his throat briskly. Then in a tone more peremptory than he intended, "I've come to see our foreign prisoners, but I need to examine their records first."

The wardress progressed down the corridor; both men were transfixed by the size of her rolling buttocks. A row of beer bottles could have comfortably balanced around her girth. David welcomed the diversion. He thought about the last time he had travelled this route, dragged naked, freshly blinded and near to death. Now he was making the return journey, uniform neatly pressed as Acting President of Gamasi.

They arrived at a small office containing only one chair, a table and a large framed picture of a blue-eyed Jesus Christ. The woman handed David a thin cardboard wallet. He slid out the eight typed sheets of A4 paper. On the top left of each a cell number had been written in thick black felt tip pen, on the right was glued a passport size photo. The pictures had obviously been taken against this office wall with a cheap Polaroid camera. Some of the faces that stared back were very scared. David looked up from the files and addressed the large wardress sharply, "Have any of these people been ill treated?"

Her eyes bulged in horror and she spluttered in dismay, "Lord no, never, I was put here to look after them and that's what I've done … anyone wanting to harm the poor lambs would have to get by me!"

David tried not to smile, "Are you aware why these *poor lambs* are here?"

She shook her head vigorously, "That's none of my business, we're all sinners, but salvation…"

David sensed an imminent sermon and interrupted, "Very good, so they're all healthy?"

She considered the question, "I guess so, in their bodies that is ... but up here." She tapped her gaudy bandana, "I'm worried about the one called Paul."
This whole conversation was heading in a direction that Colonel Churu had not envisaged, "Ah ... excuse me, I don't know your name?"

"Sorry, I never said, it's Chrystal."

David Churu stuttered, "Ok ... well ... Chrystal ... could I have a few moments to go through these?"

He sat at the small desk and examined the eight sheets of paper.

The first was a man of around forty with neat brown hair and light grey eyes. A pleasant face, but unremarkable. He read the details typed beneath, which he guessed were taken from a visa application. Johan Koeffe, nationality German, age 38, profession engineer, home town Essen, reason for visit: tourism. David stared at the basic details. This man doesn't look like a monster why has he travelled here to murder my countrymen, maybe even mutilate them?

The next was a young Russian woman, Linda Tatlina. Very short blonde hair framed dramatic high cheek bones and full lips. Large dark eyes stared challengingly into the lens. Her look contained many elements, confidence, awareness of her attraction, David felt the photographer must have been a man and he had no idea how he knew this. But there was something else; he sensed fear. At first sight, her motivation for murder was incomprehensible.

An American. Paul Henning looked like an overweight schoolboy. Pale unlined face, rather vacant eyes distorted behind rimless glasses. David re-checked the name; this must be the one whose sanity was causing Chrystal concern.

Strangely Robert Goff was smiling at the camera. A large sharp nose dominated a ruddy angular face, topped by a mass of tight curly hair. British and aged 27. Profession rather strangely stated as *gentleman*. "Sorry, planet's out of tigers Mr Goff, why not bag a nigger?" David made a mental note to

163

have this guy's luggage checked. He felt it likely there would be a photo of this *gentleman* staring at the camera, rifle in one hand and a foot resting on a dead Gamasi.

Next was an employee of the tour company. Sergeant Thomas McRae. Parachute Regiment (retired.) Scottish, aged 33, he looked the part. Square jaw and shaven head, he glared into the camera from under heavy brows. This man was every inch a killer, but he's only the tour guide; probably cultivated the persona to impress the tourists. More importantly has he ever killed here? David stared into the dark eyes. Is the man that points out the targets any less a murderer than the one who pulls the trigger?

Lorna Karrol was beautiful despite her lack of makeup and the signs of stress. Obviously terrified, she stared into the camera with the look of someone barely in control. I wonder why Chrystal didn't mention this one; she's definitely on the edge. He stared at the photo, taking in the fine bones, full lips and dark hair drawn severely back from her face. He sighed, why do I feel sympathy? Did she feel sympathy when she had my people in her sights? I guess not! He dropped Lorna's details onto the pile. Well now it's your turn to feel fear Miss America.

The following sheet was confusing. David shuffled back to Robert Goff and held the two details side by side. Robert and Fiona Goff could have been twins; he checked the two-year age difference. They shared the same features from large nose and mop of curly hair to their weather beaten complexions. Their details were identical; apart from she described her profession as *civil servant*. He assumed they were husband and wife, but nothing in their details confirmed it.

The final sheet indicated that cell seven one six was occupied by a Michael Bray. The man stared back at the camera with undisguised contempt. Like some blonde god he was confident of his place in the world. A forty-year-old New Yorker. Rich guy destined to stride the planet unchallenged. David smiled at the photo. Well you won't be striding anywhere for a while Mr. Bray.

David interrupted Chrystal as she was browbeating his driver over his lack of a balanced diet, "May I see the prisoners now?"

As the three made the short walk she explained her reason for putting them at the rear of the prison, "I have over a hundred cells to choose from, but the back ones are bigger and have toilets ... plus they're much cooler in the middle of the day." David had the surreal impression he was being regaled with the attributes of a hotel.

The driver stood to one side, his double barrelled twelve bore pointed at the floor. A large bore shotgun being the preferred weapon if one of the prisoners decided to make a break for it. Johan Koeffe was the first to be unlocked. Although he stood up quickly as his door was opened, making a break looked far from his mind.

David introduced himself, "Good evening, I'm David Churu. This is just a short initial visit. Have you any complaints?"

The German looked confused, "I am sorry, I do not understand."

David frowned, "I regret we have no German speaker who can translate."

There followed a moments silence while Johan processed this statement, "It is not a language problem, I speak English. I do not understand your question; do you mean complaints about being in prison?"

Churu shook his head, "No, I mean about your treatment in here. You're in prison because of the murders you've committed in my country."

Johan threw up his hands, "I have never murdered anyone in my life!" David turned to leave, but the German continued, "What can I do? I am innocent of any murders."

"That is my job to find out."

Johan was desperate, "Will you please contact my wife, she has no idea what has happened to me. Please for the sake of my two young sons."

David spun around; face like stone, his single eye bore into the prisoner. The silence lengthened as the German stood unsure what was happening. At last as if a spell had been broken the soldier cleared his throat, "We will inform your embassy you are here, they will contact your family."

There were three empty cells between each prisoner to prevent communication. The next to be opened was Michael Bray's. This prisoner did not rise, but sat on his mattress with back against the wall. He examined the Colonel silently, fingers linked and forearms resting nonchalantly upon his knees.

David repeated his enquiry which elicited a sneering smile, "Just complaints about my illegal imprisonment in solitary confinement and being given shit to eat, or do you want the full list?"

Churu stared down at the American, "The *shit* to which you refer is standard fare for my people."

Bray gave a derisive laugh, "I'd guess it's not what you fat cats eat."

"No, you're right, not all the time," he called to Chrystal who was standing just outside the door. Her face appeared around the doorframe, "For the next three days please give this prisoner the same rations as I received when I was a guest here."

Chrystal looked at a complete loss.

He explained, "Just plenty of water."

The next American was starkly different. Paul Henning was lying on his mattress in the foetal position with his eyes closed. David's introduction met with no response. He stared at the comatose young man. Each prisoner had been issued with two books, which in the last two cases were obviously being read. Paul's books still sat in the corner untouched. He nudged a white trainer with shoe, but there was no reaction.

THE BIG GAME

Chrystal was filling the open doorway, "He's like that all the time. I make him eat his food and then he's straight back to sleep."

"And he's not ill?"

She shook her head, "Don't think so, but a doctor would do no harm."

David turned on his heel, "At this time our doctors have more pressing matters to attend to."

Sergeant McRae appeared resigned and optimistically requested some beer and a woman.

Robert Goff seemed unfazed by his imprisonment and claimed the conditions to be similar to his old school, but without the buggery.

His sister tried to question David about their situation, but he rebuffed her enquiries.

A tremor in the Russian girl's voice betrayed her outward calm. She sat on her mattress, hugging her knees and replied to David's enquiries in little-girl-lost tones.

Lorna Karrol was in the last cell. She stood very straight with her back pressed against the far wall. David decided that the photo had not done her justice. He repeated his spiel.

Her voice was calm and businesslike, with a soft East Coast accent, "Please can you tell me who I can see to sort out this mess?"

David repeated what he had said to the others, "This is just an initial visit, and you will have ample opportunity to prepare your defence."

"Defence suggests a trial, what am I charged with?"

Despite his revulsion for everything these people stood for, David found himself wanting to prolong their meeting, "As yet there are no formal charges. You've been arrested for multiple murder, but I will not enter into any discussion about your case at this time."

167

As he watched, several emotions flitted across Lorna's face, she made her decision and gathered herself, "Then I demand to see a lawyer."

David gave her an ironic smile, "Do you really? And your *demand* is noted. Have you any preferences? Perhaps the same lawyer that represented my countrymen before you murdered them?"

As the cell door clanged shut and the steps receded, Lorna slid down the wall and all her self-restraint evaporated. She sat on the floor, chin in her hands with tears coursing down her face.

34

WASHINGTON DC

It was early morning in the capital. In a city of early risers, the two fat men sitting on opposite sides of the maple conference table were ahead of the pack. They craned sideways to read their reports as they forked up small mountains of bacon, eggs and home fries between pink wet lips.

Fatter spoke around a mouthful, "...and do you think that these new Gamiguys will ever honour a deal?"

Fat paused with his fork mid route, "Gamasis. No I guess not. Or maybe, but only as long as it suits them, probably let us set up all the technology and infrastructure then tell us to swivel."

"Mmmm. Can we buy up this new guy?" Fatter thumbed back a page, "This Churu?"

"Maybe, but it's early days. Can't tell how long he'll be in charge."

Fatter digested cholesterol and information, "Any chance of putting in a Big Mac and Coke guy instead?"

"Maybe, but there's hell of a lot of interest from the East."

"No problema, we don't care. Let 'em do the donkey work as long as we get our cut and control the market." He launched into one of his favourite diatribes, "Profits don't come from work; it's the guys doing Jack Shit that get the cream ... anyway with the fuckin' unions in this country who'd want to make stuff? Let our little yellow buddies have all the hassle of digging up this tantalite crap, let 'em make all the shiny shit our citizens crave. The guys who pay for all this," a wave of a dimpled hand encompassed the high ceilinged room and their empty breakfast plates, "Just wanna buy low and sell high ...

as long as the selling's done by spotty kids on minimum wage."

Fat had heard this sermon many times, "Yeah, but these African guys aren't stupid, they'll see we're just middlemen and cosy up with one of those eastern donkeys."

Fatter grunted his reluctant agreement. They returned to studying the files.

Suddenly Fatter smacked the table, "Hehhh, you seen this CIA report? Seems the ousted guy, Amutu, has been busy-busy with the Brits since he got kicked out."

Fat shuffled forward two pages and skim read the report, "Yeah, guess that could be a problem."

"Problem my ass." Fatter found the paragraph he sought, says here that Amutu loves the Limies, practically jacks off to a picture of Her Royal Highness, and what's more, the good ol' Limies love us."

Fat frowned, "I should point out that he's *EX* President and if you read on, you'll see the Gamasis wouldn't exactly lay on a ticker tape parade if he showed his face again."

"Yeh, yeh, yeh, I saw that, but as they say, a week's a long time in politics. This Churu will soon fuck up and they'll be praying for the old guy to come back."

Fatter sat back in his chair and grinned, "Know what? I feel a coup coming on!"

***

LONDON

The Prime Minister, Foreign and Defence Secretaries came to the last item on their list: Gamasi. The PM stopped his Defence Minister as he about to launch into his progress briefing, "Sorry Nigel, had a call just before you arrived, we're being put under a bit of pressure on this one."

His Minister frowned in concern, "Time's already tight Ian, how long are..."

The PM held up a hand, "No no, it's not a time issue. It's our American chums, they want to be involved."

"Bloody hell, why?" they both chorused.

"Feel they need to keep tantalite supplies under their wing."

The Defence Minister blew out his cheeks, "That's bang out of order; we've done a lot of work on this and in a very short time..."

The Foreign Secretary interrupted, "The Economists won't be best pleased; they've already built projected tantalite revenues into the year after next."

The PM nodded and tapped his teaspoon on the saucer as he considered the ramifications, "True, true." He came to his decision. "I'm going to tough this one out; I'll tell them it's our show and thanks, but no thank you. So press on Nigel..."

35

At the end of one week the Xtremers lives had already established a routine. Three times a day Chrystal brought them meals and filled their water jugs, they had no idea what time these highlights happened as their watches had been removed.

The meals were always the same. Breakfast was unleavened bread and a bowl of weak gruel. Lunch was rice and chicken. The evening meal was the same as breakfast, but with either a banana, or a quarter of melon.

Both their books could be changed regularly, but as they were leftovers from the Ambassador Hotel the choice was somewhat eclectic.

Every second day, at random times, two armed soldiers would appear with Chrystal at their cell door. After being placed in leg irons, they would shuffle down to the shower block. The ritual was always the same. As soon as the soldiers had unlocked the leg irons, Chrystal would order them both out into the corridor. She would then coyly retire to a stool at the far end of the room, where she was separated from the prisoner by rows of half cubicles.

After showering they would dry themselves with difficulty on a small, threadbare towel. Laid out for them would be a fresh, but dingy grey shirt and baggy trousers. As these clothes came in just one size, Lindy and Lorna had to add large turn ups, whilst the taller men looked comical.

Once Chrystal was assured that her charges were once again decent, she would bellow to the soldiers and they would all make the return trip.

On David's second visit he had given every prisoner a pad of lined paper and two felt tip pens on which to draft their defence. The way each received their task varied greatly.

Johan set to work immediately and requested a German/English dictionary.

Mike had reluctantly accepted the writing materials, "I guess whatever I put; the result will be the same?"

David considered the question, "I'll give due consideration to every submission."

The American snorted, "Oh *you* will? What are *you* then, my judge and jury?"

"Yes."

Mike was visibly taken aback and ran his hand through his hair, massaging the scar under his hairline, "Who the fuck are you then? Got any legal knowledge? What kinda system are they running here?"

David quietly considered the questions, "I told you my name yesterday, it's David Churu and in common with Solomon, I have no formal qualifications. I hope our system will be a fair one.

"Ok Solomon, just supposing you decide I'm guilty of murder; what happens then?"

"That's something I've yet to decide."

Mike let out a hiss of derision, "So no appeals in your *fair* Gamasi system, just some one eyed black guy decides your fate?"

David's single eye glinted, "Exactly, but I believe the absence of an eye, or white skin will not influence my judgement."

Sergeant Tom McRae's attitude was similar to Bray's, although not so confrontational. He appeared to be resigned to whatever was going to happen, but his major concern was the death penalty. David gave him no assurances, "I alone will decide your guilt, or innocence. Gamasi still retains the death penalty for murder."

The Scotsman shrugged, "I guess I know what the answer'll be then, life's cheap around here."

David considered the statement, "Is that what you believed when you decided to work for Xtreme Tours?"

"It's not just my belief old Pal, it's a fact."

In their separate cells Fiona and Robert Goff seemed strangely relaxed about their imprisonment and both thanked David politely when he handed them the writing materials.

Lindy was the next to accept her pens and paper. "I was only here on holiday," she said when he entered her cell.

"Just write a day by day account of your time in Gamasi and a description of anyone who can confirm what you say. It will help if you give me as much detail as possible."

She tipped her head to one side and stared up at him through her lashes, "I've spent all my time either topless sunbathing, or in bed with my boyfriend. How much detail would you like?"

David ignored the innuendo, "I mean details of any of the staff at your hotel who can confirm where you were and when; if you don't know their names, just describe them and their job."

David Churu shrugged to Chrystal as he left the materials beside a recumbent Paul Henning. She had been waiting just outside his door, "He's starting talking to me, I'll make sure he writes everything down." After Chrystal had locked Henning's cell door, she addressed David again, "Colonel, that poor boy's terrified."

David stood and stared at her for a moment before coming to a decision, "I must stress that all these people are here on suspicion of murder."

She made a dismissive face, "It's for the Lord to judge, not us."

THE BIG GAME

David hardened his voice, "Maybe eventually, but right now it's my job. You must understand that ALL these prisoners are dangerous."

It was difficult for David to keep that thought in his mind as he stepped into Lorna's cell. She appeared less scared than the previous day and was sitting cross-legged on her mattress. Today her long brown hair softly framed her face, it looked freshly washed. He held out the writing materials, "Please write down everything that has happened since your arrival here."

She frowned. David, against his will, noticed how prettily her nose wrinkled. "What, since I arrived in prison?"

"No, here in Gamasi." He cleared his throat and spoke more gruffly, "And it's no good leaving out any detail of shootings, we have many witnesses."

Lorna shook her head and the movement created highlights in the sheen of her hair, "Then your witnesses are lying, I haven't even touched a gun during my time in Gamasi. Ask Lindy the Russian girl, she'll confirm that we..."

David held up his hand to silence her, "As I just said, write everything down, don't tell me."

"So do the police or a panel of judges read it?"

"No, just me."

She looked confused, "I don't understand, are you a prosecutor?"

David considered her question, "Yes, at this time I am fulfilling that role."

She stared at the tall, slim man. Yesterday he had terrified her; after he had left she could only remember a soldier with a piratical eye patch. She studied him and found him to be an enigma. A soldier who spoke perfect English, but wore no insignia of rank and claimed to be a lawyer. But over-riding the aura of enigma was the power of his authority and intellect. Today she felt no fear, "So if you're our prosecutor, who will decide on our innocence?"

"I will make that decision as well."

175

She took a moment to absorb this information, "Is this some kind of tradition here?"

He grimaced and dropped his eyes to the floor, she sensed an overwhelming sadness, and with an effort he appeared to gather himself, "No, until very recently the tradition in my country was that people lived or died at the whim of a psychopathic despot."

Lorna thought this was not a good time to reveal that she had found President Charles Amutu to be a charming and sophisticated man.

***

With the engine ticking over, Serovec stared at the customs post. The red and white striped barrier 100 metres ahead was in the closed position. If he sat there any longer the two armed guards would become suspicious. He was leaning forward as if rummaging for some documents in the front of the Jeep, but was in fact sliding one of the seized Kalashnikovs onto his lap. He selected first gear and started down the gentle incline.

Both men were looking in his direction. Their automatic weapons slung loosely around their necks, but capable of being deployed in a second. One leant against the concrete barrier support, whilst the other stood half in the door of the customs post.

Many questions ran through Vasyl Serovec's mind as the distance closed. Were there more unseen troops nearby, but foremost was if there were any whites in the new Gamasi army? He slowed to a halt, grinned and gave the closest soldier a cross between a wave and a salute.

Weapon still dangling, the man left the barrier and stepped towards the side of the Jeep, his path would cause him to cross in front of his colleague. Anticipating the moment when the second man's vision would be blocked, Serovec dropped his right hand onto the AK47. Holding eye contact with the guard, he blindly felt for the trigger.

THE BIG GAME

Bullets spewed forth, ripping into the guard's pelvis throwing him backwards towards the lounger in the doorway. As the first man fell away the continuous stream of fire slammed into his buddy, he was flung through the open doorway before he had time to raise his weapon.

Afterwards the only sound breaking the silence came from high in the canopy as panicked birds abandoned their early evening roosts.

The Russian remained crouching by the side of the jeep as the squawking diminished. There was no sound of human activity so he cautiously stood up. He retrieved his small black case from the vehicle and set it down between the bodies. He unbuckled the first sentry's belt, dragged down his trousers and shook his head in disappointment.

Moving on from the second man, Serovec added both their weapons to his growing collection in the front foot well. He walked to the borderline painted on the road and pushed down on the concrete counterweight, raising the barrier.

The heat of the day was becoming just a memory. The evening was pleasantly cool as Vasyl Serovec drove out of Gamasi onto foreign soil.

36

WASHINGTON DC

It was a working breakfast in the early morning once again. Fatter demanded an update on the Gamasi negotiations.

Fat gathered his thoughts, "I've had talks with my opposite number in London, first time around they denied all knowledge of any meetings with Amutu. So I gave 'em times and dates; after a bit of shuffling they came clean."

Fatter slapped his wide pink brow, "What's the matter with these guys, don't they know about our special relationship?"

"They've a big problem with this one. Seems they think they've a right to first call on both Gamasi and its tantalite."

Fatter's eyes hardened, "Go on."

"Well they're thinking along the same lines as us, putting this Amutu back in charge, but having him screwed down so tight he won't be able to shut his eyes."

Fatter seemed to be expanding; gone was the folksy fat boy. His voice was low and as cold as steel, "Right, so here's what we do: get right back to those tight assed fuckers and lay it on the line."

He held up his left hand and ticked off the fingers with his right, "Number one. Put out the story worldwide that good ole Amutu, friend of the people, has been ousted by Communist rebels who by the way eat babies for breakfast.

Number two. We'll launch a COMBINED campaign to return this much loved leader to the bosom of his people. So if our dickhead Generals fuck up, we can always blame the Limies.

Number three. Expenses and troop dispositions will break down as 90% us and 10% Brits. But make sure their guys do the shitty 10%, we don't want any of Uncle Sam's boys coming home in body bags.

Number four. All tantalite revenues will be split as in number three … or close enough so they'll never know the difference.

Number five. If they even THINK of screwing us over, their so-called independent nuclear deterrent runs out of parts within the month. They can forget about keeping their planes and subs running, they'll be using fucking hand carts." He rubbed both hands together and then had another thought, "And don't let them even think they can cover it up, within days we'll leak to their media that after all those billions of dollars they've paid us for nuclear toys, they can't use them. Now go to it!"

Fat was being dismissed, but had a final question, "Do you want to run this by the boss before I talk to the Brits?"

Fatter smiled, "No, we don't wanna worry Mr President with too much detail. Anyway he's a busy man today; he's just gotten a coupla new ducks for his tub.

***

LONDON

The lunchtime London traffic was close to gridlock as the Foreign Secretary stood in his favourite position staring down. Whilst his eyes followed the inching mass of cars, taxis and busses his mind was far away in North West Africa; he was considering Gamasi. He turned around, "So Gerald, apart from this new American complication, everything is falling into place?"

"All's going well at the moment. Amutu is making his preparations. He's drawing up a list of loyalists that we can rely on when the time comes. General Gboja, his second in command, is working with our strategic chaps on the operational stuff. Actually they're quite impressed with him, looks a bit of a goon, but he's certainly got his finger on the Gamasi pulse."

The Cabinet Minister smiled, "Can't be too challenging when you've only got three armoured bicycles."

His assistant laughed sycophantically.

"And they both understand not to contact their friends back home prematurely?"

"Absolutely Sir!"

"Anything else then Gerald?"

He consulted his notes and before looking up, he hesitated, "Just one thing Sir, if I may say so, this American intervention hardly seems fair; Gamasi has always been our show."

The Politician nodded and stared into the middle distance before replying, "Yes, true enough, but there're sensitive aspects involved here. The consensus is, we have to work with our American friends for the greater good."

The civil servant thought he would push his luck, "So much for *the special relationship* then Sir."

His boss considered the statement, "There are many special relationships in this world Gerald. The bully and the bullied, the rapist and the raped, they all have special relationships."

Gerald returned to his office to prepare for his next meeting with President Amutu. His recent train trips to the teashop in Surrey had made a pleasant diversion, but this morning there was a chill wind. He was pleased that Amutu was coming to him.

He glanced at the old timepiece on the mantelpiece as it made its ponderous circumnavigation of the faded face; they were due to arrive in forty minutes. Using the heavy cast iron tongs, he placed two large lumps of coal on the fire and stood for a moment staring into the flames.

The Foreign Secretary's news that the Americans were now involved had been a bombshell. In fact not just involved, a ninety percent input made it their operation, with Britain playing a supporting role.

The civil servant sighed, politics, what a wonderful life this would be without politics! At least the brunt of the changes will be for the chaps in Defence. He smiled quietly to himself as he imagined their reaction to the news. Liberate Gamasi or *Op-Reunion* as it had been codenamed, now downgraded from a major to a minor operation.

He guessed that after the essential posturing they would be quietly relieved as they were stretched worldwide. Now with British requirement down to around one thousand men, they could deploy mainly Special Forces, meaning no tricky shuffling of troops. A thousand of our elite forces, plus nine thousand Yanks, poor bloody Gamasis won't know what's hit them. Mostly a rebel army a few weeks ago, now pitched against the best in the world.

He smiled to himself ... and the American forces will maybe help as well!

It never failed to amuse the Englishman to see the two Gamasis together. He smiled inwardly as he greeted them. President Charles Amutu so short, with General Gboja towering over him. Settling his visitors in the worn leather settee, Gerald broke the news of the changed game plan.

181

Gboja always deferred to the President and Amutu received the information in silence.

Eventually Amutu spoke, "And what do the Americans want from us?" Gerald assumed Amutu meant the "us" to mean the Gamasis, but in the interest of presenting a common front against the superpower, he included Great Britain.

"Sadly these days the markets rule supreme. In simpler times Her Majesty's Government was able to assist any of our Commonwealth colleagues without let, or hindrance..." he left the statement hanging in the air.

Amutu frowned, "Suppose I say we don't accept their offer?"

Gerald had anticipated this reaction, "Like oil and gold, your tantalite is a world commodity. In reality their offer is non-negotiable."

"I find it interesting that you just described it as *our* tantalite, *ours* but only as long as we do as we're told?"

The Englishman was a good chess player and this was another move he had rehearsed. "May I be rather blunt?" he raised his eyebrows for their permission, but continued anyway. "At this moment it isn't *your* tantalite. Not to put too fine a point on it, it's Colonel Churu's tantalite. It will only become *yours* when we have wrested it from him; our price for that wresting is American / British control."

The Gamasis were preparing to leave when Gerald brought up his final point as if it had slipped his mind, "Ah yes, one more thing. You told me the other day that you met the last party of foreign big game hunters."

Amutu frowned at the description, but decided not to question it, "the most recent group from Xtreme Tours? Yes, we both met them briefly."

The civil servant chose his words carefully, "Well two of them have distant connections with our Royals. Maybe you remember them?"

"Possibly, what were their names?"

"Goff, Robert and Fiona Goff."

THE BIG GAME

Both General Gboja and Charles Amutu nodded. Amutu replied, "Yes, I remember them, especially Fiona, a very spirited young woman."

"Some very influential people here are concerned for them."

Amutu grimaced, "Their concerns are justified; but most probably belated. I would assume by now they are both dead."

37

David Churu found that his evening visits to the Xtremers provided a welcome respite from the pressures of re-shaping Gamasi. He found the way each prisoner was modifying their relationship was proving a fascinating insight into human behaviour.

The best adapted to incarceration was Fiona Goff. David's time at Sandhurst, the British officer-training establishment, had not engendered within him any love for their upper classes. He considered them to be patronising and boorish. He was determined not to let this influence his treatment of the Goffs. During their sessions, he was reluctantly discovering that he liked her. Even after making allowances for her vested interest in placating her inquisitor, he felt she possessed an open mind and a genuine respect for others.

At their second session she handed him a balanced and well-argued dissertation on the importance of countering terrorism. Within her six pages, she had explained her reasons for visiting Gamasi and how upon discovering that the situation was not as initially described, declined to take any further active role. The comprehensive nature of her defence meant that David needed to question her no further. Despite this, he continued to call on her for a few minutes each evening. She was always cheerful, optimistic and although she never said so, David had the impression she expected the cavalry to arrive at any moment.

During the two weeks, there had been an amazing change in Paul Henning. The American was now communicating freely, the only problem being that it was solely through the medium of his wardress. David found the sessions somewhat surreal. In the beginning he had resisted this development, but finally accepted it as the only way forward. If they were ever going to resolve this prisoner's case, he had to allow all Henning's words to be routed via the gargantuan Chrystal.

Whilst David's driver remained outside the door with his shotgun, the three would sit in a semi circle on folding canvas chairs. The size of the cell, dictated that they were all very close together, but Chrystal and Paul sat with their plump thighs touching and on the last two occasions she had enveloped his hand in hers. Whilst David found this woman's ability to disrupt his agenda irritating, in the interests of progress he decided to ignore this growing intimacy. He was fascinated by Chrystal's total recall of the Californian's every thought. As she recounted every detail, the man nodded at regular intervals confirming the accuracy of her recollections. "…and Paul's happy to set all this down on paper, but he's not too good at writing."

David was confused. Extensive questioning of the Xtremers themselves, examination of their luggage, and questioning of hotel staff and guides, had created very accurate files on each prisoner. Initially Paul Henning had been the easiest to investigate. Scanning just a fraction of the vast array of internet information on him, the image of a present day cyber legend was totally at odds with the man sitting hunched opposite.

"What do you mean? He's a talented programme creator, one of the best in the world! Are you telling me he's illiterate?"

Chrystal's booming laugh was painful in the small cell. David noticed that she gave Paul's hand a surreptitious squeeze and he smiled shyly, "Lord no, it's just handwriting. If Paul had a computer, he'd do it in no time."

David ran his hand through his re-growing hair in frustration, "So he's asking for a computer in his cell, because he doesn't want to use a pen and paper like everyone else?"

"It's not that he doesn't want to; he just needs to get it right."

David pressed his point, "And he says he can't do that with the materials we've supplied?"

Chrystal shook her head, "He's not saying he can't, but that he's no good with the old ways." She fixed David with pleading eyes, "I know you're a good man Colonel, I know you would want this boy to have the best chance to write his defence."

David looked at the ceiling in frustration and took a deep breath, "Ok, ok, I'll arrange a laptop computer for just one day."

If Robert Goff's schoolteachers had been asked to describe the boy, there would have been two totally different versions. It would have been difficult to judge him on the evidence of his exam papers as he rarely did more than laboriously write his name, the date and form number.

This paucity made not the slightest difference to his future. By a lucky accident of birth he would never want for anything. A thousand years ago in the England of Kings and Barons, Robert's ancestors had chosen well.

In stark contrast, his sports masters knew a different boy. Fast, agile, a natural team player, he represented his house and school in every outdoor discipline. Were it not for his total lack of academic ability he would have gone on to play for a university. Tradition was important to Robert Goff. Psychopathic dunces with superb hand to eye co-ordination dominated his genes and he was still living off the benefits.

After many false starts, Robert had decided to adopt the style of the broadsheet rugby journalist for his defence. This decision was predictable as this was the only reading he ever indulged in. He sat back and reviewed the fruits of his labour. He had to admit that it read rather like a mismatch. In essence a list of dates, venues and his kills during a very short stay in Gamasi; he suspected it would not aid his case. As an afterthought, to even things up a bit, he credited the shooting of Wolfgang Schmidt to the opposition.

THE BIG GAME

"Still doesn't seem to fit the bill," he muttered to himself, "Pity can't get Fee to give me a hand." Then a thought occurred to him, I know, a bit of moral stuff at the end's what's called for!

Slowly he added a few more lines:

Came to Gamasy to help with there terrarist problem in anyway I cood. Desided army was best way to help as im rarther good shot. Feel jolly strongly that peepell carnt just go forsing out proper guvenments so helped out by shooting terrarists. Possabull I was wrong as Fiona seys the old sistem was pretty bad so maby Chooroo and the new sistem is good. Must say I still think it shood be done with elecsions rather than terrarist acsions.

He was unsure of some of the spelling and experimented with several alternatives for *people* and *actions* until deciding that they had to be right. He was satisfied with his efforts and felt that this footnote added just the right balance to what was a rather damning start. The final sentence illustrated that he was a man of principle and not simply trying to wriggle out of a tight spot by telling them only what they wanted to hear.

Literacy was obviously not Sergeant Thomas McRae's forte either. His defence was short and to the point. He had never shot anyone during his time in Gamasi. He was just an employee of an international tour company. Xtreme Tours had a properly negotiated and legal agreement to assist the government of Gamasi. He should be released immediately.

Johan Koeffe was struggling emotionally, but definitely not with literacy. The thick sheaf of papers he produced was akin to a company report. In perfect English he had carried out a life audit culminating in his arrival in the prison.

Starting with details of his parents and childhood, he had carried out a dispassionate analysis of all the influences that had contributed to his present situation. Without attempting to shift responsibility he illustrated how his ex boss had been one of the major reasons. A detailed domestic annual cash flow was employed to justify his need to retain his job within Schmidt's organisation.

His conclusion included a description of his wife and sons and how he was missing them. His final point was that on a personal and moral level, he could find no way to justify his presence in Gamasi.

Lindy still believed that her way out of the predicament was to seduce David Churu. He noticed that on every visit that she had neglected to secure more of her shirt buttons until she was now left with just one. Her unrestrained breasts, though pert rather than voluminous, always seemed to be on the point of total exposure.

In passable English she had set down her holiday timetable, this had been confirmed by the hotel staff. Without doubt, she had taken no active role in the killing of any Gamasis.

As David entered her cell, she dropped her book in feigned surprise and was forced to lean forward to retrieve it. She remained kneeling at the end of her mattress staring up at him from under her lashes, her lips damp and slightly parted.

He enquired about her conditions.

"I am bored," she replied, with a slight pout, "Is there nothing I can do to get out of this place?"

David looked down at her, "It won't be long before your case is decided."

He had two more prisoners to visit, each difficult in their own way. Michael Bray because of his open aggression and Lorna Karrol because it had become the highlight of his day, and that made him feel guilty.

Lorna Karrol felt exactly the same. She could recognise David's step and found herself becoming slightly breathless in anticipation of his arrival. After many hours consideration she

THE BIG GAME

still could not understand her infatuation. He had never even acknowledged in word or deed that she was a woman. His perfect English was always polite and formal. He rarely smiled and carried with him a great sense of sadness.

Her subtle questioning, suggested he had no family and was obsessed with his work. When she tried to probe too deeply he would skilfully avoid disclosing his actual job, or rank within the Gamasi army.

After his last visit she had sat and pondered why he was beginning to dominate her every waking thought. I know, I've read about it somewhere. Some plane passengers were hijacked at a Scandinavian airport ... yes Stockholm, the *Stockholm syndrome*, or maybe it's *effect*. The victims began to identify with their captors. It was the same with those terrorists and the heiress in the 70's. Yes, that's why I can't get him out of my mind ... I've got the *Stockholm effect*.

38

MOSCOW

The two detectives waited, perched on the sofa placed centrally of the huge minimalist reception area. Opposite them the immaculately groomed receptionist picked up her intercom. She listened for a moment, and then nodded to the two huge men standing silently against the far wall. Without a word, one beckoned the policemen to follow him through the double doors, the second giant followed too close behind.

Vasyl Serovec sat in his shirtsleeves. The vast pane of glass from floor to ceiling behind him framed a panoramic view of Moscow. The minarets flanking the Red Square could be seen in the distance. Both giants took up positions either side of the doorway, with their hands clasped in front of them.

The detectives were left standing in the middle of the vast expanse of onyx floor. The only item of furniture in the room was Serovec's huge stainless steel desk. He did not greet them, just opened his right hand drawer and removed a mat black metal sphere. He twisted it and placed it in the centre of his empty desktop where it began to tick loudly. "You have five minutes."

The senior detective cleared his throat, "We want to ask you about your trip to Africa."

Silently Serovec held his gaze.

"Mmm ... we believe you visited Gamasi."

Serovec just observed the policemen without blinking.

The questioner looked confused, "Well did you visit Gamasi?"

"No, Ghana."

"We have information to the contrary."

Again Serovec did not respond, just waited motionless with his large hands resting on the desktop either side of the ticking kitchen timer.

"We also want to speak to you about one of your staff, a Miss Linda Tatlina."

Not a muscle moved behind the desk, it was as if he was carved from stone.

The detective drew himself up, "Mr Serovec, your secretary told us you were prepared to answer our questions."

"You are not asking questions; you are telling me your beliefs and aspirations," he leaned forward and examined the ticking sphere, "You now have four minutes remaining."

The second policeman spoke for the first time, "Can we speak to Miss Tatlina?"

"Probably."

"Is she in the building?"

"I doubt it."

The first man joined in, "Do you know where we can find her?"

Serovec considered the question, "The answer is no. I suggest you start in Ghana."

The detective frowned, "Are you saying you left her there?"

"Yes."

"Why did you do that?"

Serovec raised the corners of his mouth, "It's a pleasant country."

"We believe you had more than an employer / employee relationship."

Serovec reverted to silence.

"Were you and Miss Tatlina lovers?"

"No, but we had frequent sex."

"Did you have an argument?"

"No."

"So to your knowledge, the young lady is fit and well?"

"Yes."

The detectives appeared to have lost the thread of their questioning.

The junior one changed tack, "We have received a request from the London Police. Did you travel from Heathrow together with..." he referred to his notes, "An English couple called Goff?"

"Possibly."

"Surely you know the names of the people you travel with."

Serovec appeared to be analysing if this was strictly a question; he decided it was, "The airline neglected to show me their passenger list." The policemen exchanged despairing glances.

The senior one spoke, "I think that will be all at the moment."

Vasyl Serovec held up the timer, "You still have one minute."

The senior man decided to round off the meeting on an authoritative note, "That will be all for now. But we may need to come back and talk to you some more about..." His words died as he realised that he was speaking to Serovec's broad back as he had turned in dismissal and was now examining the Moscow roofscape.

The detective broke. He shouted, "You think you are the big man now Serovec, but you wait, your time is coming..." His colleague plucked desperately at the arm of his boss's coat, but all his pent up frustration began to pour forth, "You think we can't touch you, that all your money, your contacts will protect you from justice. But you're wrong Vasyl Serovec ... every day, step by step we're getting closer, closer to the day when I come through that door with a warrant for your arrest. I won't rest until you're rotting in jail ... remember this day Serovec, remember it when you see me across the other side of the courtroom."

Serovec turned around slowly; the giants moved in from the wall awaiting their cue. He walked right up to the senior policeman and stood silently as the man gradually ran out of words. Serovec slowly lifted his right arm until his scarred fist was right in front of the detective's face; gradually he opened his hand. The blunt finger nails gently brushed the tip of other man's nose.

THE BIG GAME

The policeman squinted to see what rested in the palm; it was the small black timer. The two zero marks were in line.

"I have bad news for you," Serovec paused, "The lift has just broken."

The policemen stood in confusion as the man turned and mumbled a few words into his phone. Flanked by the giants, they waited as Serovec returned to the window and once more stared out across the city.

A long minute passed and suddenly from the left a vertical cable appeared on the other side of the glass. Seconds later it was followed by another, they jerked across their line of vision before disappearing at the opposite side of window. All five men watched in silence.

Serovec turned and tapped a code into a connecting door in the right hand wall. He nodded to the giants, "Bring them." Huge hands locked into the back of the detectives' collars and they were dragged along with their feet barely touching the ground.

The room next door was empty apart from a large glass case taking up one wall. Pinned onto the green baize backing were what appeared to be rows of used condoms.

The detectives were held in front of the display. In various shapes and sizes, some black, some brown and a few white; the detectives stared at rows of human penises.

Each item was neatly labelled with a time, date and location. The top row were all from 1980's Afghanistan. The trophies in the incomplete bottom row were all labelled *Gamasi* and dated the previous month. In fascination they noted that the penultimate exhibit had been shot through the glans.

Serovec pointed to the space at the end of the row, "Still room for two little ones."

He stepped to the window and entered a code. As the sheet of glass slid smoothly upwards the room was transformed by the Russian winter. Just outside, the pair of cables hummed gently as they were tugged by the wind.

The policemen's shoes scraped vainly on the polished floor as they were propelled to the window and forced to stare down into the dizzying void.

Upon a nod from Serovec, the giants took a second grip on their waistbands and lifted the pair up and over the sill and dropped them into the maintenance cradle.

Both policemen gripped the safety rail as it began its swaying descent down the side of the skyscraper. Serovec resealed the window, immediately shutting out the cold.

THE BIG GAME

39

BATU - GHANA

Hansie had done some strange people smuggling jobs, but this was the strangest. In the time of Amutu's secret police he made a lot of money moving scared people in the dead of night.

He sat at the far end of Batu's dirt airstrip building up to maximum power. His twin engined Cessna shuddered against its brakes, he squinted out of the side windows at the plumes of dust disappearing behind them. Shutting down the throttles, he stared ahead down the bumpy strip.

His solo flight from Kamba had been uneventful, apart from the very rough landing. Now taking off with three passengers, plus luggage was going to be extremely lively.

After a switchback ride of tooth jarring jolts they were up, banking high over the dense Ghanaian forest. The South African relaxed and thought about the three people he had just collected.

The whole sequence of events had been unusual. Three days ago, an Asian rich kid had approached him at the airfield. Hansie had seen the guy before in the Andromeda, Kamba's only western style nightclub. He did not know his name, but had the strong feeling his father was a high-ranking politician. Without offering a name, the man got straight down to business, "How much do you want to collect my uncle from Batu?" Batu was a coastal village just inside the Ghanaian border. Previously a small fishing community, now the Batus all shared a different profession; smuggling.

195

Hansie was equally direct, "My price depends on what your uncle's smuggling?"

"Nothing ... but there's one irregularity."

The pilot's eyebrow's raised in feigned surprise.

"My uncle also wants to bring two passengers who are without passports; his new wife and her mother."

The South African considered the well-groomed young man, assessing his Mercedes 4x4, unusual in a country of donkey carts, "Well my usual price is two thousand dollars cash. But I've got to assume your relatives are stuffed full of best Columbian which you're going to sell at the Andromeda..." He forestalled the denial, "...whatever, I want six thousand, half now, balance on delivery. Take it or leave it."

To his surprise the man had taken it.

He hadn't even turned off his engines at Batu. As soon as he touched down, his three passengers had jumped out of a dusty Range Rover with tinted windows, parked just under the tree line. As he spun around, they stood clutching one bag each as his slipstream tore at their clothing.

His two rear seat passengers were clad from head to toe in black Burkhas, even their eyes were hidden behind thick mesh. *Uncle* sat in the front next to him. A huge man with very protruding teeth, black beard and dressed in the style of a Muslim cleric. Hansie spoke only English and Afrikaans and as *uncle* spoke neither; it was a silent trip.

The South African leant against his wing and watched his passengers being driven away towards Kamba in the Mercedes 4x4. He thought again what a strange job it had been.

Not strange in that the theatrical adhesive securing *uncle's* beard, was separating.

Not strange in that *mother in law* had broad shoulders and wore men's shoes.

But strange in that they were the only people he had ever smuggled *into* Gamasi!

***

David Churu's life was slipping into a routine. He needed to keep busy, if he tried to sleep before he was exhausted mentally and physically, the ghosts of Sita and the boys took over. They were present all the time; hovering at the back of his mind, only by frantic activity could he control them.

07.00hrs breakfast with Nat Beyla began the day. Whilst eating, they would set priorities and re-schedule all matters that had not been resolved the previous day. A packed itinerary of meetings and visits filled the time until the two-hour cabinet meeting at 18.00hrs.

At 20.00hrs he would be driven to the prison to call upon the foreign hunters. Apart from two, all the cases had been completed so most cells required only a one-minute visit. As his driver negotiated the bumpy road that lead down to the prison gates, he considered the report in his hand.

Yesterday he thought that only Michael Bray's case was unresolved. Now this new evidence relating to Lorna Karrol had blown everything apart. To an uninvolved investigator the allegations would have little effect. But yesterday David Churu had finally admitted to himself that he was falling in love and today his mind was in turmoil.

Chrystal unlocked Michael Bray's cell and stood aside for David to enter. The notes showed that this was their sixteenth meeting and probably their last. Churu was not a psychiatrist, nor did he wish to become one, but he felt each prisoner should receive the sentence appropriate to their crime. In that endeavour, he wanted to understand what drove them.

Yesterday David had come to a decision - tell Bray the facts of life I've wasted enough time on this guy. Underlying

David's irritation was guilt. He knew that he had been using Michael Bray's refusal to cooperate as a way to delay pronouncing the verdicts. Delays allowed him to continue to visit Lorna Karrol every evening: this added to the guilt he felt for thinking about any woman so soon after Sita's death.

All sixteen visits to Bray had followed the same pattern. The prisoner would be arrogant and dismissive of David's efforts to persuade him to enter a plea. The American refused to recognise Churu's right decide his fate. Yesterday as David left he had not minced words, "Tomorrow will be my last visit before sentencing the following day."

Bray had sneered, "Will you be wearing a kangaroo costume for that little farce?"

David had ignored the comment, "As things are, you'll receive a death sentence for an unspecified number of murders." This statement prompted no response so David continued, "At any time up to sentencing I'll accept your plea as to why events should not proceed." He had nodded at the blank writing pad in the corner as he left the room, "Your fate Mr Bray is literally in your own hands."

As soon as David entered the cell, he saw the writing pad was untouched. However there was a change in Bray. Usually he lounged on his mattress, but tonight he stood. He was agitated, constantly running his hand through his hair.

David considered the changes, "Is there anything you wish to say?"

Bray stared at the ceiling and appeared to be searching for words.

David waited, as time dragged on he prompted, "Do you wish me to come back later?"

Suddenly Bray turned on him; his face a mask of fury, "No I don't. You're not fooling anyone, aping justice. Just fuck off back to the jungle."

David's driver, who always waited just outside the door, burst in with his shotgun levelled. Churu signalled him out of the cell, then turned and silently followed.

Chrystal locked the door and checked the spy hole. Michael Bray was leaning against the back wall with his head in his hands. His shoulders were shaking.

Chrystal led the way to Lorna's cell. Although David found the prospect of confronting her with the new evidence profoundly unpleasant, at the same time it was a massive relief. No longer would he be plagued with guilt; guilt that he could develop feelings for another woman. He held blessed proof that all the time the American had espoused honesty, she had been misleading him. Lorna's smile of welcome died as she saw David's stony expression as he entered her cell. He held up her file and came straight to the point, "Do you wish to add anything to your list of events?"

She stammered slightly, "No, I don't think so." She had a terrible feeling of foreboding.

"You told me you had met Amutu."

She paled, "Yes, that's correct."

"I think that wasn't a complete answer." He opened the file, "A member of his domestic staff has alleged that one evening you dined alone with him in his private apartment ... is that true?"

"Yes. Is that a crime?"

David studied her in silence for a few moments, "No, not a crime. But you chose not to disclose it and that was dishonest." Lorna could think of no response. Although he knew the section by heart, he referred again to his file, "The member of staff says he was dismissed as soon as he had served the meal." He flipped pages to Lorna's list of events, "Your entry for that night just details ... dinner and bed." David hesitated, "May I assume you shared both events with Amutu?"

Lorna's eyes flashed, "Who's asking? You or the Official Inquisitor?"

David turned on his heel, "Then I'll assume the answer is yes."

40

That evening's cabinet meeting had finished early as there were few items on the agenda. After the other members filed out, David Churu pushed back his chair and stretched, "Do you think the old regime's changing its ways?"

Nat Beyla made a face, "I doubt it."

David nodded, "I guess you're right. But it used to be constant battles; recently they have hardly contested a single point."

The Major considered the statement, "I've thought the same, do you think they're up to something?"

His friend grinned ruefully, "They will always be up to something, plotting our downfall, that's just the way they are."

"I guess there are many out there that would like to see us dead."

David stacked papers, "I'm under no illusions. I know my death will be no more than a bump under the tyres of destiny, but despite everything I'm not ready to go yet."

Beyla smiled, "I think the people want us around," he indicated the long table strewn with documents, "Or at least until we've sorted out this lot!"

"Yes, you're right. People-power Nat, as long as we're doing right by the people the Old Brigade will never win." Churu selected the files he would need for his next task; the Xtremers trial

***

Promptly at 19.00hrs an army truck containing sixteen soldiers appeared at the prison gates. Chrystal marshalled the five pairs of male and three pairs of female troops and issued them with handcuffs and leg restraints. In single file they followed her rolling figure through the maze of corridors.

As they arrived at the cell doors Chrystal unlocked and supervised as each prisoner was secured. Then with an escort front and rear, they were dispatched individually to the staff canteen which was to form their courtroom.

The tubular canteen chairs and tables had already been set out. Eight pairs of chairs were positioned a few paces apart as they entered the door. These faced a table at the far end of the room, behind which were positioned three more chairs. It was over two weeks since the Xtremers had seen each other. Since the night in the Ambassador Hotel yard, their human contact had been restricted to Chrystal, David Churu and the soldiers who supervised their showers.

One by one, they shuffled awkwardly in and exchanged tentative smiles. Handcuffed to their escorts, they settled in the pairs of chairs and stared around. In only seventeen days their horizon had shrunk to the size of a small cell and the size of the staff canteen appeared daunting.

At exactly 20.00hrs Colonel David Churu, Major Nathaniel Beyla and a bespectacled young Corporal entered and sat down behind the table facing them. David arranged the files that had become so familiar to him. The corporal opened a writing pad and made some notes.

Beyla cleared his throat, "This court is convened to pronounce nine sentences. Eight on the foreign nationals present, plus one in absentia. It will be conducted in English and the cases heard in alphabetical order. Presiding will be Acting President, Colonel David Churu." An intake of breath from the prisoners greeted the news that, unbeknown to them; their inquisitor from day one had been the Acting President.

David looked along the rows of seats in front of him as he spoke quietly and clearly, "The interim government of Gamasi has delegated to me the task of trying your cases. At this time no appeal system exists, so the decisions I am about to announce are final and irrevocable. During your time in custody, with the help of others, I have fully investigated your cases. We have interviewed the soldiers who accompanied you on your hunting trips, hotel staff," he met Lorna's eyes for the end of his sentence. "...And anyone who could help us provide a complete picture of how you spent your time in Gamasi. Before I commence proceedings I must state that, whilst our ultimate intention is to abolish the death penalty in Gamasi, at this time it remains the sole sentencing option for those convicted of murder in this country..."

***

The tall double gates closed the moment the Mercedes 4x4 swung into the courtyard. Its headlights picked out an array of expensive cars parked in the drive, the young Asian pulled under the portico. His three passengers jumped out and disappeared inside the open front door.

In the hallway, the owner of the house greeted them effusively. Then ushered them up the broad staircase and into a front bedroom.

The taller man entered the dressing room and began to carefully peel off his false beard in front of the mirror.

The remaining pair removed their black burkhas to reveal two short figures, a broad bearded man and slim, elegant woman.

Downstairs the dining room was packed with visitors, all chatting animatedly over drinks.

Ten minutes later the two men descended the stairs and entered the drawing room.

All conversation ceased. One by one prominent Gamasi politicians and military elite stepped forward to congratulate President Charles Amutu on his return from exile.

General Gboja left Amutu to his networking and followed the young Asian into the library on the other side of the hall. The clubber walked over to a packed bookshelf and withdrew a bulky tome. Behind the book were two brown plastic pill bottles; he handed them to Gboja.

"Here are your Roofies."

The General frowned, "the Rohypnol tablets?"

"Yes, one hundred tabs of what they call the date rape drug. They're not blues, so they can be put in water."

Gboja looked confused, "Blues?"

The young man sighed as if all this was common knowledge, "These days nearly all of them contain a dye that turn drinks bright blue. That lot are made to the old formula, no taste, no smell, no nothing; they just wake up with a headache and a fanny full of spunk!"

The General's face was a mask of disgust.

***

David selected Michael Bray's file and angled it towards the clerk beside him.

"Michael Bray," read out the Corporal clerk, "Charge: murder."

The New Yorker's escort stood up and tried to take a step, but the prisoner to whom he was handcuffed remained seated.

"I don't recognise this travesty," Bray announced in firm tones.

Major Beyla addressed two soldiers waiting at the door, "Bring the prisoner forward."

In anticipation of this occurrence, these troops had been chosen for their size and strength. They stepped forward and

Bray was held in front of the table with his feet barely touching the floor.

David withdrew the first of the nine sheets that he had completed that morning. "Michael Bray, I find you guilty as charged, at 07.00hrs Friday morning you will be executed by shooting. Take him away."

This announcement was greeted by startled cries and groans from the other prisoners, amongst which David recognised Lorna's voice. As the soldiers removed Michael he was shouted in fury, "This is murder; I demand a proper trial..."

As the sounds of Bray's abusive tirade gradually receded down the corridor, the Corporal called Fiona Goff. The charge was attempted murder.

David glanced up at the young woman as she stood in front of him. She looked pale despite her ruddy complexion. "...It is clear from our investigations that you came to this country with the intention to kill. That you did not act upon that intention does little to mitigate your original crime. I therefore find you guilty and impose a sentence of ten years imprisonment, to be served without remission."

This announcement was also greeted with audible concern. Major Beyla indicated that she be returned to the rear of the room.

Robert Goff stood to attention as his charge of murder was decided. David focussed on the man's strained features, a cheek muscle twitched under his eye. "You also came to Gamasi with the intention to kill, an intention that you carried out on numerous occasions, apparently without remorse. I therefore find you guilty as charged."

In the background David heard a chorus of *nos*. He ignored the interruption and continued, "You are a young man of extremely limited intellect. I suspect that at the time you carried out these acts, you genuinely believed you were combating terrorism. I am giving you the benefit of that doubt.

I have commuted your death sentence, to twenty years imprisonment without remission."

Paul Henning was also supported by soldiers as he was brought forward to answer his charge of murder. Not through unwillingness to cooperate, but because his legs would not support him.

Major Beyla requested a chair for the prisoner.

Chrystal stood at the back of the room with a handkerchief pressed to her mouth.

"Paul Henning, you also came here to kill. That you are patently unsuited to that task does not serve in your favour. I sentence you to ten years imprisonment without remission."

Rather strangely the decision was greeted with a cry of delight from Chrystal.

The plump Californian smiled enigmatically.

David refused to meet Lorna's eyes as she stood in front of him; instead he focussed on her file, "Lorna Karrol, it is clear that you came to this country with no knowledge of the evil intentions of some of the other prisoners..." he paused for effect, "However, you made no attempt to discover the nature of your trip prior to your arrival in our country. Had the intention been the killing of our endangered wildlife rather than our citizens, you were equally disinterested..."

Lorna opened her mouth to interrupt but he silenced her with a wave,

"...For this omission I am fining you one thousand US dollars for every day that you have been in our country. This money to be paid to our local orphans' home here in Kamba."

As soon as the charge of attempted murder was read out, Johan Koeffe seemed to expect his sentence. His shoulders and head dropped as he received the ten-year blow.

Sergeant Thomas McRae stood to attention as his charge of conspiracy to murder was read out. As David examined the man's rigid features, the eyes fixed on a spot near the ceiling, he guessed this was not the first time the Scotsman had answered a charge. "McRae your case was particularity hard to decide. You have been in Gamasi over a considerable period and during that time have been instrumental in the deaths of many of our countrymen. Although we can find no evidence of you actually pulling a trigger I consider you to be equally culpable. I therefore sentence you to twelve years without remission."

The Corporal clerk read out, "Vasyl Serovec: murder," and glanced up, his eyes scanning the room for movement. Then in confusion he returned to his list and added, "...In absentia."

David read clearly, without looking up, "I find Vasyl Serovec guilty as charged: the sentence being death by shooting. All evidence suggests that this man is no longer in Gamasi, but efforts will be made to find him and carry out the decision of this court."

The final prisoner to be presented was Linda Tatlina. In her oversize grey prison clothes and without makeup, she appeared smaller and younger to all the other Xtremers. Over a week ago she had abandoned her efforts to seduce David and had recently just calmly awaited her fate. "...You also made no attempt to determine the nature of your visit. I impose a fine of one thousand US dollars a day, to be donated to the same orphanage."

Lindy gasped dramatically and clutched her chest, "I no have much money."

David had expected the response, "Then you can work there as a volunteer, until you have paid off your debt," he allowed himself the only smile of the proceedings, "At their wage rates, you could be with us for many years."

Colonel David Churu stood, indicating his job was complete. He addressed all the prisoners as they sat chained to their escorts, "I have one final task. Tomorrow all of you with custodial sentences will return here in the afternoon for details of how you'll spend your coming years."

He turned to leave, but as an afterthought, raised his voice," I'll leave you with one thought. In a poor nation such as ours; do not expect it to be a period of leisure!"

41

Not much surprised Cedric Farringdon, but the top secret communiqué he held in his hand had done so.

He stared across the desk at his Trade and Military Attachés. "You remember I said the other week that the days of gunboat diplomacy were over? Well it appears that I was wrong. Though this is probably more along the lines of gunship diplomacy." He waved the thin sheet of paper, "it appears that the forests hereabouts are crawling with our special forces."

Giles and Jonathon just raised their eyebrows and awaited the Consul's explanation.

"This information is strictly restricted to the three of us, but in the early hours of Thursday morning, and I quote" he focused on the information, *"a substantial combined US / British force will secure strategic targets with a view to assisting the return to power of the elected President, Charles Amutu."*

Both young men grimaced in silence as Farringdon continued, "Nice of London to give us thirty six hours warning before we discover these chaps crawling around in our shrubbery."

The Trade Attaché could wait no longer, "I assume it's the tantalite Sir. Churu is still playing hard to get."

His boss nodded, "Must be. Anyway to resume." He peered through his reading glasses once more, "Instructions are to keep our heads down until all the fun is over. London will let us know when we're to greet the prodigal upon his return ... if it all works out that is."

After his assistants had filed out the diplomat re-read the communiqué.

He puzzled over when Charles Amutu had actually been *elected*. Must have somehow missed that event, he thought to himself.

***

Chrystal dragged back the heavy door and stood aside. Lorna and Lindy stepped, blinking into the early morning sun.

The first shock of the day had been their luggage waiting on the bleached wooden bench when they arrived in the showers. Their bags had been returned from the hotel and Lorna felt like a kid at Christmas as she unpacked all her familiar possessions. Despite the creases and musty smell, it was wonderful to get dressed in proper clothes again. The feeling of her own shoes and soft underwear next to the skin was delicious. She struggled to apply her makeup as tears coursed down her cheeks.

The second shock had been the freedom to walk unaccompanied from the showers to the front hall. Lindy had been waiting for her and Chrystal stood back smiling as the women embraced, laughing and crying in each others arms.

An army staff car awaited them, with two women soldiers sitting in the front.

Now they were bumping along the road from the prison gates, staring hungrily at the views denied them. It seemed inconceivable that life had been carrying on just the other side of those concrete walls.

Lorna stared as a woman swept the ground outside her front door. Two men worked on an old truck and a boy with only one arm drove three goats ahead of him with a stick.

209

Accustomed to constant disinfectant, the smell of the city was overpowering. The fumes, the dust, the animals, even the sewage smelt good. Their driver weaved and hooted through the throng of carts, cars, dogs and bicycles.

Dragging her eyes off the chaos, Lorna turned to Lindy, "Any idea where are we going?"

The Russian woman grinned back, "No, but I think it is good." They both roared with laughter and the front passenger turned and laughed with them, though plainly she had no idea what the joke was.

Lorna stared at the teeming street, "I guess we're probably going to that orphanage. Do you think you will be ok working here?"

"Me? Work in Kamba?" She hazarded a guess, "Are you are speaking of the fine?"

"Yes, paying it off by working in the orphanage."

This statement was met with a huge gust of laughter, "Lorna, are you always believing everything? I have money; I charge it to my credit card today."

The car swung into a quieter side street and pulled up at the entrance to a courtyard of a very dilapidated colonial house.

Both soldiers got out and indicated that Lindy and Lorna should follow them under a tall archway. As they entered, their ears were assaulted by the screams of hundreds of children, they echoed from side passages and off the high stonewalls.

Children burst from every opening around the huge quadrangle and hurtled towards them. Under the guidance of the adults, the chaos of dark blue and white uniforms and black skin gradually settled into excited lines. The orphans were formed up in order of size, ranging from early teens at the back, to silent, wide-eyed tiny ones in the front.

A tall man approached the women as they stood with their military escort. He shook their hands and addressed them in halting English, "Welcome, I am the director of the Amu..." He caught himself and hesitated," ...of this orphanage. We only just hear that you give us a big gift." He smiled hugely,

"It is our wish to thank you. In your honour the children want to sing for you … an English song." He turned, spoke two words and began to conduct.

The American and Russian stood in the bright sunshine as around two hundred voices engulfed them in *Away in a Manger*.

Neither woman moved when their car stopped outside the front door of the Ambassador Hotel. Both the driver and her colleague turned around and looked at them. The driver smiled and nodded at the massive door, "Hotel!" she nodded again.

Lorna and Lindy looked at one another in silence and then in unison grimaced and shook their heads. Lorna addressed the couple in the front, "ANOTHER HOTEL?"

Five minutes of drawing pictures on an old envelope, elicited the information that the capitol city of Gamasi had only one other hotel besides the Ambassador. Many hostels, but just two hotels.

They swung out of the Ambassador's gates and back into the traffic on their way to Kamba's other hotel. The women in the front kept up a voluble conversation, punctuated with screams of laughter.

Lindy looked puzzled and nodded to the front, "I wonder what's so funny?"

The Hilton Honeymoon Hotel was painted bright yellow with electric blue woodwork. It seemed unlikely the renowned international hotel group was aware of their branch in Kamba.

It was built in 1970's style block work. Under its red and white hand painted sign was a smaller green and white item announcing: *GOOD ATENDANCE. SPEAKIN IN FRANCE – GERMANY – INGLISH.*

Mystified, Lorna re-read the smaller sign. After a second reading she was still unsure if it boasted of its staff quality, or popularity. If it means the staff, they must have telephone links to the other countries. Moments later her assumptions were proven wrong.

Thanks to her UN training Lindy was proficient in all three languages, however she soon discovered that the colour-blind owner was only a tri-lingual smiler.

Despite communication difficulties she soon established there was a problem, "I really don't think we want to stay here Lorna."

The American frowned, "So it's not the best, but McRae once told me there's not a lot of choice. At least there are no ghosts, like at the Ambassador!"

The Russian considered her point, "Ok ... how to say this? This hotel charge honeymoons by the hour."

Lorna was surprised, "By the hour? ...Oh I see ... are you sure?" She looked back through the front door and saw the soldiers in the front of the car were wiping away tears.

Lindy nodded, "Total sure. Trust me, I know this stuff!" She turned to the owner, standing behind his orange quilted reception desk. Creating a circle with her left hand she mimed the internationally sign for sexual intercourse, followed by a vigorous shake of her head.

The owner smiled, this time in Gamasi, and shrugged eloquently. As they turned and picked up their bags, he suddenly became animated and beckoned them to follow him.

The women looked at one another in indecision.

"What do you think Lindy?"

She shrugged and smiled, "we can look."

They followed the man along a narrow corridor and emerged into a bare, concrete yard. In the centre was a large timber chalet. Suspended over the door was a sign bearing the words: *HONEYMOON SWEET*. The women dared not risk looking at one another.

"At least it'll be quieter," observed Lorna, in a strange muffled voice.

THE BIG GAME

As soon as the owner closed the door behind him, both women collapsed on the pink candlewick bedspread screaming with laughter.

Suddenly Lorna stopped laughing and sat up, "Lindy what the hell am I doing? Mike's due to be executed in the morning and I'm acting as if there's nothing's wrong." She rolled off the bed.

Leaving the Russian and her bags, she sprinted down the corridor and out of the front of the hotel. The army car that had brought them was just pulling into the traffic. Ignoring the horns and brakes, she dashed into the road and pounded on its rear panel. The shocked soldiers pulled up sharply, blocking the road. Above the cacophony of horns Lorna shouted at the driver, "Please, please take me to Colonel Churu."

***

General Gboja handed out the twists of paper to all the men grouped around the room. He returned to his seat and scanned the faces to ensure they were all paying attention.

"Remember, timing is crucial. Depending on the size and weight of the victim, these pills should be effective for around twelve hours. Now, apart from your own targets, you're all supplying approximately twenty others contacts in your chain." He paused once more to ensure each man's full attention, "I cannot stress strongly enough that every one of your contacts must understand that their target has to drink between ten and eleven o'clock tonight.

If any one of you has a problem, then I need to know about it before midnight. Any final questions?" Again he scrutinised the ring of faces. "Then leave this house one at a time, at fifteen minute intervals. Good luck my friends. Tomorrow we shall greet each other in a re-born Gamasi."

213

42

The Corporal clerk tapped on Colonel Churu's office door. David looked up from the sheaf of papers he was reading.

"Sorry to bother you Sir, but that American woman is demanding to see you."

The Colonel frowned, "Demanding? Do you mean Lorna Karrol?"

"Yes Sir."

David had just returned from an official reception with the Chinese trade delegation. He was still wearing his best formal uniform and did not know if he would have time to change before this evening's cabinet meeting. He was desperately trying to catch up with his paperwork.

The Xtremers' trial had put him way behind. He looked at the large pile yet to be completed and the small file he had so far processed. He sighed to himself, who would imagine a revolution would generate so much paperwork! He felt pulled in two directions. He glanced up at his clerk, "What the hell does she want?"

"She say's it's a matter of life and death, Sir."

Churu considered the statement, "It has to be about that damned Michael Bray. Tell her she can have ten minutes at..." he glanced at his watch and then at the food import projections in front of him. "Oh show her in please ... but tell her she's only got ten minutes!"

Lorna took David Churu's breath away as she walked into the room. He had never seen her dressed in anything but prison clothes and without makeup. She looked stunning and for a moment he was unable to speak.

Lorna had sat outside the Colonel's door and rehearsed what she was going to say; assuming he agreed to talk at all that is! The last time we spoke, if you don't count the trial,

THE BIG GAME

when only he got to speak, it had been a row. I'm a fool! Why didn't I put dinner with Amutu in my statement? Guess I didn't want to appear like a collaborator. But why didn't I just tell him nothing happened, apart from having dinner?

Anyway, it was his fault for assuming I couldn't have dinner with a guy without jumping into bed with him. What century does this man inhabit? I knew Mike all of ... all of ... at least, five hours before I slept with him. My God, what's happening to me? And I bet he keeps me waiting for hours, just to boost his precious male...

"Miss Karrol?" the Corporal was standing with his hand on the door handle. "The Colonel will see you now. But he's very busy so he can only spare you ten minutes."

Lorna followed the clerk into the office and felt the blood rise into her cheeks. Colonel David Churu was standing silently behind his desk wearing white formal uniform. Lorna took in the beautiful tailoring; the stiff high cut collar, the gold epaulettes and felt her knees weaken. As she stared at his dark complexion, black eye patch and fine hawk like nose. A Pirate Prince. She could not speak.

They stared one another in silence.

Lorna broke the spell, she coughed, "I want to talk to you about ... about ... err ... Mike ... Michael Bray."

David tried to reply, he swallowed, but was mesmerised by the flow of her neck, the cascade of her hair as she stood...

Lorna suspected he was doing the old wrong footing trick. You bastard! Putting me under pressure by saying nothing. Making me do all the running, easier just to blank my pleas for clemency. She flushed, but kept her tone level, "I need some time with him."

David shook his head as if to clear it, "I see, I believe you are ... partners."

"No, or at least, not any more."

He considered her statement, "So you are now separated?" He paused as if considering the point, "...And were you together for many years?"

Lorna flushed. To say one month did not seem to aid her case. "No ... not very long ... anyway it's not important. He's

215

still a person I care about and I need to talk to him. Find out why he won't help himself."

David shrugged, "It's rather late for anyone to help him, he's due to be executed..." he glanced at his watch, "...in around sixteen hours."

"So nothing will effect that decision? Your decision? You say he has to die at seven tomorrow ... and that's what'll happen ... come what may ... it's that simple?"

"It's not simple at all. I believe it's what Bray himself wants."

"What do you mean? I think you're wrong." Lorna was losing all the control she had mustered outside his office, "So suddenly you're a shrink as well as President?"

"I think you're wasting both our time, Miss Karrol."

"I'm sorry. I just need to talk some sense into him."

"I gave Michael Bray every opportunity to ask for clemency."

Lorna became conciliatory, "I'm sure you did, but it's different ... for me."

David pursed his lips, deep in thought, "He was informed of the deadline."

"And you won't even let me see him?"

He considered her request, "You may visit him this afternoon; under supervision."

"And if he pleads for his life?"

"It is not to you he must plead ... it is to the people of Gamasi."

Lorna tossed her head, "And how exactly does he do that?"

"I am their representative in this matter, so it is to me."

She felt her calm deserting her again, "We both know that'll never happen. So you sit here and people have to come and plead with you? Is this what you get off on? Westerners pleading for their lives? You disgust me. Is there something in the water around here that breeds fucking tin pot despots?"

He stood and stared at her in silence, his single eye boring into her, "Shall I tell you what disgusts me Miss Karrol?" He continued without waiting for a response, "It's rich westerners and their ... women, coming here and murdering my people.

You treat the rest of the world like an air-conditioned theme park, created just for your amusement. But maybe now your partner understands the amusements are real ... they can bite back. And tomorrow morning he'll discover that the bullets are just as real as the ones he used to kill my countrymen, and do you know what Miss Karrol?" He stepped from behind his desk, "I believe this planet will be enriched by the death of Michael Bray."

Lorna wrung her hands in frustration, "I'm sorry, I'm sorry ... all I want to do is try and save his life," her shoulders slumped and she hung her head in silence.

The seconds dragged by, eventually Colonel Churu spoke. "You're thinking solely of Bray, but when a person is executed many others suffer; innocent people. Let me explain. In Gamasi, when we have an execution to carry out, we ask for two marksmen to volunteer. Both these men now have sixteen hours in which to mentally prepare for their task. One rifle will be loaded with blanks and one with live rounds, so neither will ever know if they have killed a man in cold blood." David Churu paused, deep in thought once more, "Tell me, by coming to see me today you obviously believe yourself to be a persuasive talker?"

Lorna frowned, "I guess I am, but..."

He spoke over her, "Then I'll offer you a deal; let us call it *the despot's deal*. If it is solely Bray's arrogance that is preventing him pleading with me, I'll accept a letter from him to the people of Gamasi, apologising for the wrongs he has done them. This letter must explain why he came here to murder their fellow countrymen. Upon its receipt, his sentence will automatically be reduced to twenty years imprisonment."

Lorna began to thank him, but he stalled her. "Don't be too hasty with your thanks; there's a sting in its tail. If however I'm right and Mr Bray does wish to die; and you're unable to persuade him to accept this concession; then you must agree to be one of the marksmen at his execution."

Nat Beyla was waiting outside as Lorna Karrol left the office. He walked in and raised an eyebrow.

David Churu frowned at his friend, "Don't ask Nat." He nodded towards the departed American, "Have you completed all those foreigners' work allotments?"

The Major separated a single sheet of paper from his sheaf and placed it on the desk. The Colonel ran his eye down the names and the plans of how they were to serve their sentences. When he reached the end, he nodded.

***

The prison canteen was less crowded today. The five prisoners had two escorts each. As soon as his clerk was settled, Major Beyla started talking as if he was addressing troops on parade, "Yesterday Colonel Churu handed down your sentences. Today I'll explain how you'll repay your debt to Gamasi. Our country has need of your skills, so during your time here you'll contribute to the growth of our nation.

If your contribution is made willingly, then there's no reason to believe your time will be unpleasant. Throughout your sentence, the option will always remain for you to serve it in prison. I'll now call your names, there's no need to stand. But be aware this is not the time for questions."

He referred to his list, "Fiona Goff." He focussed on the young woman; she looked relaxed and appeared to have returned to her normal demeanour, "You'll spend the next ten years helping to develop our tourist industry."

Fiona looked startled and began to speak, "I'm sorry, I don't..."

Major Beyla ignored her interruption, "As I said this is not the time for questions. The full extent of your task will be explained to you later. Initially you will all work with our people during the day and return to custody every night. It will be a learning curve for all of us, but gradually your situation may improve." He returned to his papers, indicating Fiona's time was over.

"Robert Goff. With a sentence of twenty years you'll be with us the longest. It has been decided that you're to work with your sister, but with special responsibility for encouraging eco-tourism."

The Englishman looked as if he had just been given a school prize.

"Paul Henning. Our vision is that Gamasi will be the first truly interactive democracy in the world. We intend there to be no government, parties, or politicians. Any group of one hundred citizens will be able to propose changes, or additions to our laws or constitution. We want everybody's vote to really count. It is your task for the next ten years to conceive, develop and refine a secure system that will allow every person to decide on every issue. "

Paul Henning half turned and smiled shyly at Chrystal. Then behind his glasses, his eyes took on a far away look; he had already begun drafting the system.

"Johan Koeffe. Gamasi needs an engineer with your expertise. For the next ten years we expect you take an influential role in a project that will transform the economy of this country."

The German needed to speak and sensed that he would be refused. He attempted it anyway, "My family, my wife and sons, is it possible that they could join me here?"

Beyla nodded, "Not immediately, but possibly in some months."

A weight seemed to have been lifted from Johan's shoulders.

"Thomas McRae. The dramatic changes to our economy means that we will be under constant threat of invasion. You'll spend your next twelve years training our young people to resist those incursions when they occur."

Major Beyla looked at the five prisoners in turn, "So in conclusion, your sentences will be what you make them. You're all part of the experiment that is New Gamasi, a country where traditional prison will be consigned to history.

We're going to build a unique country here out of the ruins bequeathed us by ex President Charles Amutu. We believe that by the end of your sentences, people from all over the world will want live and work here." He allowed himself a rare smile, "It is possible some of you may even choose to stay on!"

***

It had been the hardest decision of her life, but Lorna had agreed to *the despot's deal*. The moment they unlocked Mike's cell she regretted her decision.

Mike had not slept for days. His eyes were sunken and his face had aged ten years. He constantly massaged the scar under his hairline. She considered how their lives had changed in a few weeks. From ardent lovers to near strangers. He was no longer the man she had left New York with one month ago. They were unsure how to greet each other.

"How are you Mike?" as she spoke the words she recognised the crassness of the question.

He simply shrugged in response.

She continued, "I think we can get you out of this."

He sneered and nodded at the half open door, "Who's the we? You got Superman out there?"

"No, I meant us; you and me."

His grin was haunted, without a hint of humour, "Ah the old team. Did you come here so we could get it together for one last time? The condemned man…"

Her eyes were cold, "Do you want me just to walk out? It's your call."

A succession of emotions flitted across his face. Then he rubbed his eyes, "I'm sorry. Guess I'm under pressure. Not myself…"

Lorna considered her next question carefully, "Mike, will you answer me something and you've got to promise to be one hundred percent honest?"

"Not much point in lying at this late stage of my life."

"I agree, but it's a tough one that you might find easier just to blow out ... but believe me it's the most important question of your life ... and probably mine as well."

Her personal afterthought stirred his interest, "Ok, I promise; go for it."

Lorna took a deep breath, "Mike is there some reason ... I don't know how to put this, but do want to die tomorrow?"

He looked at Lorna in a mixture of confusion and irritation, "Is that your big question?"

"Yes, at least part of it."

"I hope the other part makes more sense. Of course I don't want to die."

She released her breath, "Well I've been talking to David Churu..."

Bray snorted in derision, "Bet that shit can't wait for the morning."

She shook her head, "You're wrong Mike. I don't believe he wants your execution to go ahead."

"Lorna, you're a good person, but you're living in a dream world. His type ... it's their thing. He probably believes that he gains power from killing me. He probably had to stab a lion or something before he became a man."

"He's a highly intelligent, sophisticated man..."

Mike turned away from her, stared at the wall and furiously rubbed his scar.

Lorna tried again, "Look Mike. All you have to do is write a letter..."

"Saying what? What do you think he would he like? Sorry I shot your little black buddies ... promise it'll never happen again..."

She stared at him in silence for a moment, "Actually yes, something like that."

He grinned broadly, "Well why the hell didn't he say so before? Not a problem. One letter equals no execution? That's my kinda deal. Let's get started. Where's my pad?" He rushed forward maniacally, scooped up the pad and pen and settled on his knees, "How do you think I should start? Dear Mr President or Dear David?"

Lorna looked down at him, "I don't understand why you're acting this way. You have the chance to live and you seem determined to blow it."

He slung the pad and pen so they bounced off the far wall. "Then let me explain … it's really simple Lorna, It's because I don't believe it. Any of it. It's all a load of bullshit. That Churu guy, and all the rest of them, they need to kill us, humiliate us, for a thousand reasons, right down from the slave trade to … to job discrimination. I've been there. I've stared it in the face. I've seen their hate this close." He held one quivering hand an inch from his nose and with the other, jabbed his chest.

"Mike, this makes no sense. Nothing like this has happened to you here."

"Did I say here? Let's get real … just for once tell it how it really is? No more fucking PC crap! We both know it's the same the world over. Them and us, black versus white. It's the same back home; the strutting young warrior out to prove himself … out to get his first lion. Believe me Lorna, you can take a savage out of the jungle, but you can't take the jungle out of a savage."

Mike pressed his face so close to hers, she could smell his stale breath and unwashed teeth. He stabbed at his own chest with both forefingers, "Let me tell you something about this guy, Michael Bray is never going to play anyone's lion again, just so some fucking native can prove himself!"

Lorna felt she needed time out and tapped on the cell door. She was embarrassed that Chrystal and the soldier waiting outside must have heard every word.

She sat in the small office and gathered her thoughts. There had to be an answer to the situation, but she had no idea what it was.

Ten minutes later they let her back in his cell. Mike was sitting on the mattress, slumped against the wall. His head hung forward so his long blonde hair obscured his face. Lorna went over, kneeled down next to him and put her hand on his shoulder. She spoke gently, "Please let me help you Mike. I know you need help and time's running out."

He nodded silently.

Lorna watched as one by one, dark drops appeared upon the thighs of his light prison trousers.

His voice was quiet, choked, "They held me, three of them..."

When she realised he could say no more, she waited. Eventually he gathered his voice, "Two held my arms, while one..."

Lorna held him to her as he shook, "You can tell me Mike. Here in this cell?"

He shook his head and took a deep breath, "No, back home … nearly twenty years ago, after a party at one of the guy's apartments. He was broke, cheap part of town. I was new in the city and didn't know where to avoid, where you had to take a cab, where the street gangs ruled."

She waited again as his voice tailed off, just stroking his hair.

"I'd had too much to drink. They were only young punks, if I'd been sober I could have … anyway they dragged me into an alley … pinned me against some railings, took my cash and cards. Then they..." His voice broke once more.

Lorna realised she was rocking him like a baby and making low crooning sounds.

"There was a street light at the end. It showed his face. Acne, bad acne. His face was a mass of spots, some ready to burst."

It was as if he was speaking to himself, a monotone that Lorna had to strain to hear.

"Both my arms dragged back though the railings … forced behind me … then the knife, in the street light … everything so slow … he reached forward … I had to look into his eyes … with one hand he pulled my hair … his knife in the other." He could say no more.

Lorna soothed him. In the end she broke the silence, "Was it … sexual?" she felt him shake his head.

"No, he tried to … to … to scalp me."

43

David Churu re-read the lined A4 sheet. I wouldn't describe it as an abject apology, but it'll do for a start. He picked up his phone and spoke to his clerk, "Is Miss Karrol still there?"

The effect of seeing her walking into his office was the same as the first time. He invited her to sit down. The strain she was under was written clearly upon her face. "I've just read Bray's statement. Whilst all three of us know his grudge to be illogical. I now understand more."

Lorna hardly dared ask the question, "And will it suffice?"

David looked at her with his head on one side, "It is an apology and although he sets out a flawed reason, it is a reason of sorts."

"Please, don't play with me. Will his execution go ahead?"

"Miss Karrol. You are not home yet; there was never going to be an execution."

"What? ... I don't understand."

"We don't approve of murder, whether by the state or individual."

Her eyes flashed, "So you put me through all that ... that elaborate charade?"

"The old homicide law in my country is quite unequivocal; the death penalty exists for murder. It's simply that I used my discretion."

She visibly shrank, "So Mike was never going to die ... all that pain for nothing."

"No, not for nothing." He nudged the A4 sheet of paper, "Michael Bray has come a long way in a short time. Gamasi now has the next twenty years to build him up. He's a top commodity broker; we need him ... and just maybe he needs us."

THE BIG GAME

Lorna stared at Churu in silence, her head a whorl, "Do you enjoy playing God Colonel? You've put us through hell and for why?"

He considered her words, "God ... let me see ... I try to do the best for the maximum number of people; if that's God's game then maybe I do. But as far as hell is concerned Lorna Karrol, you know nothing. By the weekend you'll be back in America with the best dinner party story of your life."

He picked up his phone, "Please see Miss Karrol out of the building." He stood up to signify the meeting was over. As she reached the door, he spoke. "Ah, an amusing postscript to tell your Direct Debit Liberal friends over their coffee and liqueurs ... let me see, how would you put it? ...*Know what? And the tin pot despot actually fell in love with me.*"

Lorna was in the street, before she understood what he had said.

***

Cedric Farringdon looked up from his desk as Jonathon ushered the women into the room.

He stood up and shook their hands before escorting them to the easy chairs. An attractive pair, even if the Russian was a trifle obvious, the American was damned pretty. "...So Ms Karrol, as far as you're aware all your party are alive and well, albeit languishing in jail?"

"Apart from Wolfgang Schmidt, the man who was shot on the hotel roof."

Farringdon shook his head sadly, "Yes bad business about Schmidt. His body is now on its way back to Germany."

Lindy added, "And we know nothing of my partner Vasyl Serovec. When we are captured he just disappear..." She swept her hands prettily as if performing a magic spell.

225

Jonathon Forbes spoke from the other side of the room as he took the tea tray from the maid, "No worries there Miss Tatlina."

Lindy flashed him a smile, "I no worry Jonathon."

The Trade attaché decided to ignore the strange response, "We have received information on Mr Serovec from the Russian Police. He is in Moscow; in fact he arrived back there just a few days after your imprisonment."

The Russian giggled, "Then I think they must be happy police, without Vasyl they are very boring."

Farringdon cleared his throat, "There's a lot of concern back in the UK about the young Goff couple. How were they coping?"

Lorna grimaced, "Very well. In fact they coped better than all of us."

"Good, good," murmured the Consul. He accepted his tea cup and moved on, "As you know we look after American interests in Gamasi, as your Government doesn't maintain an official presence here. So if there's anything you need, I'm sure Jonathon here will be able to help."

The younger man smiled winningly over the rim of his teacup as he desperately tried to ignore the expanse of shapely Russian leg.

The Consul turned to Lindy, "And the same applies to you, Miss Tatlina. Please just ask." He seemed to be considering a difficult point, "Now accommodation. Can't say I'm familiar with this Hilton place," he raised a bushy eyebrow to his attaché who was now standing behind the women, but had trouble attracting his attention. He coughed loudly and Forbes jumped, "Have you a view Jonathon?"

"Sorry Sir, a view of what?"

The Consul frowned in irritation, "A view on this Hilton place where the ladies are staying."

The young man pursed his lips and shook his head, "Not suitable at all. Frankly the sooner we get the ladies out of there the better."

"There's only the Ambassador and that's a no-no, "said Lorna firmly.

Farringdon adopted his no nonsense tone, "I appreciate your problem with the Ambassador Hotel, but I think you should stay there just until we can arrange flights out."

"Thanks for your concern," replied Lorna. She exchanged smiles with Lindy, "...but we really like the Hilton."

Cedric Farringdon became the kind but firm uncle, "I'm sure you do my dear, but these are strange times. You will be safer at the Ambassador and I'm assured it has been fully refurbished since your rather unfortunate stay."

Lorna laughed, "Oh don't worry, I think we've survived the worst that Gamasi can throw at us."

Farringdon saw this was one he could not win. He concluded with great feeling, "Just remember Africa's a funny place. Very ... unpredictable."

The British Consul looked up as Jonathon Forbes returned from seeing the two women to their taxi. "That's a nuisance Jonathon, last thing we need tonight is those two wandering around loose."

"Exactly Sir, but if we'd gone any harder on the point it might have let the cat out of the bag."

"Yes tricky. No one will care about the Russian girl, but the Americans can get very touchy about their people. Probably sue us or something!"

"Could put a couple of our chaps in there tonight to look out for them?"

"Good idea. After all can't be the worst way to spend a night – watching a couple of pretty girls!"

"Indeed not Sir. Venue may not be perfect though, they could be in the middle of a war zone," both men chuckled at the thought.

***

Lindy removed the complimentary bottle of Indian champagne from the hand basin of cold water, "It is in the price, so must drink it."

"Alcohol? I've forgotten what it tastes like."

They sat half propped up in a nest of pillows wiggling their bare toes in front of them, sipping the wine and luxuriating in the softness after prison mattresses.

Lorna broke the companionable silence, "It's been the strangest day of my life. Life changing even."

Lindy smiled at the thought, "I look forward to be back in Moscow with my family. If not tomorrow, then day after for sure."

Lorna looked dreamy "Yes, I can't wait to get home." She hesitated as if unsure how to put her next point, "...But I'm coming back soon."

The Russian woman swivelled her head in surprise, "Back here ... to Gamasi?"

"Yes, like I said, today was life changing."

"Explain please!"

Lorna frowned as she assembled her thoughts, "This morning when we were at the orphanage, I decided it wasn't enough."

"Enough what? Money? Give more then; I think they will not say no."

"No, not money. I'm giving up my life in New York and moving here. I'm coming to Gamasi to work with those kids."

Lindy looked bewildered, "Ok, if you think it will be good for you. What do the orphanage people say?"

Lorna grinned, "They don't know yet, but I won't take no for an answer."

"I think that your life will be ... Lorna I want to be nice ... but it will be ... be difficult."

"I'm not a dreamer Lindy. I know some of it will be shit ... maybe a lot of it, but it's I want to do ... do some good. Anyway it's not the only reason, there's a man here as well..."

The Russian grimaced, "You still care about Mike?"

Lorna looked horrified, "No not Mike ... another man."

THE BIG GAME

Lindy bounced onto her knees, slopping both their drinks, "This is SO, SO romantic. This is like Hollywood movie. You give up life in America for love. And I have no idea who it is. Who is he? Do I know him? How did you meet? Since hotel we have been only in prison!"

Lorna laughed. "Yes you know him. You have met him many times."

Lindy screamed, "I have no idea!! Is it Johan the German? No, no that is not right. Lorna you are BIG SHIT BASTARD. Tell me now."

The American could not help grinning, "Look it'll probably never work. If it does it could be years before ... we have said a lot of bad things to each other, at this time he probably hates me. If I work here, maybe one day..."

Lindy held a slim fist under Lorna's jaw and growled through gritted teeth, "You tell me now!"

Lorna hesitated, "...It's David, David Churu."

The Russian leapt up and down on the bed like a trampoline, " Lorna you are FANTASTIC woman ... two presidents in one month!"

The strains of the day, plus Indian champagne had taken it's toll and they soon settled down for the night. When the lights were off Lorna lay in the reflected glow from the honeymoon hotel opposite and thought about her Russian friend. She propped herself on one elbow and addressed the back of the tousled head, "Lindy."

"Mmm?"

"Do you think you'll ever settle down with a man?"

There came no reply as if she was considering the question. Then Lindy rolled over. There was a twinkle in her eyes, "Lorna I'm sorry, I should tell you before we share a bed, but I, how do you say it? ... Play for this other team."

Lorna was surprised, "Play what? ...Oh, oh wow, do you mean you're really a ... a lesbian?"

229

Lindy wet her lips with the tip of her tongue and slid sinuously closer. Her voice became husky, "Yes Lorna … kiss me."

Lorna sat straight up, "Look Lindy, I really like you, but I've never really..."

The Russian roared with laughter, "You must see your face!"

When the punching was over, they settled down to sleep again.

Lindy stared wistfully at the ceiling, "No, you no good for me without big fat dick."

Lorna considered her statement for a moment, then hung over the edge of the bed and began to rummage noisily in her luggage. Her voice was muffled, "Well it just so happens…"

Lindy turned to her in horror, "No, I speak of man..." She caught sight of the other woman grinning at her from under the crook of her arm. She kicked Lorna on her hip, tipping her onto the floor where she lay helpless with laughter. It was not going to be good night's sleep.

***

Xtremer duties over and tonight's cabinet meeting cancelled, David had the rare luxury of an evening off. He sat looking at the remains of their Chinese take away meal, thinking about his day. As usual he was missing his family, but at the same time could not wipe away the image of Lorna Karrol in his office.

Nat Beyla called through from his kitchen, "The meal came with a free bottle of wine, what do you think?"

"I think it'll not be a good vintage."

From the kitchen came the sound of a popping cork. Beyla walked in holding two full glasses and a bottle of sparkling wine in his huge hands; he raised an eyebrow in enquiry.

David Churu had little tolerance for alcohol, but thought that tonight he might need some help sleeping. He nodded then voiced the subject on both their minds, "Strange so many

THE BIG GAME

members calling off at short notice tonight. Are we missing something? A big match for example?"

Neither of them were football fans, so the Major shrugged his broad shoulders.

David continued, "Whatever, it's good to spend some time off together, proper time. It's been too long."

Nat grinned, "That's the problem with saving your country; it steals your life."

They raised their glasses and tapped rims, "To Gamasi."

They sat and chatted, suddenly David shook his head, "Is it me, or is this wine very strong?"

His friend just smiled, "You've only had one glass..."

David felt the room begin to spin and put out his hand to steady himself. He stared across at Nat Beyla, but he could not focus. The Major's features were swirling. He tried to put down his glass, but it slipped from his hand, "What the hell is..."

He felt himself sliding over and tried to save himself, but was unconscious before he hit the floor.

44

There was only a very slight roll as the Atlantic swell lifted the enormous bulk of the US aircraft carrier Hartford.

The American General in overall command of Op-Reunion was drawing the meeting to a close. He glanced at the British Colonel in charge of Special Forces, "So your guys are all ready for us Tim?"

"Yes Sir, all strategic beacons in place; your boffins have confirmed they're transmitting ok. Diversions all wired and running. My chaps are now moving into position for their snatch targets."

The General cast a hard look down the length of the table, "So no excuses for friendly fire, or getting lost – OK?"

There was a chorus of approval from the assembly.

He checked the multi-faced clock opposite and focussed on the only black man present, "No bad news from your people, General Gboja?"

The Gamasi soldier ran his tongue over his prominent teeth, "It's half an hour past the deadline and no calls" He glanced at the satellite phone in front of him, "I believe that all the foremost rebels will now be drugged."

***

Lorna came half awake. She sensed breathing next to her and for a moment thought it was Michael, and then she remembered Lindy.

But what had woken her? A huge ceiling fan. She laid in the dark and tried to remember; she was sure there was no fan. Confirming her suspicion, there was no air movement.

She snapped awake, it wasn't a fan. The throb was a helicopter and it was becoming louder! Then she picked up another sound, a distant popping and crackling. It was small arms fire. Further off, the dull thump off an explosion made two glasses rattle together. Lorna sat up in bed and listened.

Next to her Lindy stirred, sighed and spoke to her in Russian. Realising where she was, the woman swapped languages, "What is going?"

"It sounds like a war out there?"

Lindy groaned, "I think you make joke again. Is it like this Scramble game ... go straight back to prison ... do not collect two hundred dollars?"

"I'm not joking, there really is shooting out there. And the game is called Monopoly."

Lorna threw on her jeans, leaving Lindy with a pillow over her head grumbling about *Scramble* and *Monopoly*. The American pulled back the corners of each curtain and peered out. The only views were of plain walls and the rear of the hotel. She padded to the front door, slipped off the chain and peered out. "Shiiit!!" she exclaimed, "Lindy this is for real, get your ass out of that bed!"

Dawn was just lighting the sky and the sound of distant firing came from all around. There were now three helicopters circling high above the city. They hovered in a pattern, their banks of powerful white searchlights sweeping the streets.

Lindy appeared on the door step scratching her head. She wore only knickers and was using the candlewick bed spread as a cloak. As the women stood and stared into the night sky, two shadows separated from a corner of the yard.

"Miss Karrol?"

"What the fuck..." Lorna leapt backwards for the door, colliding with Lindy who had the same idea. They clung onto each other to avoid falling.

"Sorry to startle you ladies. We're with the Consulate; personal security." The shadows materialised into two young

Englishmen. Although in jeans and tee shirts, they had assault rifles swinging from straps over their shoulders.

"What? ... What are you doing here? ... And what's going on?" Lorna swung her arms to indicate the gunfire and helicopters.

The second man spoke, "Nothing to worry about. Just a bit of local trouble."

Lorna clung onto Lindy and started to smile, "Oh, just a bit of local trouble. No problem then. Know what? ... For a moment, we were worried."

Lindy grinned back, "Not me ... I used to be with the UN."

The Englishmen exchanged bewildered looks as the woman hung onto each other howling with laughter.

Epilogue

It felt as if the hair on the back of his head was glued to the floor, then he realised it was.

David Churu fought his way to consciousness. One by one his senses kicked in: each was familiar. He could not move his head one millimetre; he began his inventory.

He was naked and spread-eagled on smooth concrete. Restraints pinned his wrists and ankles. Hard pegs were forced into his ears. The only smell was disinfectant. He had a view of a single bulb hanging from the ceiling; so the scaffold board and nails were missing.

He lost consciousness again.

He awoke to the sound of footsteps approaching. There was a third tapping as if the man walked with a stick. They stopped, out of his range of vision.

"Good morning David."

The voice was familiar, a voice from the past. Churu swivelled his eye. Although close, the man stood on his blind side. He got the blurred impression of a dark suit and a long pole on his right hand side. He cleared his throat, "Good morning … Charles"

Amutu chuckled, "Yes, but we must stop meeting like this. What am I saying? This will be the last time."

David realised he felt no fear, just an immense tiredness, "You are here to kill me?"

Amutu, when he answered, sounded regretful, "Yes David, some jobs one cannot delegate. I'm here to thank you and to kill you. But it will be warrior's death; in the traditional way."

"Then release me, a warrior doesn't die pinned to the floor."

The deep laugh boomed around the plain concrete walls, "Do you think me a fool, release a man with nothing to lose? Whereas you David are a fool, you have strengthened my position and at the same time exposing all the traitors."

Although David dreaded the answer he had to ask the question, "Nat ... Nathaniel Beyla, was he one of..."

"Major Beyla? A good man and sadly one of yours..." he glanced at his watch, "...or rather *was* one of yours, right to the end."

Amutu remained silent as if making a decision. Finally the desire to boast was overwhelming, "Actually I should thank you for something else ... you performed another service that was impossible for me."

Despite the lethargy, David had to know how he had unwittingly assisted his killer, "What did I do that you couldn't?"

"You've allowed me to negotiate with the western powers from a position of weakness. They now believe I'm their puppet, their dog. Before your temporary incursion they didn't trust me, they would have trussed me up like a Thanksgiving turkey. Now they feel secure. Confident as they spend their millions on developing Gamasi's mineral wealth. Secure right up to the moment I nationalise their infrastructure and sell our tantalite on the open market."

"You'll never manage it; they'll freeze you out."

Amutu was smiling as he replied, "They'll try, but their sticks and carrots won't work. We have no further need for World Bank loans, or their aid packages. Gamasi has an essential world commodity and they know they can't control the Eastern buyers. Ok, they'll always be searching for my replacement, but we both know I'll recognise him when he comes."

Charles Amutu stepped forward into David Churu's line of vision. In his right hand he held a long antique spear. He placed the tip carefully on Churu's chest exactly over the heart. Its weight caused the point to pierce the skin and a small pool of blood formed around the tip.

Amutu's gaze locked onto Churu's remaining eye, "Sorry David, you were a good soldier, but you never did understand THE BIG GAME."

He linked his fingers and placed his cupped hands over the end of the shaft; took a deep breath and drove down with all his weight.

The End

Author's Note

Tantalite is a black, heavy mineral that is a vital ingredient in the manufacture of electronic goods such as cell phones and computers.

Found in sub-Saharan Africa it's uncontrolled mining has serious implications in terms of conflict escalation, displacement of communities, human rights abuses and environmental issues.

Its discovery in the Congo has led to the invasion of natural parks - causing destruction of forests and the decimation of endangered species like the gorilla, okapi and forest elephant.

As the enormous worldwide demand for consumer electronics put a strain on the supply of tantalite ore, prices have soared to hundreds of dollars per kilogram.

The import of legitimate tantalite cannot be properly controlled but the recycling of electronic goods can alleviate additional pressure on the resource.

About the Author

From the time he left school at fourteen Duncan has had a varied career; ranging from professional racing driver, private detective and Oklahoma cowboy, to President of an outlaw bike club, taking him from homeless to multi-millionaire and then flat broke again.

His writing is influenced by his diverse experiences including, natural healer, international trucker, director of a rainforest charity, and his mistaken imprisonment for a triple homicide.

240

0778265 9454

CPSIA information can be obtained at www.ICGtesting.com
Printed in the USA
LVOW13s2021080813

346999LV00021B/673/P